Twelve Feet Down

The Twelve Feet Series:

Twelve Feet Down

Twelve Feet Up *The First 5.6 Feet*

Twelve Feet Up *Somewhat Sideways*

Twelve Feet Up *All the Way Up*
(Coming Soon)

Twelve Feet Down

A Novel

John Penteros

Published by Green Sombrero Press, LLC

First Edition: September 2016
ISBN: 978-0-9979046-0-4 (ebook)
ISBN: 978-0-9979046-1-1 (paperback)

Visit the author's website: www.JohnPenteros.com

Cover design by Christian Fuenfhausen
Editing by The Editorial Department
Ebook formatting: www.ebookconverting.com

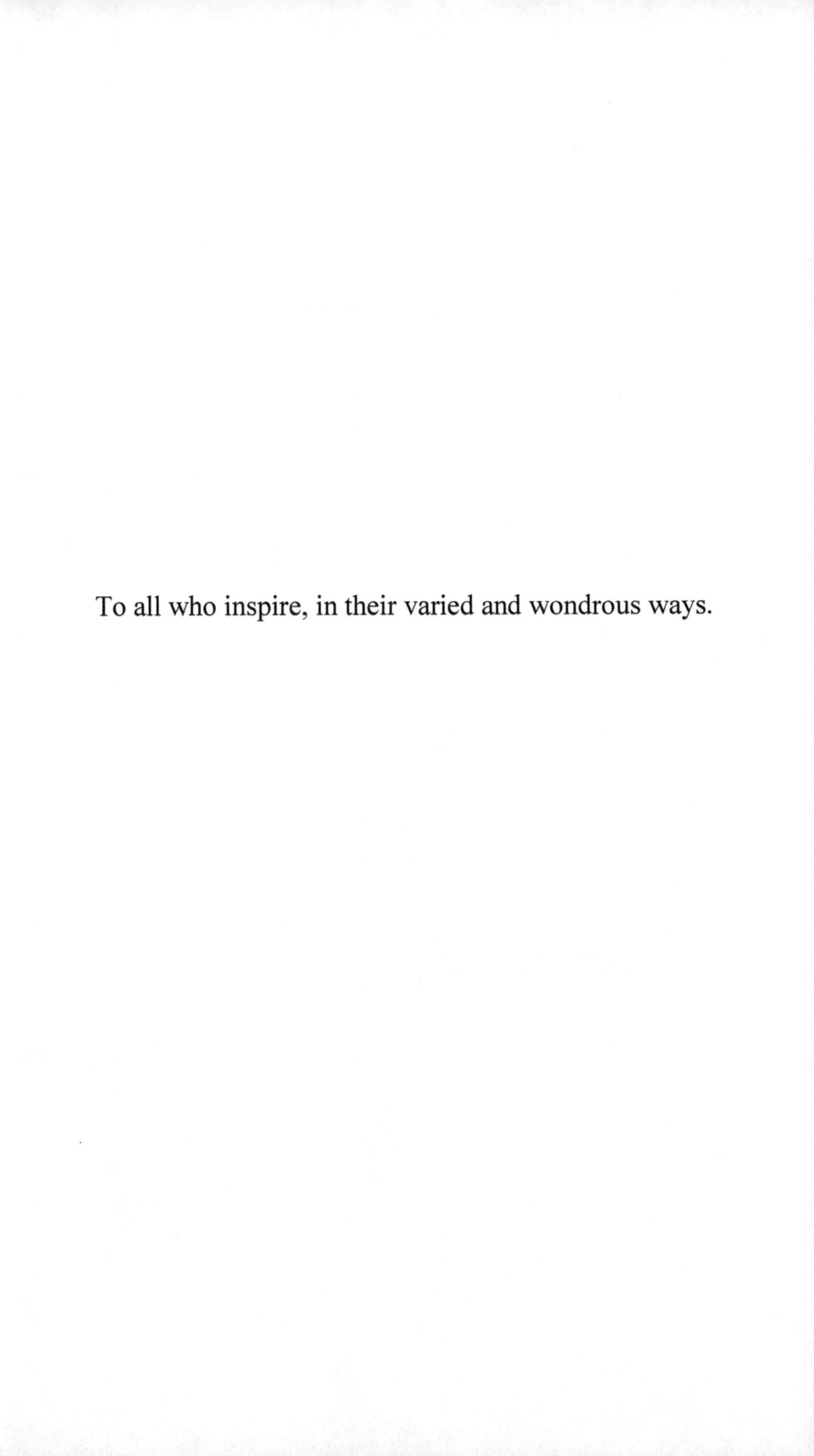

To all who inspire, in their varied and wondrous ways.

What you own is your own kingdom
What you do is your own glory
What you love is your own power
What you live is your own story

Rush, "Something for Nothing"

1

Backhoe

IF HE GOT CAUGHT, he'd be dog meat. No doubt there was a stiff penalty for digging a twelve-foot-deep hole in a forest preserve. By the time he finished, he'd be able to park a full-sized pickup like his dad's big Ford completely inside it with the doors open and a canoe on top.

If he didn't get caught.

The first line of defense consisted of pink insulation and plywood tented around the backhoe's engine and held in place with U-clamps to keep things quiet. He'd also painted the backhoe and the sound-muffling rig in army-green camo colors. He'd done all this in his backyard. Surely Mom had seen him, but she'd said nothing. Probably heeding Dr. V's advice *to set tangible boundaries for Joe, but within that structure to allow him harmless outlets that, under normal circumstances, you might question.* Ha!

In addition to the stealth backhoe, several months ago Joe had created two rings around *Ground Thirteen*—the name *Ground Zero* was already taken, so he figured naming it with his age was the next best choice.

The inner ring consisted of carpet remnants screwed onto two-by-fours sunk into the ground between trees. The back side of the carpet faced away from the dig, toward the ears of tootling neighbors just a hundred or so yards away.

For the outer ring he'd nailed signs to trees or secured them to metal posts every twenty feet or so—signs from Home Depot that said "NO TRESPASSING" and "WARNING: SECURITY CAMERAS IN USE." The best deterrents, though, were three signs that said "U.S. Government NO TRESPASSING." He'd "borrowed" those the day he and

Fred went fishing for radioactive-tumor bass near the Fermilab atomic accelerator plant.

He wondered if stealing government signs would buy him even bigger trouble. Of course Fred hadn't objected; the people who posted those signs were the same people who took a large chunk of his paycheck.

When Joe planned for reducing noise, he'd thought the rumbling of the backhoe's engine would be the biggest problem. But now, as he dug, it was obvious that its creaking joints and hissy hydraulics, along with rocks clunking inside the metal bucket, were much more likely to attract attention.

Oh well. At this point he'd just have to hope for the best.

Joe worked the backhoe as easily as any construction-site veteran, stretching the boom and bucket past the center of the dig with every scoop, just as he'd been taught.

Start at the farthest point away and work toward you, so you aren't wasting time pulling dirt across places you've already dug. Use the ground you haven't dug yet as a wall to help push dirt into your bucket.

Dad had always been the sultan of practical advice.

Think of it this way: if you only fill your bucket seventy-five percent full, then every fourth bucket you'll be one bucket behind. A job that could be done in three days will end up taking four. Time is money, Joe.

Dad was economical, too.

Aside from roots, the soft forest dirt cut easily under the force of the backhoe. In a short time, Joe had a hole big enough to bury his bed and all his possessions, if he'd been so inclined.

But that wasn't what he had in mind.

The dirt he dug up had to be moved far enough away that it wouldn't attract attention, and he had a dump site picked out. However, this place required him to cross the main trail that led down to the creek, which meant higher risk of human contact.

He had a plan for that, too: when it was time to haul, he'd first scout the haul path on his bike to make sure nobody was around. Then, he'd pull up the outriggers, load up the front bucket, and slalom through the woods until he came to the creek trail—a short stretch that took him to a wide, stony area where he'd turn right.

Finally, he'd travel a couple hundred feet or so to an embankment that marked the descent to a remote part of the creek, a place called Spooky Acres by all the kids and even by a few grown-ups he knew. Depending on whom you asked, it was home to Bigfoot, El Chupacabra (the midwestern variety), escaped serial killers, the ghosts of a young couple killed while hitchhiking after the Kennedy High prom of '72, or the restless spirits of soldiers ambushed by the Potawatomi Indians during the war of 1812 at Fort Dearborn (these ghosts had packed-up and moved to the suburbs).

Regardless of which story a person believed (if any), nobody ever went to Spooky Acres. That made it the perfect place to drop dirt.

On his way back from dumping, he'd stop and rake over any backhoe tracks around the trail. An experienced tracker would notice, but no city dope would ever recognize the overturned leaves or branches with bits of dirt on them.

And he had backup plans. If he got caught emptying a load, he'd say his mom was widening her garden and had extra soil to get rid of. If he got caught digging the hole, he'd say he was hired by an NIU professor to dig for artifacts, as this area was a known historic location of a Potawatomi Indian community (which it probably wasn't). In case anyone needed more convincing, he kept some arrowheads his grandpa had given him a few years ago in his pocket.

Joe soon figured out how many buckets he could dig out before it was time to haul. If he hauled too often, he wasted time pulling up and resituating the outriggers. If he didn't haul often enough, too much dirt fell between the trees, making it harder to scoop up later. And after a while, he spent less time verifying that the coast was clear and only covered the deeper tire tracks. His efficiency improved.

Time is money.

At the start of the first day, Joe had felt like he'd gotten himself in way over his head. However, as the hours rolled on and his work progressed, uncertainty was replaced by confidence.

Man was an explorer by nature, right? Humans had always found new lands, cleared them, farmed them, built on them. Ground Thirteen was merely a speck in a vast expanse, and he figured he had as much right to stake his claim as past settlers did.

And besides, it wasn't like he was doing this for selfish reasons. He needed a private space where he could think … and invent.

How else was he going to make the world a better place?

2

No More Fathers

WHEN DAD WAS STILL HERE, Joe and his parents had gone to mass every week. But that changed after the accident. First there was Joe's stay in the hospital, and then Mom had to sort out what to do with Dad's business. Somehow they just never went back to church.

At times he missed St. Andrews, even though the mass and the meaning behind the sacraments were somewhat lost on him. But there had been something reassuring in the rituals, something soothing in Father's voice as he gave the homily. Mass was a time when the people around you took a break from being mean and selfish.

Still, there was one benefit to skipping church: he'd have the whole day to work on his project.

Sundays were perfect: Mom would be sleeping in, and there was no need to wake her up to tell her where he was going since he'd already told her Saturday. He'd said he was doing landscape work for someone in Palos Crest, a newer upscale development where people had big houses on big lots, though not as big as the lots in Joe's neighborhood.

Maybe he was still a kid, but he'd gotten jobs doing everything from a pool dig and yard grading last summer to snowplowing in the winter. He was gaining a reputation for being just as good as a professional, but at a much lower price.

Joe awoke at 5:15 a.m., eager to get back to the woods where his dew-bathed backhoe awaited him. He'd finished breakfast and was packing a lunch when his mom called out from her bedroom.

"Joe?" She'd stopped calling him Joey last fall at his request.

"Yeah?"

"Why are you up so early?"

Joe slouched. "I'm doing that job—the one in Palos Crest, remember?"

"At 5:40?"

"I won't get there until six. That's when I told them I'd get started." He wished she hadn't woken up, but he had his lies lined up just in case: what the job entailed, the customers' names, how much they were paying him. The only way he'd get busted was if she went there to look for him. But she'd never shown up on the job site before, and he was counting on her to be consistent.

"Honey, I'm glad you're such a hard worker, but nobody wants to hear a backhoe engine at six a.m. on Sunday."

She had a point. Joe thought for a second.

"I'm not firing up the backhoe right away." Joe folded up his lunch bag. "Mr. Doersma said I could get there early and do quieter stuff like putting in some plastic border and hand-digging plant holes … stuff like that."

"Come here, honey."

Joe sighed and limped to his mom's bedroom. He stopped at the door.

"Yeah, Mom?"

"Come lie next to me."

"Mom, I really gotta go."

"Come show me love before you go."

To walk away would have been cruel. She lay on the right side of the bed—her side. There were still pillows on Dad's side, along with a dad-sized dent in front of them. It had been a year and four months, and it was still Dad's side.

Joe sat next to his mom.

"How's your leg?" she said.

"Gone."

She smiled. "I told you if you sprinkle it with Miracle-Gro, it might grow back."

"Ha ha. That's so funny I forgot to laugh."

His "souvenir" from the accident was a missing right leg, cut off just above the knee. Mom had a grab bag of one-liners in case either of them started taking things too seriously, including "Throw away the prosthetic and you'll save me fifty percent on shoes." And his favorite: "If you're ever attacked, just pull off your leg and beat the guy over the head with it."

"Is your prosthetic bothering you?"

"It's fine, Mom."

And it really was, except for the occasional sweating and itching on his stump. Fred had even put a leather pouch on it for holding his house key, money, and Fred's phone number. He'd shown Joe how to wrap the prosthetic foot with athletic tape to make his shoe fit tighter. Fred had also attached a rat trap to Joe's right bike pedal to keep that foot from slipping off, since his fake foot couldn't feel when it wasn't centered on the pedal.

"Doesn't make you sore anymore?" Mom said.

"Nope." He leaned over and gave her an awkward hug. "Gotta go now."

"Okay, but before you go …" Her eyes began filling with tears. With the back of her hand she caressed the side of his face. "You're going to be a good man. I'm very proud of you."

Just what I needed. It's hard to have fun with a guilty conscience.

"You need anything … um … before I go?" Joe said. *Please ask for something so I don't feel so bad, but not anything that takes too long.*

She thought about it. "On your way home, can you stop by the store and get a gallon of two-percent? Just take five dollars out of the jar … and Joey?"

"Huh?"

"I love you. Be careful. Ask to use their phone and call me sometime. I'll be home all day."

"Okay. Bye Mom. Love you too."

He left, pondering how it was that moms could make you feel everything from good to bad to amusement to guilt in the space of just three minutes.

3

Spooky

APRIL MORNINGS WERE CHILLY in Illinois, and in his haste to leave Joe forgot his jacket. But going back inside was out of the question—his mom might think of something else she wanted. He'd just have to deal with it.

Joe headed off in a direction opposite the woods, toward Palos Crest, in case any neighbors were watching. That way, if they happened to run into his mother, nobody would say, *Palos Crest? That's not where I saw him going ...*

He'd take a series of left turns around the block using the theory that while two wrongs don't make a right, three lefts do. And he wasn't worried about anyone on the next street spotting him because nobody there knew him.

It was calm at this hour. The only signs of life were a pudgy jogger in a Purdue Boilermakers running jacket, and a terrier who ran alongside Joe for a good fifty feet before the dog's fenced-in yard forced him to give up and deliver a final exasperated woof.

The sky's dim gray hue hinted at the approach of sunrise. Although he wore a long-sleeve shirt, Joe's arms were cold; it was probably only forty-five degrees outside. At least his dark-green backpack gave him some warmth.

Inside the backpack were his steel-toed work boots. Dad had always insisted Joe wear them when they went to jobsites together, and Mom was still willing to purchase them since he did backhoe work. He also packed peanut butter sandwiches and a handful of granola bars. Three bottles of water were more than enough for this weather. And he brought a first aid kit with tweezers, gauze, tape, bandages, and hydrocortisone cream for poison ivy. He kept Dad's old bowie knife in the middle compartment by itself, so he could find it fast if he needed to.

Joe approached the deep water-drainage ditch that separated civilization from forest preserve, dug out fresh every other year by the Ditch Witch machine. Some unknown trail guardian always came by after a fresh digging and reconstructed a dirt-and-gravel bridge high enough to cross without flipping over the handlebar.

Crossing the ditch from this side of the block meant going through the fields before entering the woods. Here, weeds and saplings were tall enough to hide a small child walking, or a thirteen-year-old on a bike bending low over his handlebar. The trail was wide at first but quickly narrowed into a rutted tire path.

Joe always wore his Levi's out here, even on the sweltering days of summer, to avoid being scratched by overhanging milkweeds and stickers or stung by insects. But today the only life on the trail was Joe and a few birds chirping in the new day.

The woods approached. Even at midday they weren't very bright, but at the brink of dawn they looked downright dismal. To make matters worse, he'd be taking a poorly lit path to a point just yards from the turnoff to Spooky Acres before he turned left and headed to Ground Thirteen—which meant that as he made the turn, he'd have his back to the scariest spot out there.

He stopped at the woods' edge, giving his eyes time to adjust to the dark. When he could see the path, he began pedaling, hating every clank of his chain and crack of a twig. He could've brought a flashlight, but figured that would just make it easier for someone to find him.

The woods were quieter than the field—no birds calling here. His own breathing sounded so loud he might as well be yelling. At least the woods were somewhat warmer than the open air of the fields. The trees' canopy was a tent, and the forest bed was a thick wool blanket.

As he rounded that left turn, something grabbed his right leg.

His other foot slipped off the pedal, but momentum kept him going until he lost his balance, plummeted to the ground, and came to rest lying face up—his backpack under him, the bicycle on top of him. His prosthetic had pulled partway off.

"What the …"

Joe lifted his head and looked toward his feet only to discover his right pant leg was caught in the chain. He tried to pull it free, but it was wedged tight between the chain and sprocket. Next, he tried lifting himself up to stand, but the angle was wrong. He lay back down and let his body go limp.

His heart pumped adrenaline. He breathed heavy.

Why didn't I just stay in bed where it's warm and safe? Or snuggle up next to Mom? This is stupid.

He closed his eyes. What would Dad say?

Things worth doing usually aren't easy. If they were, everyone would do them, and all the world's problems would already be solved.

Joe felt his throat tighten.

But how do I know if it's worth doing? Tears began to fall. *Why aren't you here to tell me what I should do?*

Time passed as he lay there tangled up and sniffling. Self-pity was something he'd thought he was done with after surviving last Thanksgiving and Christmas without Dad. As much as he hated to admit it, Dr. V was right: if he held it in, it would come out at times he least expected or wanted it to.

Gradually, light seeped into the forest and the dark-gray world became greener and friendlier, more alive than it seemed a few minutes ago. Joe pulled a sleeve across his nose and dabbed his eyes with the other. The birds chattered in full force now, and the whole idea of spooks and ghosts seemed ridiculous.

Joe opened his eyes and swallowed. Time to get to work.

***

By mid-morning, digging had become rote and the fear of being caught had declined to a manageable paranoia. With the hole's perimeter marked by a narrow trench, the only brainwork required now was to not surpass the twelve-foot depth limit his design required. If he dug too deep, he'd have to backfill with dirt or extra gravel.

Time is money.

Ground Thirteen was a relatively large clearing where the sun shone through and low ground cover thrived. Only the stump of a felled oak abutted the dig site. Who knew why such a massive tree had been cut down and carried off? Maybe the forest rangers took it down because it was diseased, or maybe a lawless woodworker pilfered it to make a houseful of furniture. Regardless, the stump was one of the reasons Joe chose this location.

The other trees were at least eight feet from the hole, but they still sent some rather large roots toward where he was digging. The backhoe lifted when it encountered one of these, requiring him to cease digging and go into the hole with a saw.

Joe hoped his exterior-wall design, using pressure-treated two-by-eights braced with four-by-fours, would be strong enough to resist the forces exerted by such roots. His design allowed three inches of clearance between the barrier wall and a completely separate interior wall, so if the pressure of roots or dirt did bend the two-by-eights, the inner walls would remain intact.

The backhoe's engine breathed out light puffs of sooty smoke as Joe jostled around in its bird's-view throne. He exhaled an unheard sigh. Months of preparation just to get to this point—just to get to the beginning.

And next came an even bigger hurdle: Fred.

4

Call from China

JOE HAD ALREADY TOLD FRED the plan—sort of. What he'd really said was, "I'm going to build a fort in the woods. Could you help me get a few pieces of wood and some screws and stuff?" To which Fred had replied, "Sure buddy, just let me know what you need and I'll bring it out to you." The time had come to find out if Fred would come through.

When Joe had called Fred earlier in the morning, he'd said he had something kind of important to discuss. So Fred swung by during his lunch hour, which for Fred was any twenty-minute chunk of time he could find between ten and three. And now Fred's black Dodge Ram 4X4 Quad Cab pickup stood in the driveway with the door open—a habit formed by years of stopping at one jobsite after another, sometimes for just a few minutes, and often going back into the truck to get papers or a measuring tape or a lighter.

It was Friday, and Mom was working at the library, probably helping someone who didn't know if the letter C came before or after the letter D.

"Remember I asked if you could get me some supplies for my fort?" Joe said.

"Yup," Fred said. "Sure do."

Fred was about six feet four in actual height, but in presence he was twelve feet tall. Occasional grays peppered the long brown hair he kept tied in a ponytail, and a seldom-trimmed mustache and goatee buried his thin lips.

Joe reached into his backpack, took a deep breath, and pulled out a folder that pictured the Chicago Bears in action.

"Ah, The Refrigerator," Fred said.

"Huh?"

"William *The Refrigerator* Perry. That guy right there, number seventy-two, defensive lineman—bigger'n one of me and two of you put together." He squinted. "Looks like they're playing the Patriots. Probably that Super Bowl where Chicago smeared New England." His voice lowered. "Wasn't a good game. Even Bears fans turned the TV off after a while."

"Oh."

"It's your folder," he said. "You didn't know?"

Joe studied the folder as if he were seeing it for the first time.

"I asked Mom if she had a folder and this is what she gave me. It was in Dad's office."

"Oh." Fred always got quiet at the mention of Joe's dad.

"The bill of materials is inside. In the left pocket." Joe handed the folder over to Fred.

"Bill of …" Fred's bushy brow furrowed, then he smiled. "Cute."

"And the specs are in the right pocket."

Fred glanced at the right side while pulling the stapled sheets from the left.

"The action plan or whatever you call it is behind the design specs," Joe said. "There's separate drawings for framing and electrical—no plumbing—and the money for the materials is in the envelope—twenty-eight hundred dollars— I think I added it up right—and there's extra for gas and delivery fees and all that …"

"Electrical?" Fred's smile was gone. He pulled out the envelope, opened it, and thumbed across the bills. "Where'd you get this kind of money?"

Joe shrugged. "Got about seven hundred dollars in pity money for Christmas this year—or I guess it was really last year," he said. "I saved up the rest from doing jobs."

Fred looked around as if there might be enemy agents lurking nearby.

"Joe, I …" He shook his head. "You got a building permit in here too?"

"Don't you just bribe someone?" Somehow it had sounded funnier when his dad said it.

"I can't—I mean *you* can't build something like this," Fred said. "A fort is supposed to be a private little space made with leftover plywood, all banged together with nails stickin' out everywhere, and just enough space for you and your buddy and a few girly magazines. Not a—what is this …" he pulled out a drawing. "Not a twelve-by-sixteen-foot luxury suite with twenty-amp wiring. Why twenty-amp?"

"Dad always said workshops ought to have twenty-amp wiring for shop tools that use lots of current."

"Your dad was right about that," Fred said. "Man, this ain't a fort, it's a condo! Whaddya gonna do with shop tools in there?"

"Don't know," Joe said. "Just have some ideas, I guess."

"I got an idea you're fixin' to make an atom bomb, what with those signs you took from Fermilab."

Joe cocked his head and kicked at grass growing through a crack in the driveway.

"I don't think I'm that smart."

Fred held up the folder and pointed at it.

"Oh yes you are."

"Before you say no—"

"I already *did* say no."

Joe put on the most pleading, pathetic look he knew.

"Before you say no *again*—would you at least come and take a look at where I'm gonna build it?"

"You mean where you *were* gonna build it." Fred hemmed and hawed for a moment. He pulled out the envelope containing the cash and slapped it against Joe's chest. "Put this somewhere safe." He threw the folder into the front seat of his pickup. "I assume that's my copy?"

"Yeah." Joe threw extra sadness into his reply. *If I have to, I'll shake my prosthetic loose and fall over.*

"Aw, what the hell," he said. "I got another twenty-five minutes to kill before I gotta be somewhere."

***

Fred looked funny on Dad's old Specialized Rockhopper mountain bike. Joe could picture him more on a hard tail chopper like Biker Man Jerry's down the street. Biker Man had given Joe a ride on his Harley a few months after Dad died, but when Mom found out, she told Joe not to do it again. That was fine with Joe, since the cruiser seat required him to lean forward onto Biker Man's back to keep from sliding down onto the lower seat where Biker Man sat. Biker Man was a cool guy and all, but Joe didn't like being that close to some man who wasn't Dad.

As he and Fred got close to the ditch where the woods trail started, it was Joe's turn to look around for enemy agents. Fred was swerving the bike in an S-pattern, obviously enjoying something he hadn't done in years.

This is it. This is do or die.

They went through the short section of the field, into the woods, and made the left turn from the main trail—the spot where Joe had fallen last Sunday. With Fred there, it wasn't Spooky Acres anymore … it was just another part of the woods.

Joe dropped his bike and climbed onto the old stump at the edge of his hole. Fred ambled up at his own pace, peering over the edge like he'd never seen a hole before.

"Man, you're serious, aren't you?"

The hole was finished. The sides were straight, with a layer of clay visible about a foot below the surface. Hairy roots hung off the sides for the first few feet. The bottom was as flat as anyone could possibly hope to make it.

Suddenly, Fred looked concerned. He leaned his ear toward the hole.

"Hey, wait a minute—what's that?"

"What's what?"

"Those voices."

Joe looked panicked.

"Where?"

"Down there." Fred pointed. "They're speaking Chinese."

Joe laughed. "C'mon, whaddya think?"

"I think your dad taught you how to dig a proper hole." Then he whistled. "Man, how long you been working on this—where's the dirt?" He looked around. "There's no way that's all that came out of *this* hole."

"I emptied it off a ravine down by Spooky Acres," Joe said. "Whole thing took me a week."

"How long you reckon it'd take you to fill it back in?"

Joe's face sank.

"I won't waste my time telling you how much trouble you could get into for what you've done here," Fred said. "Your dad and I got into a lot of trouble for doing less than this." He stroked his goatee. "Nobody saw you doing this? Nobody else knows?"

"Nope."

"What about your mom?"

Joe's eyes widened. "Hell no!"

"You know the only reason this didn't cave in is because of all the tree roots holding up the sides. You're lucky to be alive."

"Yeah, I kind of figured that."

"You couldn't have got so deep without that extended boom either."

Joe hoped Fred's interest in the details would override his caution, which might eventually turn "no" into "maybe."

"All right," Fred said. "Digging this hole without anyone noticing is one thing …" He walked over to the backhoe and studied its sound reduction and camouflage, then looked at the wall of carpet Joe had erected around the site and shook his head. "But do you actually think you could get all the lumber and whatnot in here and bang it all together without anyone seeing or hearing you?"

"It's in the plan," Joe said.

"You don't think someone will run across this thing eventually?" He stared at Joe, all the humor gone from his whiskered face. "I mean, you ain't the only one that ever comes out here, you know. You've just been lucky so far."

"It'll be covered up with that dirt there, once it's been built. I'll even re-cover it with leaves and branches, and plant a few vines like those over there."

"I meant while you're in the process of building it. Don't you think the odds are that someone would catch you before you could get 'er buried?"

Joe shrugged. "Not if I get it done before school lets out for the summer."

"And how were you gonna get in? You'd need a trap door or something."

"I'm sitting on the entrance," Joe said in a matter-of-fact tone.

"A tree stump for an entrance, huh? And a secret push button hidden in that tree over there to open it, I'm sure." He took another look in the hole. "You got a Bat-phone to call Commissioner Gordon down there?"

"Come on, Fred," Joe said. "I'm not some stupid kid pretending to be Batman. I really know how to do this. I've been planning it since last summer."

"And where do you plan to get the electricity from?"

"From a streetlight." He pointed in the general direction. "Maybe a hundred yards away."

Fred winced. "That's a hell of a cable run—not to mention another six months to a year in the pokey for stealing electricity. And now that *Fred* knows about all this, guess which one of us will be doing time?"

"You won't get in trouble, I promise."

"You can promise all you want, but they'd *know* you didn't get those materials all by yourself, Joe! You don't even drive yet. I take that back—from what I've seen here, you probably *do* drive, and fly jets too, but the cops will be looking for whoever helped you out, and that would be me." He was

18

using the same voice he used with workers at construction sites. No wonder they usually did what he wanted them to.

He sighed. "Couldn't you be happy with a four-by-eight fort up in one of these trees?"

"No privacy in the trees. Everybody would use it."

"What're you gonna be doing that you need … never mind, don't answer that." He held up his hand, then reached back and scratched the back of his neck.

Joe waited for a final answer, but all Fred did was shake his head.

"Sorry kid, I gotta get back to work now. You riding back with me?"

"Nah, I'll just hang out awhile." Joe slouched on his stump perch.

"All right," he said. "See you later. Tell your mom I said hello—if your plan allows it." He smiled, but Joe didn't laugh.

5

"HELLO RAMESH"

ON SATURDAYS, JOE VOLUNTEERED at the Palos Springs Public Library, where his mom had worked for the last eight years as the principal librarian. Usually Mom went in with him, trying to "catch up on things," although as far as Joe could tell, she never did catch up. There were always a hundred things that needed to be done: books to cover, spine and pocket labels to create, and stamping—always stamping. Catalogue records were continuously added, deleted, and corrected. There were books to mend with ripped pages, broken spines, or worn covers. There were overdue books whose borrowers needed to be warned and sometimes fined. Boxes of new books arrived in need of processing, and outgoing boxes contained books that had once served their purpose, but were now obsolete and often laugh-worthy.

Mom had shown him some of the books they weeded out. One that stood out in his memory was a 1970s book of pop-tab art which showed everything from vests to wall art made from soda-can pull-tabs. Computer books were always good for a chuckle. One pictured a guy with feathered hair and a clunky keyboard peering at a bulky monitor which displayed **10 CLS; 20 PRINT "HELLO WORLD"** in green pixilated text. Yep—these books needed to go.

The latest big project was to replace all the older barcodes with newer ones. Replacing one barcode was easy enough, but pulling fifty-five thousand books off the shelves was taking a lot longer.

The first time Joe helped out at the library, he'd thought it had to be the most perfect place he'd ever seen, with countless rows of books neatly aligned. Library workers knew where everything belonged and could point to just about anything in a snap, and what they couldn't answer they could usually find out from another staff member or the computer within seconds.

Seeing Mom answer questions concerning spreadsheets and presentation software, and watching her solve printer networking issues impressed Joe, especially since she didn't use the computer much at home.

Joe liked the people who worked there too—like Helen and Liz and Ramesh. They treated him like a member of the team, even when he was there without his mom, like today.

Joe's work was voluntary, which meant no pay: just many words of appreciation. There was something satisfying about library work, such as seeing books freshly fitted with protective covers, labels, and barcodes get entered into the cataloguing system then wheeled out to the stacks for shelving, ready to be checked out for many years to come.

Lately though, Joe was here not because he wanted to be, but because he felt he had to be. He was stocking up on good deeds to counteract the bad ones: namely deceiving his mom and eventually (as Fred pointed out), stealing electricity from the city. On the Saturdays he didn't show up (such as last weekend), he felt a twinge of guilt, and this guilt drove him to work harder than usual.

One of the library technicians was Ramesh, a college-aged expatriate of India. His business-casual shirt and pants hung on his frame the same as they would on a clothes hanger. He approached Joe with a smile.

"Joe, if you keep working so fast, they will not be needing me here anymore."

"Just want to get these books done." Joe pointed to the double-sided cart loaded on both sides.

"I see. You have many books to barcode there."

"Uh-huh."

"Tell me, after you are done with those, what will you do next?"

"Um … give them to Liz or Helen to enter in the system, and go get another cart." It was obvious, wasn't it?

"I see. And after that you will do another cart, and another, and another. Perhaps not so many carts today, but at some point, between you and me, we will be done with changing all the old barcodes. Correct?"

Joe liked Ramesh's clear and calm way of expressing himself, but today he wished he'd just get to the point.

"That's right."

"Then, when we are finished with the changing of the barcodes, will you step back and look at the work you did and say *that was a fine job we did changing all those barcodes*?"

Although Ramesh wasn't trying to be funny, Joe couldn't help cracking up a little.

"Yeah, sure, I guess."

"I want to tell you …" Ramesh pulled up an armless wheeled stool to seat himself and rested his arms on its back support. "I can think of some memorable things that happened on days when you were changing the barcodes." He used smooth hand gestures. "Please tell me if you remember them too."

"Okay …? But I sorta need to get these done. I won't be able to come in on Saturdays for a while."

"Are you taking a leave of absence from volunteer work?" Ramesh raised an eyebrow.

"No … well, sort of." Joe looked away—it wasn't a total lie, but closer to it than he'd like. "I have this other job I need to get finished."

"I understand," Ramesh said. He folded his hands together. "So tell me if you remember this: one day, just a few months ago, a couple of boys walked into the library with balls of snow and threw them at another boy sitting at a table. Then the two boys ran away. They carried on quite loudly."

"Yeah, I remember. The kid who got nailed ran out after them, and then Helen ran outside and yelled at all of 'em."

"Precisely. And another time, one of the shelves in nonfiction suddenly collapsed, and the sound of it startled Liz so bad, she screamed very loudly."

Joe chuckled. "That was a good one."

"It was," he said. "Now Joe, you tell me two things you remember during the time you were changing barcodes."

"Well, you brought us all some Indian food to try, and after the spicy soup we had to keep drinking water for like, the rest of the day."

"Ah, the lentil curry soup. Your face was sweating quite a bit, but you were brave and ate it all."

Joe blushed. "And uh … I don't know. I can't think of anything else."

"How about the pizza and soda we ordered a few weeks ago when we all ate lunch together."

Joe shrugged. "Nothing really special about that, though. We've had pizza lots of times."

"But you do remember?"

"Yeah, sure."

"Then please ask yourself this …" He paused. "Which memories will you most likely share with your future wife and children: the memory of your barcoding achievement, *or* the memories of the snowball fight, the spicy soup, sharing pizza with friends, and the librarian who jumped and screamed?"

As Joe thought about it, Ramesh dismounted the chair and went out to the floor, where he was quickly approached by a patron with a question.

Joe gazed at the book cart for a moment before going back to his barcoding—at a bit slower pace than before.

6

Speech! Speech!

JOE HAD TURNED IN HIS REPORT on the Potawatomi Indians some time ago, and he'd received it back the day before spring break. As Mr. Zelnicki handed back the graded papers, he'd instructed his students to use spring break to practice delivering their speech on the subject.

"Don't just read your speech from your paper," Mr. Z had said. "Nothing puts an audience to sleep faster than a speaker who reads words off a paper. You might as well just hand the paper to the audience and tell them to read it themselves."

Joe, who had sunk into his seat at the word "speech," glanced up.

Good idea! Can we do that instead?

"And remember …" Mr. Z held up three counting fingers. "There are three steps for conveying information to your audience. Number one—tell them what you're going to tell them. Number two—tell them. Number three—tell them what you told them. Now, practicing by yourself in front of a mirror is a start, but practicing in front of people is better. Get your mom or dad to listen to you, or better yet, get the whole family together. Brothers and sisters are a tough audience. If you can survive delivering your speech to *them*, you can probably survive speaking in front of the class."

That had been the Friday before the break. Today was the day: sixth period, language arts—right after lunch.

Great. Make sure the stomach's good and full so I can blow more chunks on the front row.

The late bell rang.

Joe sat there like a convicted man awaiting his sentence. There was always the chance Mr. Z would forget about this speech nonsense and move on to something else. Maybe a test—one that covered everything since the beginning of the year. Or if Mr. Z got good and sick over spring break, and there was a sub for the next few weeks …

But Mr. Z walked through the door.

"Well hello, class. How was everyone's vacation?" he said.

Super! I dug a hole in the woods big enough to bury everyone in this class, but right now I'd just like to throw myself into it.

"Good, glad to hear it," Mr. Z said. "I trust you're all rested and practiced up for your presentations?"

There was a collective moan. Joe was slightly comforted knowing he wasn't the only one dreading this.

"Oh come on, it won't be that bad," Mr. Z said. "Think of this one as practice for your persuasive speeches you'll be doing at the end of May."

The class groaned even louder.

"Here's the podium," he said. "You can use the overhead if you have pictures, graphs, any support materials. But don't put your typed pages up there; this is not a read-along. Okay—who wants to go first?"

Joe felt a flicker of hope. There were always the show-offs, the brave hearts who threw up their hands when the call was made. Then there were the *Gee, I'm not sure, I don't really want to, but I think it would be better to get it over with* types who held their arms at half-mast. But the majority slouched, attempting to go unnoticed. Joe was a sloucher, and if things played out as they should, he might not have to present today.

"Okay Julie, let's start with you," Mr. Z said.

Julie Silverstein approached the podium with the confidence of a politician. She opened her folder and began speaking.

Joe entered a trance-like state, ignoring the content of Julie's speech but noting the quality of her voice, where she inserted pauses, her use of eye contact. He'd been hoping she'd falter, her voice would start to shake, she'd lose her place, become flustered, and break down in tears. But she didn't. On the contrary, all she needed was an unflattering suit and an ugly hairdo and she'd be ready for Capitol Hill.

This was a bad start. He was hoping that if divine intervention didn't cancel his appearance at the podium, at least the other speakers would be lousy enough to make him look good by comparison.

When Julie stepped down, the class applauded. Mr. Z made a few comments on her excellent use of eye contact, perfect speed of delivery, and good organization. For improvement, he said she just needed to put a bit more animation in her voice to make it less monotone.

Heh, wait till you hear me—I'll have everyone sleeping after just four syllables.

"Alrighty then, who wants to be next?" Mr. Z searched the room, and for a fraction of a second, caught Joe's eyes. Joe almost pulled a neck muscle he turned away so fast, but it was too late.

"Mr. McKinnon?" he said. "You look all fired up and ready to go—would you like to be next?"

"Yeah, I guess so," Joe said.

The shaking began before he even left his seat. As he walked up the aisle, Joe's heart rate doubled as if he'd just been sprinting. He stepped up, placed his notecards on the ledge, and clutched the podium—his lifeline.

He looked out at the familiar faces—friendly faces, mostly—kids he'd gone to school with for years. They looked into his eyes and Joe knew they saw the fear in him.

He dropped his eyes back to the safety of his notecards.

"My rep-p-p-port is on …" He swallowed hard and gasped for air, "the Potawat … the Potaw-w-w-watami Indi—" Another swallow. "—ans."

He glanced up to survey the damage so far—just long enough to see some of the kids chuckling and others whispering to each other, no doubt taking bets on how long before he hit the floor. Mr. Z sat at the back of the room taking notes on a legal pad. Some of the kids wouldn't look at him. He felt hurt, ashamed, embarrassed. He had laid his true self out for everyone to see, and it was an awful sight.

"The P-p-potawatamimi Indi—"

"Joe, Joe, let's hold up for a second." There was compassion in Mr. Z's voice, and concern on his face. "Let's do *this*. Close your eyes."

Joe obeyed.

"That's it. Now take a few deep breaths, and relax."

With his eyes closed, Joe saw this was worse than disaster. His face flushed and his whole body shook. A trail of sweat ran down the side of his face and dripped from his chin. Any chance of regaining composure and having his nervous first words forgotten was gone.

He heard Mr. Z shush the class; then a chair squeaked. The class was so quiet, Joe began to wonder if they'd all left.

Suddenly a hand pressed against his forehead.

"Good Lord, you're burning up!" Mr. Z said. "I could tell you were sick the moment you took the podium."

Joe opened his eyes, confused. None of his classmates were smiling anymore. Those whose eyes had avoided him now looked concerned.

"Let's get you down to the nurse right away and see if we can't get you home in bed where you belong."

And with that, Mr. Z swept him away. As they were heading through the door he bellowed out to the class, "I want silent sustained reading while I'm gone. And if I hear *any* talking when I step back in this room, there *will* be a three-page essay due tomorrow!"

As soon as they were far enough down the hall, Mr. Z put his hand behind Joe's back and steered him toward the cafeteria. Joe had to walk fast to keep up with Mr. Z's long strides. Along the way, Mr. Z called out to Mrs. Lee, the sixth-grade administrator. Just before she turned into the office he asked if she wouldn't mind sitting with his students for a few minutes while he took care of a minor emergency.

***

Only a custodian and a few cafeteria workers were there, cleaning up the fallout from four hundred sloppy middle-schoolers. Suddenly Joe found himself seated at a lunch table with Mr. Z directly across from him. He felt like he'd just woken up.

"You were terrified, weren't you?" Mr. Z said.

Joe kept his arms to his side and stared at a French fry six inches in front of him.

"I understand your fear, Joe. It's nothing to be ashamed of. And I know it doesn't seem possible, but this *is* something you can work through."

"I can't do it," Joe said to the French fry.

"Yes, you *can*," Mr. Z said. "Public speaking is a common fear. Most of your classmates are afraid of it too."

"Not Julie."

"I said *most*, not all." Mr. Z paused. "Everybody's born with a different deck of cards up here." He tapped his temple. "So, for example, one person's math card is an ace, while the next person's is a deuce. We all have our deuces. One of yours is speaking in front of a group. One of mine is being in confined places."

Joe looked up at his teacher.

"I had an MRI a few months ago," Mr. Z said. "That's a medical procedure where they make you lie down in a narrow tube and take pictures of your insides." He looked away for a moment. "You know how you were up at the podium, all shaking and heart going a thousand miles an hour? That was me in that MRI tube. I thought my heart was going to burst. I needed to shower and change my clothes when I got home. So trust me, I know how it feels."

Joe's trembling had ceased. His eyes tracked his teacher's, searching for signs of truth in his statement.

"But you don't have to live with it," Mr. Z said. "You can make it go away, or at least learn to manage it."

"But you would still get nervous if you had another MRI?"

"I manage being in elevators and crowds," he said. "It just so happens that getting an MRI is about the worst type of confinement you can imagine. Besides, being very confined is something I can avoid most of the time, so I don't feel it's …" He searched for the right words. "I've made the decision that I can manage my fear by avoiding those situations as much as possible."

"So … can't I do that?" Joe said. "Just avoid it?"

Mr. Z squinched up his face. "I wish it were that easy, Joe, but your particular deuce happens to be a very important one. We're all called upon to do public speaking from time to time throughout our lives: weddings, funerals, church … most any career you choose will require you to stand in front of people to make a project proposal, or discuss your findings, or train people on something you've become an expert at."

"I'll just get a job that doesn't make me do that," Joe said.

"Do you really want to limit yourself any more than you already are?"

Joe returned to contemplating his French fry.

"I didn't mean it to sound like that," said Mr. Z. "I just mean that by not conquering your fears, you'll make your life harder and less fulfilling than it ought to be."

They were both silent for a moment.

"Having fear does not make you a coward, but running from your fear does," Mr. Z said. He leaned in closer, recapturing Joe's eyes. "And what I saw a few minutes ago was a young man who was terrified out of his mind, but had the guts—the *fighting courage*—to stand up there and face his fears even if it meant passing out. And I think you were just about ten seconds away from that."

Joe managed a smile.

"If you can arrange to stay after school tomorrow, I'll work with you. You can lick this thing."

"Do I have to?"

"You don't have to take my help, but you do have to do two speeches before this year's over, *with* or without me." He leaned back and lifted up his hands. "Your choice."

Joe considered, then nodded. Mr. Z reached out his hand, and Joe showed him that *his* was not the handshake of a weakling.

7

What Fred Said

IT WAS FRED WHO PICKED UP JOE from Halverson Middle School. Mrs. Atkins, the school nurse, called Joe's mom, who in turn called Fred. It was easier for Fred to get Joe since he could just throw Joe's bike into the back of his truck. Mom had put Fred on the pickup list in the school records along with Grandma and Grandpa McKinnon and Grammy Jeanne, but she'd only added the grandparents as a formality since they all lived hours away in Indianapolis.

Joe felt a certain power when he rode in Fred's Dodge Ram pickup. It was a rugged construction-worthy vehicle, with beefy off-road tires, a chrome-plated industrial tool box, and an aerial view of the lesser vehicles on the road. It was the perfect fit for Fred, who said there were two types of animals on the road: wolves and sheep. Fred had his occasional matchups with other drivers, but those who tried to take him on usually backed off once they got a closer look at him. Part of Joe cheered for Fred the wolf, but another part of him wished he would just chill out.

"So you're sick?" Fred said.

"I don't know."

"Hmmm. What's the problem then?"

"Teacher thought I had a fever, said I should go home."

"And you didn't argue with that, did ya?" Fred laughed.

"Of course not." Joe grinned.

Fred hit the brakes hard at a light with a short yellow: Central Avenue. Three beer bottles rolled forward from under Joe's seat. Joe heel-kicked them back under.

"Are you well enough to answer a question?" Fred said.

"I guess."

"I've known you since the day you were born …"

He honked and waved to two guys in a utility truck crossing the intersection. A sign on its door said, "J & J Plumbers." The driver threw Fred a peace sign, and the passenger waved over the roof.

"Yeah?" Joe said.

"You're an honest kid and I need an honest answer."

Joe swallowed. "Okay."

Fred turned down the radio and looked straight ahead. With his reflective side-wrapping shades, Joe couldn't tell if he was eyeballing him.

"Here's the deal. I don't care what else you do in that underground condo you're gonna build, but you have to promise me you'll never EVER use it as a place to smoke or drink or do drugs."

He stared down Joe as if he'd already committed a felony.

Joe was caught off guard. He didn't care about any of those things, and even if he did, he wouldn't need to build a bunker in the woods to do them.

"Yeah, sure Fred. I promise."

"In fact, I want you to promise me that you won't do *any* of those things *anywhere*. Because if you do, I'm coming out to that condo with a cement truck to fill it in."

A car gave Fred a wake-up honk and he punched the gas to make up for a couple lost seconds of green light.

"And that ain't all," Fred said. "If your grades start dropping. I'll go out and put a padlock on it until I know you're back up to speed again. Got it?"

"Yes!" Fred might be reading him the riot act, but along with it, he was giving Joe the go-ahead.

Fred smiled and reached out for a shake. Joe smacked his much smaller hand into Fred's and shook it with vigor.

"One last thing," Fred said. "I could get in a boatload of trouble for this. We're talkin' police, forest rangers, lawyers—the whole works. I don't expect you'll go around bragging about your secret hideaway, but if you get caught, we don't know each other. Right?"

"Right!"

Fred glanced at Joe. "You don't look so sick to me, homey."

Joe raised the back of his hand to his forehead.

"Fever … feeling faint … need a doctor." He coughed. "Take me to the hospital!"

Fred laughed and stepped on the gas. "Roger, headin' to the ER—stat!"

<h1 style="text-align:center">8</h1>

Getting to the Point

HAVING TO WAIT UNTIL FRIDAY for his building supplies was worse than trying to fall asleep the night before Christmas. On Tuesday and Wednesday Joe had his speech to keep him preoccupied—as if that were any consolation. Tuesday he stayed home from school, using the day to practice his speech alone, then he rode to school just before the final bell and waited in the office where Mr. Z came to fetch him.

At first, Joe felt uncomfortable. Even though it was only Mr. Z watching, spewing a stream of rehearsed words to an audience seemed so phony. He was self-conscious of every syllable, and felt like each sentence he spoke was under scrutiny.

He wondered why he never felt that way during everyday conversation—even with a group of kids he was fine. Why should he feel so different just because there was a podium in front of him? Shouldn't it be easier when you already know what you're going to say?

But repetition helped remove the weirdness, and soon his nerves began to settle. The words started flowing more smoothly and automatically. Mr. Z also told him things that made a lot of sense: he said part of the nervousness comes from feeling like you're some bogus imposter, trying to fool people into thinking you're an expert. But he made Joe understand that although he wasn't an expert on the Potawatomi Indians, he knew more than the other kids, even more than Mr. Z himself—and that was good enough. Joe laughed when Mr. Z said how every day, politicians *talk out of their butts*, and how the audience usually doesn't know better.

Mr. Z also helped Joe loosen up at the podium, to not speak until he was ready, to slow down (yet still get to the point quick), to throw in humor for breaking tension, to use hand gestures (but not too often), and when feeling stared at, to defocus his eyes.

At the end of their session, Joe felt a lot better. He hadn't realized there were so many things to consider when giving a speech and how ill-prepared he'd been on Monday, like a soldier going into battle with a sling-shot. Tomorrow would be okay … he hoped.

***

On Wednesday Joe delivered his speech … and it wasn't bad. He was no Julie Silverstein, but the words came out and the shaking was minimal—he survived. And when he finished, other kids gave him positive comments. Even Julie said, "I could tell he really knew what he was talking about."

What's more, Mr. Z gave him a thumbs-up.

Joe smiled. He began to feel like, with a little more practice, he might be able to manage his deuce after all.

***

Without the speech to keep him occupied, the next two days crept by slower than a grandma texting for the first time. Fred would dump the first load of supplies Friday at Drop-Point Charlie (DPC), the place Joe had picked out for deliveries.

DPC could be found as follows: Woodside Lane ran parallel to the field; its adjacent ditch was the same one Joe crossed whenever he headed to the woods. Joe lived on Oak Street. If he took Oak south to Woodside, then turned left and followed the ditch toward the woods, he came to a dead end. At the dead end was a swinging bar gate with a padlock and beyond that was a gravel road, only accessible by the forest rangers. Just two hundred yards up the gravel road (which curved to the right) was an open flat area spray-painted with an orange "X." This was Drop-Point Charlie.

Of course Joe had a plan for getting past the padlocked gate. First, he went there in the wee hours of Thursday morning and cut off the padlock with his dad's bolt cutters—he'd had to put extension pipes on the handles for extra leverage. He then replaced the lock with his own similar-styled lock, which he left open for Fred and the forest rangers. With a little luck, any ranger who found it open would assume he forgot to close the lock last time and keep Joe's padlock there. It wasn't a perfect plan, but if they replaced the lock, he could always cut it off again.

And neighbors shouldn't be a problem. It was infrequent, but not unheard of, for trucks and trailers to pass in and out of the woods.

Now Joe's only concern was coming across a ranger or a work crew while he was fetching a load of materials from DPC. And since this was Fred's concern as well, Fred planned to dump the eight tons of ABC gravel and other supplies before six a.m., when there would surely be no forest preserve workers around.

9

Mom-Woman

JOE USUALLY MEANDERED through neighborhoods on his way home from school, but today he took the shortest trek he knew: the express route along 127th Avenue. He didn't like going this way because it had almost no shoulder to ride on and he felt like cars were just inches from hitting him, but he wanted to get to Ground Thirteen as fast as possible.

From 127th, he turned right on Merrimack Street, relieved to be away from cars whooshing past him. Up ahead was Brain STEM Preparatory Academy, a charter school for extra smart kids who wanted to become rocket scientists and nuclear engineers. Ahead of that was Algonquin Hill Elementary, Joe's alma mater.

Brain STEM Prep (nicknamed "The Brain") had opened just a few years ago after much controversy over it being built right next to Algonquin. In its first year, The Brain offered only kindergarten through fifth grade. Joe's parents would've liked him to go there because it emphasized math and science, but Joe was starting sixth grade when it first opened. He could've switched to The Brain for eighth grade since they'd added sixth through eighth this year, but by then, what was the point?

Many Algonquin students in grades below Joe had transferred to The Brain, and it was widely believed Algonquin Hill would soon close its doors for good. But for now, it was still open and kids spilled onto the streets from both schools. Joe felt a small surge of pride: he was at the top of the grade school food chain, about to enter high school. And what's more, he'd be a high-schooler with a place of his own.

Happiness isn't always a smile on your face or a song in your heart, Joe. Sometimes, it's a hard day's work with a result you can stand back and look at. Either way, when life seems wonderful, be alert, because odds are it's going to change.

At 128th Joe had a stop sign, but crossing traffic didn't. In his excitement, he entered the intersection without checking, forcing a woman in a Volvo to slam on her brakes. Startled, Joe jammed his right pedal backward, breaking his prosthetic free from its stump and sending him off balance to his right. Before he could compensate, he hit the pavement and rolled.

He came to rest with his left leg crammed against the front tire of the Volvo and his prosthetic lying next to him. His backpack lay askew beside his bike.

The Volvo's door flung open and a mom-aged woman flew out. She caught sight of Joe's wayward prosthetic and froze, her eyes widening as she covered her mouth with both hands, letting out a short screech.

Joe began to hyperventilate and checked his head for blood, which he found. Although he'd suffered worse cuts from a piece of cardboard, the sight of blood confirmed what the mom-woman's scream told him: he was going to die.

His lip quivered. The mom-woman, realizing her mistake, kneeled at Joe's side and put a soothing hand on his cheek.

"No, no, no, you're all right, honey." She cradled the back of his head and gently pushed down on his forehead. "You just relax, it's only a scrape."

Spectators had begun to gather. Among them was an Asian girl he knew from his days at Algonquin, though now she went to The Brain. The sight of her, along with the mom-woman's embarrassing mothering, helped Joe pull himself back from the edge of unmanly emotions.

"Please just stay down for a few minutes," the mom-woman said, but Joe was already working his way back onto his remaining leg.

"I'm okay lady, really."

And he *was* okay, except for the raspberry on his forehead and a sore spot on his back. He grabbed his prosthetic and hopped over to his backpack.

A car crept up. The driver rolled down his window and asked if he could help. The mom-woman thanked him and said everything was under control. As the car drove away, she pulled out a pen and pad from her purse and began scribbling. Then she walked over to Joe, peeled off the paper, and handed it to him.

"Here's my number. Have one of your parents call me to let me know you're okay—or they can call if they have questions about what happened," she said. "How about letting me give you a ride home? I could fit your bike in the back."

"Uh … it's okay, I can still ride." Joe tucked the paper in his pocket. "It was my fault. I wasn't paying attention."

"Well, it *is* Friday. I'm sure you were in a hurry to get home."

Joe nodded. *You have no idea.*

"Are you sure you're not hurt? Did you hit anything hard? Are you hurting inside or anything? Do you feel funny at all? Are you dizzy? Nauseous?"

Jeez lady, get a grip! "No, I feel fine. Just a scratch, like you said." The spot on his back ached, but if he complained, his mom would get called and she'd force him to lie around and take it easy for a few days. That would be worse than the pain he felt now.

By the time Joe put on his backpack, tucked his right pant leg into his front pocket, slung his prosthetic over his shoulder and mounted his bicycle, nearly a dozen spectators had gathered.

"Can you ride with just one leg?" the mom-woman said.

"Watch me." And with a modest effort, he propelled his bike forward with one leg. Joe leaned to the left, knowing from past experience if he lost his balance to the right, it would be a painful fall onto his stump. Once he built up enough speed he was able to keep his momentum going.

Turning left toward his neighborhood, Joe looked back and saw the Asian girl still watching him, holding her flute case in front of her with both hands. She smiled.

Joe continued pedaling, feeling flushed.

Hope you enjoyed the freak show!

10

Drop-Point Charlie

SPRING BREAK HAD GIVEN Joe whole days devoted to digging, which was why he'd waited until then to start. The hole-dig was the riskiest phase of the project and he'd needed to barrel through it as quickly as possible. Mom's rule was that until Joe got into high school, he wasn't allowed to work during the week (she wanted him to focus on schoolwork), but breaks and holidays were the exception.

Although it didn't get dark until about seven, Mom was usually home by six fifteen, so Joe tried to be home by six most days. Still, thinking that too much timeliness might look suspicious, he'd sometimes get home *after* Mom. He also tried to make his coming and going from the house look normal to his watchful and talkative neighbors.

Tonight Joe would get home after Mom. Moving the supplies and gravel was a big task and he needed the extra time. He decided to get the backhoe first since he needed its front bucket to haul everything from DPC to Ground Thirteen. A nervous anticipation soared through his body as he plopped himself into the backhoe seat. This was it. This was the *real* beginning of his dream. As he went to put the key in the ignition, he found a note taped on the steering wheel. It simply read:

Near DPC in a hole in a tree in a bag

The excitement was almost too much. Joe fired up the backhoe, turned the front bucket right side up, and was about to release the clutch when suddenly he shut off the engine.

I can't be a stupid little kid. I have to ALWAYS check first!

He hopped back onto his bike and followed his paint markings to DPC. There it was: the pile of gravel at the end of the rainbow. Alongside the gravel were stacks of lumber, plywood, and drywall; a heavy metal tamper; a generator; a tank of gas; extension cords; a miter saw; a circular saw; a jigsaw; two drills; a tool box; two wonder bars; multiple boxes of decking screws, lag bolts, and washers; a twenty-foot extension ladder; rope; two plastic tarps; and more.

"Wow!" Joe's eyes widened. What a huge heap of treasure! The tools were just to borrow until he finished construction, but the rest would become a condo.

Suddenly he felt a pang of guilt. *If anyone catches me, Fred will go to jail.*

Joe was pretty sure Fred had already spent time in jail; he was, after all, a tough guy with tattoos. But Fred was his best friend, and he didn't want to lose *him* too.

Joe stiffened his lips. He turned the bike around and began heading back to Ground Thirteen, when he remembered the note. *Near DPC in a hole in a tree in a bag.*

In no time, Joe found the tree with its hole facing away from the road. In it was a lunch bag.

Cool hiding spot! There was a note written in black marker on the bag:

Call me right now

Joe opened the bag and discovered a box with a cell phone. The phone was already turned on.

This is like double-oh-seven! Joe had never owned a cell phone before, but he'd used his mom's and his dad's, and he knew Fred's number—he'd called it often since the accident.

"Hello?" Fred said.

"Hey Fred, it's me!"

"Me who?"

"It's Joe, you left me a note to call you."

"How do I know it's you? What nickname did I used to call you?"

"Ummm …" Joe thought for a moment.

"The name your mom told me to stop using."

"Oh yeah, Peg Leg!" Joe laughed.

"Okay, you're clear. Here's the deal, kid. That's your phone now—but it's just for you and me to talk to each other, nothing else."

"Got it."

"I want you to keep it on whenever you're out there in the woods. You never know what might happen out there. If you get hurt or feel threatened, call me. In fact, you call *me* before you call 9-1-1. Those guys won't know where you are—I will. And if you really need 9-1-1, I'll call them for you, besides coming out there myself. Got it?"

"Yeah, I got it." Fred was starting to take the fun out of it, like grown-ups always did. "I'll be okay though."

Fred was quiet for a few seconds before he let out a big sigh.

"I have my reservations about all this, but I'll feel a little better knowing you can call for help if you need it."

"Okay, thanks."

"And I'm not big on telling you to hide things from your mother, but if you want to keep the condo a secret, you'll probably not want to tell her about the phone either. Does that make sense?"

"I promise. I'll hide the phone real good. Can I go now? I really need to get this stuff moved."

"Just a couple more things. If I try calling and for some reason you don't answer, you need to get back to me as soon as you can. Don't blow me off and leave me worrying."

"Got it."

"And the last thing—you remember about building inspectors?"

"Yeah?"

"Well I'm yours. You don't hook wires to streetlights, or backfill dirt on top of the roof, or enclose anything unless I give you the okay. Even if I'm outta town, you wait. I'm gonna give you a list of every point where I check before you keep going. Remember, if I don't like what you're doing out there, I have a direct line to that cement truck. Got it?"

"Yeah, okay." Joe felt scolded again.

"Look," Fred said. "I don't mean to be a jerk and take the fun out of this for you. Hell, you have no idea how jealous I am that I never got to do something like this when I was your age. I just want you to live long enough to go to college."

"I get it, Fred. I promise I'll stay alive."

"God, I hope so. Talk at you later, kid."

"Later."

As he hung up, Joe wished it were possible to do this project on his own, without Fred's help. But he had to admit, there was something reassuring about having that lifeline. It was like having Dad there watching over him.

I'll always be there for you, Joe. Always.

11

Offer

SATURDAY MORNING BROUGHT light rain. April showers were common in the Chicago area and Joe realized he'd been pressing his luck, so he decided this morning's first task was to put the tarp over the site. It was big enough to keep the supplies, the hole, and some of the surrounding ground dry. Using rope, he strung it up as high as he could from the trees, making sure to slant it enough for water to run off.

Yesterday he'd dumped the gravel directly into the hole, so today he went down and spread it to a depth of more than eight inches, then compacted it with an iron tamper. Afterward, his shoulders and arms ached.

Joe spent the rest of the day working on the outside dirt retention walls. He'd wanted to build the floor first, but Fred insisted he get the outer walls finished for protection against a cave-in. And since those walls would sit directly on the gravel, and weren't connected to the floor, it *was* okay to build them first.

Joe lowered the generator and the chop saw into the hole, where they'd be quieter during use. Within a short session of cutting boards to their proper length, Ground Thirteen looked and felt like a real construction site, complete with sawdust, wood stubs, cords, and boxes lying all over.

By late morning, Joe had measured and cut quite a bit of lumber, but he still had a lot to do. He'd just sat down for a drink when his phone began to vibrate.

"Hello?"

"How's it going kid? Still have all your fingers?"

"So far. I'm cutting the two-by-eights right now." He proceeded to tell Fred about his progress, being careful to sound optimistic despite any worries he had.

"Not so easy doing a project that big by yourself, is it?"

"It's not bad. Taking a little longer than I thought, but it's moving along okay."

"If you want, I can come out and help you get going—just to get the walls and floor all banged out in a day or so?"

"Um, that's okay. I think I can handle it, but thanks."

"All right, well don't forget to spend some time with your mom too. I think she gets lonely."

"Okay I will." *Mom's a grown-up. She doesn't need me to take care of her.* "Bye."

Break time was over. Time to build some walls.

12

Dumb

DR. VANDENBERG SAT IN HIS wide leather chair facing Joe—wide because Dr. V was what Mom called "circumferentially challenged." But by far his most distinguishing features were his eyebrows. The ends were waxed into a point, giving him a look that said *I see more than you'd like me to*.

Joe sat stiff with his hands folded together on his lap.

"So, Joe—what's going on in your life?" Dr. V said.

Well, let's see ... I'm building myself an underground condominium, I'm breaking multiple laws in the process, and my accomplice gave me a cell phone of my very own.

"Nothing much." Joe blinked several times in rapid succession.

"How's school? I hear your grades are still top-notch." Joe hated how Dr. V was always probing for a place to get in.

"School's fine."

"Good. What's your favorite subject these days? Mine was always recess—still is." The doctor smiled.

Please God, not the first-grader treatment. "I guess I like math best."

"Really. Why is that?"

"I don't know. It just makes sense, I guess."

"I see," Dr. V said. "Don't other subjects make sense to you?"

Joe pondered this for a moment. "Maybe some. I mean, with language arts, sometimes you think you have it right, and it turns out you don't. Other times you write something you think is just okay, and the teacher makes a big deal out of it, like you're a genius or something."

Dr. Vandenberg laughed his boisterous laugh—the kind that makes littler kids grab onto their mommy's legs for protection.

"Yes, I remember it being like that. So you like things that make sense, then?"

"Yeah, I guess so." *Doesn't everybody?*

"Many people don't think *math* makes sense. You're one of the lucky ones, Joe. I wonder if you could tell me what it is about math that makes it so sensible to you?"

Joe hadn't thought about this before and had to think for a second.

"I guess … probably because the answer's always either right or wrong. And if it's wrong, you can explain why it's wrong."

Dr. V leaned forward in his chair, poking his pen toward Joe.

"You know, Joe, I think you've hit the nail on the head," he said.

No nails, just two-and-a-half-inch exterior-grade decking screws—they hold better.

"Wouldn't it be nice if all of life was like math? It's either right or it's wrong, nothing in between?" Dr. V. used hand gestures a lot to emphasize his points.

"I guess," Joe said with a shrug. He was careful not to give 100 percent yes-or-no answers. He'd fallen into that trap before.

"But life's not like that. Much of it is somewhere in between right and wrong."

Oh boy, here we go. In Joe's mind, he rolled his eyes.

"Like the time we spend working and the time we spend playing," Dr. V said. "It's not right to play all the time, but it's not right to work all the time either. The right answer is somewhere in the middle." He leaned back again. If Dr. V were a smoker, Joe figured this would've been the time to light up.

He shrugged again.

"What I'm saying is that everyone needs to have balance in life, Joe. I won't keep any secrets from you; your mom tells me you spend all your time outside of school either doing homework, or landscaping work, or shoveling snow—"

"Plowing snow."

"Yes, I'm sorry, plowing snow—you don't drive a snow plow, do you? You're only twelve, right?"

"Thirteen. Fourteen in two months."

"Yes, thirteen, forgive me Joe. When you started here with me you were twelve, and time has gone by so quickly."

There was an awkward pause.

"Anyway, as I was saying, your mother says she's concerned you work too hard, that you don't seem to find time for recreation. She says she doesn't see you hanging out with other kids or even playing video games."

It occurred to Joe that his mom could save a lot of money if she'd just tell *him* these things instead of paying the doctor to tell him for her.

"What do you think Joe? What would you say to her about that?"

"I don't know." Joe kept his poker face. "I guess just … don't worry." *Be happy*.

"You know, that's exactly what I told her. I said, 'It's just a phase everyone goes through. He'll decide for himself when he's had enough of working so hard, and he'll start having some fun.'" Dr. V smiled. "I also told her that soon enough she'd be saying, 'Gosh, I wish he'd stop goofing around all the time and do some work for a change.'"

Joe pretended to be amused.

"So here's what I think, Joe. Just for your mother's sake—so she doesn't worry all the time—maybe once in a while you could stay home and, just as an example, play a video game. Or better yet, see if your mom will play with you—or at least watch you play. And maybe you could find a friend at school to invite over to the house to play ball or something. Your mom tells me you have a pretty big backyard."

"Sure Dr. V, no problem." *Anything to get you off my back.*

"Very good, enough said then." He settled back into his chair. "Let's move on, shall we?"

13

Time Management

JOE'S STRESS LEVEL WAS DEFINITELY on the rise. He had to get the condo concealed before school let out, waste time being a normal kid to please Dr. V, study for finals, and start preparing for his persuasive speech.

I wish I were a grown-up. All they have to do is work and make money, then spend it on whatever they want.

Joe rearranged his schedule and reduced his sleep time to accommodate everything he needed to get done. Late-night web-surfing was first to go, since he had to be in bed by nine so he could get up at five to do his reading. The first couple of mornings were a drag; studying before school seemed about as natural as hot wings and soda for breakfast. However, Joe soon found that the morning's peace and quiet along with a freshly rested brain were a good formula for efficient studying. And doing his written homework (like math) the night before eased his mind so he could sleep better.

Mom was worried the first time she woke up and found Joe sitting at the kitchen counter already dressed (except for his prosthetic, which he put on at the last moment) and doing his homework. She'd lectured Joe that he needed to get his homework done the night before so he wouldn't have to rush to get it done in the morning, and he had to reassure her that he wasn't rushing, he was just trying something new.

"Well, as long as you're getting enough sleep and keeping up the grades," she said. "I guess it doesn't matter when you do your homework."

To satisfy Dr. V, Joe spent time with Mom playing chess or cards, or watching TV shows like *Extreme Engineering* and *Megastructures*. Although not a big TV-watcher, Joe liked these; the massive projects they undertook intrigued him, and made his own project seem tiny and doable by comparison.

In one episode, an entire island was created off the coast of Dubai just so someone could build a luxury hotel shaped like a yacht's sail. Mom thought this was ridiculous.

"I don't get it," she said. "Why would they waste so much time, energy, and resources to do such a thing?"

"Because man always has to do bigger and better things than he did before. Otherwise life's boring."

Mom gave Joe an accusing look.

"You men are always trying to prove something, aren't you?"

Joe swallowed. "Whaddya mean?"

"Bigger buildings, faster cars, rockets that go farther and farther into space—why can't you guys just chill out like us women?"

Joe thought for a moment.

"Because you women need us to build you bigger shopping malls and more makeup factories?"

"That's it, buddy!"

Mom launched an all-out tickling assault on Joe. He screamed for mercy, barely able to draw air, and when he could find an opening to speak, threatened to get his fake leg and fend her off with it. Mom replied that the smell of it alone would drive her away.

Joe retaliated with his own tickling attack. Mom screamed and laughed like Joe hadn't seen her do in years.

Thank you, Dr. V—for once your advice was useful!

14

The Rise of Inspector Fred

TWO WEEKS INTO MAY, Joe had the outer and inner walls up and the floor laid. The floor consisted of three-quarter-inch plywood on top of two-by-eight floor joists. The joists were centered at twelve inches, with spacers to keep them solidly aligned. One sheet of plywood remained unscrewed at Fred's request so he could inspect the floor joists.

"Not bad, kid," Fred said.

He'd arrived on site Friday afternoon for the first inspection. His hat had a logo of a largemouth bass jumping from the water, and he wore his hair in a ponytail with a flat carpenter's pencil perched behind his ear. A chrome measuring tape clung to his belt and he carried a clipboard.

"Tent over the hole was a good idea."

"Thanks," Joe said. *So far, so good.*

"Don't thank me yet." Fred climbed down the ladder and as soon as both feet were on the floor, he readied his pencil and pad.

"Inner walls need diagonal strapping," he said as he wrote. "Since you only have studs with no plywood. Outer walls are okay, as long as you put the dirt back evenly all around, and don't completely fill one side at a time."

"What's diagonal strapping?"

"You've seen it before. Take a strip of metal and nail it across the studs at an angle. You should nail it to every two-by-four it crosses, one going this way, one going that way," he said moving his arms to illustrate. "Do it on all four walls. I'll get them for you—on the house."

"Huh?"

"No charge," Fred said. "They cost nearly nothing."

"What're they for?"

"Keep the walls from swaying."

"They're solid. They won't sway."

"I see." Fred stepped closer to one of the walls and began to push in successive heaves.

The inner walls rocked back and forth. Joe winced and Fred stopped.

"Don't argue with the building inspector."

Joe looked away, somewhat embarrassed. To him, a 120-pound one-legged schoolboy, the walls had seemed solid enough.

Fred continued. How deep was he planning on running the main electric cable? How was he going to feed it through the outer wall and keep it watertight? Where was he going to put the grounding stake? How was he planning to wrap the outer walls with moisture barrier?

Joe winced again. "But the outside wall is pressure-treated lumber. It doesn't hurt it to get wet."

"Are all the cracks sealed between those two-by-eights? Hmmm? Water may not hurt the outside wall, but it can get through to your inside wall, your drywall, your flooring. Do you want that?"

"How will I get moisture barrier on those walls now?" Joe said. "I can't get in that narrow gap."

"You're a bright kid—I'm sure you'll figure it out." Fred tapped his pencil on the clipboard. "Rule number two: don't argue with the building inspector."

Joe kicked a scrap of wood and sent it spinning across the floor.

"What's rule number one, then?"

Fred's eyes narrowed and his muscles tightened as he moved to within a few inches of Joe's face, breathing stale-beer vapors on him.

"Who brought you all this stuff?"

"You did."

"Wrong! Who brought you all this stuff?"

Joe faltered. "I … I … I found it."

"Well that's one hell of a find—a generator, power tools, and all this lumber. Where, Joe? Where did you find it?"

"I don't know." Joe wanted to go curl up in a corner.

"You'd better know!" Fred was shouting now. "When the man's looking you straight in the eye and asking who helped you get all these materials, you'd better know. Did Fred Fergussen help you get this stuff?"

Joe stared at him with a blank expression.

"Answer the question, son. Did Fred Fergussen help you get this stuff?"

"N-no."

"You sure? You don't sound too sure."

"Yes!" There was a hint of frustration in Joe's voice.

"Yes what? Yes, Fred Fergussen helped you with this project? It was his idea that you deface forest preserve land? That you steal electricity from the city and violate numerous building codes in the process? He's the one who endangered your life both building and inhabiting this structure? Is that what you're saying?"

"NO!" Joe stomped his foot. "It was my idea! I drove my dad's truck at night and picked up stuff from construction jobs that Fred worked on. He used to work with my dad so I knew how to get it. I left him an envelope with cash to replace what I'd taken because I didn't want to be stealing it. *I* hooked up the wire to the streetlight, but I volunteer at the Palos library to make up for using that electricity. Fred Fergussen had *nothing* to do with this!"

Joe was breathing hard now, his face hot, on the verge of tears.

Fred looked surprised. "That's why you've been volunteering at the library?"

Joe nodded, still panting.

Fred's expression softened. He tore off the sheet he'd written on and handed it to Joe.

"Fix these," he said. "I'll come back to check again, then we'll move on."

Joe glared.

You did that on purpose. More humbly than before he said, "What *is* rule number one?"

"Rule number one," Fred said, "is that it's wrong to only be looking out for number one."

"Huh?"

"Google it. I'll have more stuff for you tomorrow morning at Drop-Point Charlie."

15

That Day

AT THE LIBRARY, JOE BARCODED BOOKS. His hands worked fast, but his mind was elsewhere. He looked up and noticed a familiar face among the stacks. It was the Asian girl—the one he went to Algonquin with.

What's her name?

He watched as she pulled books from the shelf, flipping them over to read their back covers. He'd known her since he was in first grade, when she was in kindergarten. Joe didn't know the names of many kids in other grades, but he'd seen *her* name on the artwork and stories stapled up outside her classroom, and more than once he'd heard her name called out in the school's hallways.

What was it though?

She rounded the corner to the next aisle and Joe lost sight of her. He turned his attention back to the non-fiction books stacked in front of him and pulled out *The Modern Skier's Bible*. The front cover pictured "modern" ski equipment featuring lace-up leather boots attached to straight skinny planks of real wood.

This was just the sort of book Mom would want to weed from the collection. Normally he'd bring it to her attention, but skiing wasn't a subject he wanted to bring up around Mom.

***

Almost a year and a half ago, he and Dad had gone shopping for Mom, six days before Christmas. It was one of the rare times Dad drove Mom's little red Honda instead of his full-sized pickup. Dad was Gigantor in the Civic; even after he put the seat all the way back and tilted up the steering wheel, he still had to squeeze in. They would have taken Dad's pickup, but Mom needed it for some "big" Christmas shopping of her own.

Mom wasn't easy to shop for. Dad knew better than to buy her books, or anything book related. With Mom being a librarian and all, everyone's bright idea was to get her "booky" gifts. He also refused to get her a gift card. Dad said that was just another way of saying "Here … I'm too busy to put much thought into a gift for you, so go get it yourself."

Mom wasn't a big jewelry person either, and perfume bothered her sinuses. Clothing? Too complicated. Kitchen gadgets and appliances? According to Dad, they were sometimes a hit and sometimes a disaster. He said one day he'd explain how bra-burning and Helen Reddy made it harder for men to shop for women.

So that day, Joe and his dad ended up at a ski shop. Dad had a great idea to get Mom a complete ski outfit: jacket, bibs, gloves, hat, and goggles. It was clothing, but Dad felt they could hardly go wrong with ski clothes. Joe suggested getting her a pair of skis too, but Dad said it wasn't worth the investment since they were lucky to ski once a year. Besides, you could always rent ski equipment, just not ski clothes, and Dad said what Mom wore the last time they went skiing was too frumpy for a woman of her *elegant beauty*.

***

When Joe looked up, he saw the girl again, this time at the checkout counter with Helen. Her eyes were big black dots with lush upper eyelashes and modest lower ones. Her hair was cut in thin jagged bangs over her forehead, revealing soft whispers of eyebrows. Shiny black hair flowed alongside her face and splashed gently onto her shoulders. Joe thought she looked like a girl from a Japanese anime book.

She laughed at something Helen said and her whole body bounced. Seemed like she'd changed a lot the past couple years.

Helen pointed to the bookmarks on the counter and the girl picked one. Through the office window, Joe could see her lips form "thank you" and "bye" as she waved to Helen and Liz and turned to leave. He wanted to ask Helen her name, but that would be embarrassing, and her name would be erased from the monitor by the next customer.

Joe breathed a heavy sigh. *Elegant beauty.*

***

Going to the ski shop had been more fun than he'd expected. Whereas shopping for normal clothing made him feel tired all over, ski clothes were bright and sometimes weird. Within a few seconds, Dad was in an aisle full of hats. He put one on that sported Rastafarian dreadlocks and proceeded toward women's wear.

"Ya, Joe, we must go to da jaa-keets now." Dad did a pretty decent Jamaican accent and Joe laughed. It was good to see Dad smile after all he'd been through with the lawyers—the anguish and the money he'd lost for something that wasn't even his fault. Maybe things would be okay again.

Together, Joe and his dad picked out a sharp white-and-powder-blue ski jacket with something like fifty tags hanging from it. That was when Dad said something that still stuck with him.

"It takes two men to figure out the taste of one woman." And as he made that statement, he'd looked Joe in the eye, taking time out from his silliness to make it clear to his son that he *did* view him as a man.

That meant a lot to Joe, since Dad's emotions were like rare coins: mostly kept in the safe and only displayed on special occasions under tight guard.

***

Joe applied another barcode to a book spine and leaned back, looking at the cover without really seeing it. Dad trusted him and could count on him.

I'm doing the right thing Dad. It's worth doing.

Mom made her way over.

"How's it going, honey?"

For the first time in a long while, Joe really looked at his mom. There was nothing frumpy about her black side-buttoned cashmere turtleneck and stonewashed jeans, or the round rubies set in silver dangling from her ears. She *was* a woman of elegant beauty.

"Good, Mom," Joe said with a smile. "Doing good."

16

Not as Dumb as He Looks

DR. V WAS WEARING THE SAME orange Hawaiian flowered shirt he'd had on two weeks ago, probably size XXXL. The folder labeled "McKinnon, Joseph" lay on the desk behind him and he held his dark cherry-wood pen with gold trim poised over his legal pad.

"Your mom tells me you've been spending more time together—that is, you and she have," Dr. V said.

"That's what you said to do, right?" Joe said.

"Yes …"

The way the doctor stretched out his reply told Joe he hadn't answered properly.

"Did it seem to you like a chore?" Dr. V said. "Like something you *had* to do?"

"No, it was okay."

"Just okay?"

"Actually, we had a lot of fun. We watched TV and played some games." Joe tried to sound extra upbeat to make up for his earlier tone.

"Good! That's exceptional, Joe."

What's so exceptional about playing games and watching TV?

"And I bet your mom was pleased you chose to spend more time with her as well."

"Yeah, I think she was."

"How about spending time with your friends?"

In reality, Joe didn't have close friends anymore. Before the accident, he'd hung out with Nick, who lived across the street, and some other kids he'd sometimes played with after school. After the accident, more kids than ever had wanted to be his friend, which he'd chalked up to either pity for his missing leg or curiosity about his prosthetic. What grade-schooler wouldn't want bragging rights for being friends with a one-legged kid? But Joe didn't want to be around anyone (except Mom—and sometimes, Fred), especially now, when he had important things to do.

"I hang with kids at school." *Not a total lie.*

"Oh? Who are they?"

Dang. Think fast. "Well, there's Nick, and Uriel, and … Andy, and the other Nick, and Jack, and Antonio, and Jun …" *Jun—that was her name!*

Nothing escaped Dr. V. "Tell me about Jun."

"There's not much to tell. She plays the flute. I think maybe she's from China."

"That's interesting. What's her last name?"

C'mon, c'mon, what's a Chinese name … "Wong. Jun Wong."

"Yes, that would be a Chinese name," Dr. V said nodding. "You and Jun—do you have a lot in common?"

"I s'pose." Joe was offering nothing extra now. Dr. V was a bloodhound.

Silence.

"Such as?"

"We both like to play chess."

"Excellent! I happen to love the game myself. Maybe we'll play sometime during one of our sessions."

"Sure." *Beats talking.*

"Do you hang out with any of your friends *after* school?"

"Sometimes." This was getting tricky. "Me and one of the guys go shoot some hoops after school sometimes, while Mom's still at work."

"And how often would you say you do that?"

"I don't know. Maybe two or three times a week. Depends on what my friends have going on, you know—homework, piano lessons, stuff like that." *Sounds believable to me.*

"Well good. I'm glad to hear you're spending time with people your age. It's very important to do that. Tell me Joe, do you ever sit down and talk to your friends about your feelings?"

Joe laughed. "No way. That's totally gay."

Dr. V flinched. "Even grown men need to talk about their feelings, Joe, and even big strong men sometimes break down and cry … and that's okay. That's quite normal."

Joe squirmed.

"I'm sure your friend Fred has cried. And I'll bet you your father shared some of his deeper feelings with your mom and maybe even with his best friends."

Dr. V studied Joe for a response, but there was none. Whenever Dr. V mentioned his father it made his insides ache. All those sessions being probed and prodded, while someone tried to unlock his secret compartments—drilling holes in his psyche to relieve pressure—trying to prevent some future emotional cancer with psychological broccoli. Maybe there was some benefit, but Joe just wanted to sort it out by himself.

"Do you ever tell Fred how you feel?"

Nope. "Sometimes, but that's different."

"Why is that different?" He scribbled on his pad, underlining whatever he'd written.

"He's just Fred. You know."

"You mean he's easy to talk to?"

"Yeah. He doesn't tell me I'm stupid. He doesn't tell me what to do." *Unless he's the building inspector.* "He just listens."

"Not many people have that talent these days." Dr. V sighed.

"Uh-huh."

"If you don't mind my asking, Joe, do you and Fred ever talk about your father?"

"No, but he understands."

"Understands what?"

"I can't really explain it. He just knows."

"I see." Dr. V looked troubled and wrote some more.

"Did Fred go through a similar experience, losing someone he loved in an accident?"

"Probably," Joe said.

"Did he tell you so?"

"No, it's just … I think just about everything that can happen to a person happened to Fred." Joe almost smiled.

"Joe, I'm going to be blunt here." Dr. V straightened up in his chair, then leaned toward his patient. "Do you ever tell Fred, or anybody else, how much you miss your father?"

He flinched. "No—I mean yes."

"This is important, Joe, is it yes, or is it no?"

"I … uh … forgot the question."

"Do you ever tell anyone how much you miss your father?"

"Yes."

"Are you sure now? At first you said no."

A tear dribbled down his cheek.

"Yes."

Dr. V handed Joe a box of tissues.

"Who?"

"Fred."

Dr. V sighed.

"Joe, I know this isn't easy for you. Talking about feelings isn't easy—especially those that come from painful experiences. But it's important that you *do* talk about them."

Dr. V put the pad on his desk and folded his hands together.

"You've been through a lot more than most kids your age. When you were only twelve, your father died right next to you in a serious automobile accident. And to make matters worse, you lost your leg. And if *that* wasn't enough, all this happened just a week before Christmas. Those memories are still there, and your mind wants to process them."

The memories *were* there. That light-spirited moment driving home from the ski shop replaced by that kid's Nissan pickup crashing through Dad's window. The pressure of Dad pushed hard against him, making it difficult to breathe. Cold pain in his leg. People who'd stopped to help, who he could hear but couldn't see—the concern in their voices. A woman crying—not Mom—Mom wasn't there. Flashing blue and red lights. Voices scratching in and out on police radios. So many "Oh My Gods." Someone yelling, "I think *this* guy's okay." Then sirens, followed by the rumbling diesel engines of the fire trucks—the hiss and squeal of their brakes as they pulled up. The smell of the Nissan's hot engine coolant leaking into the Civic—onto Dad. Wanting to turn and look at Dad, but not being able to. *Dad? Dad are you okay?* The firemen talking to him: "It's all right son, we're gonna get you out of there. It might be a little loud." *Dad?* Metal crunching, squealing, tearing. *Dad?*

Dr. V was still speaking. "… so even if you *try* to ignore them, your mind won't let you. It may let you ignore it for a while, but someday it will *make* you pay attention."

"I don't want to tell you." Joe began to shake.

"Why not?"

"I just don't." He shoved the tissues back. "It's not important."

"Joe, when I see someone crying over a question they were asked, I tend to believe it was important to them."

Joe turned away, wiping his eyes with the backs of his hands.

"If not Fred, then who? Who do you tell how much you miss your father?"

"This is such bullshit." The sound of his own words made him even madder. "What difference does it make? I don't have to tell you anything!"

"That's it Joe, letting out your anger is better than—"

Joe jumped from the couch, leaned toward Dr. V, and clenched his fists.

"Go eat a dozen donuts and leave me alone, you fat-ass!!" Then he bolted out the door.

"Joe … wait! Please, don't go." Dr. V was not quick to follow.

Joe ran past his mother in the waiting room.

"I'm not coming here anymore!" And he flew from the office.

***

"You want to talk about it?" Mom said as they followed the rush-hour current on Cicero Avenue. She took a sip of her Sprite and kept it ready for another.

"No." Joe leaned his head against the door's window.

"You had the doctor a little flustered. What did you say to him?"

"I told him he was fat and to go eat a dozen donuts."

If Mom had been taking a drink at that moment, it surely would have sprayed everywhere.

"You didn't!" She tried to suppress her laugh.

"I did." Joe perked up a little.

It took a minute for Mom to settle back down.

"Well if you decide you need to talk about it, I'm here for you, honey."

Joe stole glances at his mom. The ski outfit he and Dad had bought for Mom would have looked good on her. Didn't matter; he doubted he and his mother would ever go skiing again.

I miss you Dad. Mom misses you too.

17

The Stump, the Call

AS SOON AS THEY GOT HOME, Joe asked if he could go out for a while. Mom agreed, on the condition he'd be back in an hour for dinner.

He hopped on his bike and pedaled with a vengeance to Ground Thirteen. The site was just as he'd left it, with the addition of a few tree sheddings and a puddle of rain water on the tarp.

Joe dug up the cell phone in its plastic bag, powered it up, and set it on the backhoe seat. Its boot-up welcome tune played as he climbed into the hole. He had no desire to speak to Fred, but rules were rules—the phone *had* to be turned on.

And of course, there was rule number one: *don't always be looking out for number one.* Joe had gone online to look up the phrase as Fred had suggested. He found multiple songs with that title, and an interesting mathematical formula for calculating the percentage of time that a number begins with a certain digit. But he also found the phrase's meaning: "to act in a manner primarily advantageous to oneself."

In other words, it means to be selfish.

Joe had spent much of the weekend making the changes Fred dictated. Nailing up the diagonal strapping was a piece of cake, and covering the outer walls with moisture barrier turned out to be easier than he expected; he just stood the roll up on end and unrolled it, pulling it around the walls and taking it slow so he didn't tear it.

The next order of business was the stump entrance—one of Joe's biggest concerns. The thirty-eight-inch-diameter oak stump would have its top sliced off to lid-thickness, then hinged on later after hollowing out the stump.

He'd enter the condo by lifting the top and climbing down a ladder affixed to the inside of the stump. Narrow, yes—but at least he wouldn't have to worry about Dr. V visiting. A secret catch would keep it latched when shut and at the bottom there would be a regular door with a key lock leading into the condo so that anyone who happened to stumble upon the stump entrance still couldn't get inside.

Joe had studied tree root systems on the Internet and learned that some trees had taproots growing many feet below ground. Digging had revealed that *this* stump had a taproot nearly five feet long. It would be tough to remove, which was why he'd decided to wait until later to deal with it.

Later was now. Joe surveyed the task ahead of him; he'd already been planning how to tackle this. First, he'd hand-dig to expose the big taproot and the other roots as much as possible. Then he'd cut away what pieces he could with the reciprocating saw. He'd repeat this process until it was cleared underneath. Joe knew it would take time, but he felt confident he could do it.

Hollowing out the stump would be even tougher. The best Joe could figure was to do a combination of drilling, cutting, and chiseling. He guessed this would be time-consuming, but there was no way to know just how hard it would be until he got into it.

He started digging his entryway with different sized shovels, hand-diggers, and the reciprocating saw, throwing his diggings and cuttings into the backhoe's lowered bucket. The tap root was nearly the diameter of the stump at ground level, so Joe cut it below the surface where it was only about a foot across. The piece (which nearly fell on his foot) was almost too heavy for him to lift into the bucket.

He didn't accomplish a lot in an hour, but it gave him a chance to test the methodology and get a better look at the stump he'd soon be hollowing. His concern grew about how much time this thing would take to finish.

Joe went up to the backhoe and brought it to life. He pulled up the bucket, emptied it on the dirt pile, and readied the backhoe for shutdown, calling it quits for the day. He climbed down with the phone in his hand, but before he could shut it off, Fred called.

"Hi Fred."

"Peg Leg! What's goin' on?"

Fred sounded more jovial than Joe wanted to deal with right now. And what was up with calling him Peg Leg again?

"Eh … not much. Just digging under the stump."

"That's easy. You oughtta be done by Labor Day!" Fred sounded different—like the way people talk after getting a cavity filled, before the Novocain wears off.

"You just get back from the dentist or something?"

Fred laughed.

"Naw," he said. "Just tired from a tough day at work, buddy."

"Oh."

There was loud music playing in the background, a lot of people chattering—a woman's scream of laughter. Fred took his mouth away from the phone and said something Joe couldn't make out. Then he started having a conversation with someone, covering the phone so Joe couldn't hear it, but he heard it anyway. Some of the words coming out of Fred weren't nice.

"I … I better go. Mom wants me home for dinner now."

No answer.

"Fred?"

Still no answer.

"Fred?"

"I'm here buddy, what can I do fer ya?"

"Uh, nothing. You called me, remember?"

"Oh yeah!" Fred laughed again. "Just checkin' that I'm okay buddy. I mean …" He chuckled. "I mean that *you're* okay, pal."

"I'm fine. Thanks for calling. Bye, Fred." Joe hung up and turned off the phone, afraid Fred might call back. He put the phone back in the bag and went to where he kept it buried.

Joe remembered a time not too long ago when he'd walked past Biker Man Jerry's garage. He'd seen a bunch of guys hanging out there with Harley emblems on the backs of their denim vests and oversized wallets and chains on their jeans. The way they talked to each other was how Fred sounded: animated, obnoxious, laughing at everything.

Beer makes people crazy.

Joe tried to put it out of his mind as he spread leaves over the spot where he buried the phone. He didn't want to think about his dad's friend—*his* friend—drinking.

Son, troubles run the fastest races. It's no good to try and run away from them ... they'll always catch up to you.

18

Mom-a-roni and Crawdads

"WHERE'D YOU GO IN SUCH A HURRY?" Mom said after they'd nearly finished one of Joe's favorite dinners: macaroni and cheese with slices of hot dog and bacon mixed in. Joe knew his mom made it to soften him up.

"Just down to the creek," he said.

"Anything interesting down there?"

"Crawdads."

He couldn't look at his mom when he lied so he peered out the back window at a family of deer foraging in the garden. Mom said Palos Ranchos was the opposite of the rest of the planet: while the rest of the world was losing its forests, their neighborhood was turning into a suburban woodland.

Last July, after the annual neighborhood picnic, old Mr. Pruitt set up an eight-millimeter projector and screen. While swatting man-eating mosquitoes under the canopy of Mr. Pruitt's mulberry tree, the neighbors watched a jumpy, flickering, lint-spattered panorama of Palos Ranchos in the fifties. Huge empty lots, almost an acre each, were sparsely populated with the neighborhood's first few homes and freshly planted saplings—Mr. Pruitt's mulberry had been no taller than Joe. There were also weeping willows and silver aspens in their early years, easy prey for a harsh Illinois storm.

Back then, the Evans' house was lonely and under construction. Its most prominent features were a mortar-splashed cement mixer in a gravel driveway and stacks of brick waiting to be laid over the plywood walls. Oak Street and Woodside Lane were just gravel roads, and one could see all along 127th Avenue, two whole blocks away, with nothing to obstruct the view.

This snapshot of Palos Ranchos had fascinated Joe. The neighborhood back then was open and sunny, a completely different landscape.

Then the movie switched scenes, and there were "ahs" and "ohs" among the neighbors as someone said, "Look—it's Nancy!" Mr. Pruitt smiled as the camera focused on his young wife with her blue-rimmed cat-eye sunglasses, waving at the camera. She wore a babushka so only her curved bangs showed. Mrs. Anderson's lips began to tremble and Mom comforted the elderly woman as she dabbed at her eyes with a napkin.

While Joe was reminiscing, Mom spooned the leftover macaroni into a plastic container.

"When was the last time you went to the creek with Nicky?" she said.

"He doesn't like to be called Nicky anymore."

"Well then Nicholas, or Nick. How come you don't see him anymore? You used to be such good friends."

"We're still friends. We just like to do different things now. He's really into sports."

Mom frowned. "Sometimes people go in different directions, honey. It happens to grown-ups too."

"Hmm." Joe scraped his macaroni remnants into a cheesy collage.

"Joe?"

"Yeah?" His eyes barely held on to hers.

"You don't have to go back to Dr. V right away."

She reached across the table for his hand, and he let her take it.

"Okay." He tried swallowing away the lump in his throat. *That nosy fat-ass.*

"I'd like you to go back when school starts up again, after summer, but if you decide you want to go back sooner—"

"When school starts is good."

"That should give you some time to reflect, and I know you'll enjoy your summer more if you have a break from *everything*."

"Okay." Joe pulled back his hand.

Mom took the cue. "So what *do* you want to do this summer?"

"I don't know. Just hang, do a few jobs. Maybe go fishing. Maybe we could go camping at Lake Shelbyville?"

As soon as he said it though, he realized how awkward it would be. Moms and sons didn't go camping and fishing together—not unless dads were there to protect them.

"That sounds like huge fun, honey. Can you teach me to build a fire and clean fish?"

Too late—she was serious. "Yeah Mom, no problem!"

Dad was born to camp. Missing a tent pole? Dad would tie ropes from nearby trees to hold the tent up. Forgot the lantern? Dad had a light in his tool box that he'd hook to the extra car battery. Fish don't bite on worms today? Dad knew why: maybe the lake was too high, which meant you needed *this* kind of minnow rig, or maybe the water was too low, which required *that* kind of spinner jig reeled in a certain way. There was nothing to worry about when Dad was there.

Mom could hold her own here in the city, where all you needed were helpful neighbors, nearby stores, and the Internet, but if they went camping this summer, it would be up to Joe to keep Mom safe.

He considered saying Fred should go too. But the thought of Fred sleeping near him and his mom, even in a separate tent, was too weird. Besides, Fred had been drunk on the phone. What if he brought beer and drank too much around the campfire? Not good. Fred was fine as a prosthetic father figure—good for day-long fishing trips and help with the condo—but there was no way he was going camping with Joe and his mom.

"Joe?"

"Mom?"

"I know how much you miss your father."

"You miss him too, Mom."

She smiled. "But not as much as you do."

Joe gave her a quizzical look.

"Every time I look at you I see your father," she said. "So for me, it's like part of him is still here."

"But everyone always says I look more like you than Dad."

Mom smiled.

"It's what's inside of you that makes you like your father. And *I* know what's inside of you better than anyone else."

Dad was fearless and honest and had a solution for every problem.

Does she really think I'm like that?

All of a sudden he wanted to tell his mom everything— about the condo, Dr. V, all his fears and worries … what would she think about her son then?

"I'm kind of tired," he said. "Think I'll go to bed early tonight."

"You do look tired, honey. But you should shower first— you don't want to put that dirty face on your pillow."

Joe felt his face. He'd used the hose outside to rinse his arms, but didn't think his face had gotten dirty too.

"Those crawdads must've been pretty big to splash up so much mud," Mom said.

"Yeah, they were monsters." Joe kissed her on the cheek. "I'm tired, gonna go to bed after my shower. Goodnight Mom."

***

In the shower, Joe brooded over his persuasive speech, which was just two weeks away.

Mr. Z said they could use props if they wanted, which was a great idea as far as Joe was concerned—something to divert the class's stares. He'd thought about doing a presentation on his future invention—the whole reason he was building the condo—but the complexity of those props would require too much time, and that was something he couldn't afford right now.

However, another idea was coming to the forefront of his thoughts: solar power. He got the idea from the solar science kit sitting on his shelf. The kit could even be one of his props, but somehow that didn't seem cool enough.

Whatever he was going to do, he'd have to come up with a plan fast. In just two days, they had to tell Mr. Z their topic choice.

Mom knocked. "Save some water for the fishes!"

"Okay!"

He turned off the water and stepped out of the shower, thinking about the condo as he dried himself off. The last day of the school year would've been the Friday after Memorial Day, but six snow days in January and February added six days to the end of the year, giving him a total of four more weeks until school was out. He was probably the only kid at HMS happy to have those extra school days.

When school let out, there'd be lots of kids in the woods looking for something to do. Some would be down at the creek using the rope swing, fishing, or building dams. Others might be searching for a prime spot to build a fort. His perimeter warning signs might scare off one lone kid, but a pack of kids would just see them as a dare.

Right now, the biggest obstacle to getting the condo covered was the stump entrance. Time was running short. Some sacrifice would have to be made … and the more he thought about it, the more he knew what that sacrifice would be.

19

The Ditch, the Hole

AT 1:59 PM ON TUESDAY, in the back of Mr. Z's class, Joe unfolded a piece of paper bearing the McKinnon Contracting LLC logo and gave it a final once-over. He refolded the note and slid it back into his front pocket just as the bell rang.

When the late bell for seventh period rang at 2:05, the other kids were already changing into their PE uniforms. Joe stood in front of Mr. Lomas, listening to his own words being read back to him.

> To Whom It May Concern,
>
> Please excuse my son Joseph McKinnon from PE for the rest of this week. He has discomfort with his prosthetic. He will be getting it adjusted on Friday after school and should be able to participate in PE again by Monday. If possible please let Joe go to the library instead so he may work on his report for his language-arts class.
>
> Thank You,
>
> Lori McKinnon

Mr. Lomas pulled a pen off his clipboard, clicked it into operational position, and wrote on Joe's note:

He tore off the makeshift pass and handed it to Joe.

"Give that to the librarian, and get yourself taken care of so you can join us Monday. We'll be starting softball next week." He said it with the most cordiality he'd ever showed, which is to say, he wasn't berating or yelling at Joe.

"Thanks, Mr. Lomas."

Wearing his backpack, Joe limped away from the gymnasium the same way he'd limped in. He glanced back through the door's wire-mesh window to see if Mr. Lomas's eyes were following. Convinced he was in the clear, he turned the opposite direction of the media center, scooted down the hall, and exited through the school's side entrance.

He'd left his bike chained to a tree behind the school because there were no windows there. Within minutes, he was past the farmer's field and cruising through the parking lot of the grocery store where Mom shopped.

He didn't feel too bad about skipping PE; he'd get way more exercise working on the condo than doing calisthenics. Plus, PE was the last class of the day, so he wouldn't miss anything important like assignments or tests. What's more, HMS wasn't doing end-of-day homeroom this year—a district middle school experiment meant to add teaching time to the school day—and there was no attendance taken in the library.

All of which added up to an extra hour and fifteen minutes every day to work on the condo, and one less kid crowding the school exits at three fifteen. It was what grown-ups called a win-win situation.

Joe bypassed his neighborhood, entering the field from the edge of Palos Estadas near the golf course. He pedaled past a dead-end barrier, between dirt-pile moguls, and onto the trail that led to the woods containing Ground Thirteen. This part of the trail was straight, smooth, and overgrowth-free. It was a bicycle freeway.

He hadn't noticed how windy it was until he approached the woods and saw the upper branches of the mighty oaks swaying rhythmically. There was a constant, low *whooooosh* from the canopy; part of Joe wanted to lie back on the forest's cushiony floor and be hypnotized by the theater of leaves that swayed and flipped in the rush of spring air. But he hadn't risked getting in trouble just to mess around playing Huck Finn. There was a tangle of roots to deal with and time was precious.

Ground Thirteen had survived another day without vandalism, for which Joe was grateful; it seemed like whenever people found something unattended, they had to deface it in some way. Each day he worried he'd find the hole filled in, the tools stolen, or the condo burned.

He dug up the cell phone, but left it turned off. He'd turn it on at three thirty, the time he usually arrived at Ground Thirteen.

Soon, fresh sawdust sprinkled the dirt. The shovel sliced into compacted soil, making a thunk whenever it hit a root. He worked at a solid pace, knocking away the dirt, prying at the roots, cutting away that which hung free. It was a mesmerizing process. He breathed with a runner's cadence, unaware of the energy he was expending, the sweat that doused his shirt, or even the progress he was making. His end goal was now incidental to his journey.

Three hours passed as the pile of excavated dirt and roots grew, and the hole beneath the stump got deeper and wider.

"Hey!" said a stern voice from the other side of the hole. "What're you doing?"

Joe turned so fast he forgot to move his prosthetic with him, lost balance, and fell. He looked up and saw Fred, thumbs hooked in his jean pockets. He seemed amused.

"Oh crap, the phone," Joe said. He only now realized just how hard he'd been working as his lungs worked to catch up with his body's oxygen demand.

"Yeah, 'oh crap, the phone.'"

"I just ..."

"I know, I know." Fred waved it off, then stroked his goatee as he peeked past Joe at what he'd accomplished under the stump. "It was bound to happen. Everyone makes mistakes you know. It's even been rumored that *I* made a mistake once." There was no sign of humor in his expression.

Joe decided not to mention Fred's last phone call.

"You're really goin' to town on that secret entrance of yours. How much digging you got left?"

"Maybe another day or two. Then I start hollowing out the stump."

"Any idea on how you're going to accomplish that, Einstein?"

"I think I know what to do."

"Enlighten me."

"Drill, cut, and chisel."

"Sounds pretty tedious. What year did you say you were planning to finish this?"

"What would *you* do?" He knew Fred was about to suggest something he wouldn't like, so might as well get it over with.

"I'd probably yank the stump altogether."

Figures. "No, really."

"I'm serious—I'd pull it." Fred smirked. But if the boss said I *had* to leave it there *and* put a hole through it, I'd use a chainsaw."

"You didn't bring me one of those." Joe resumed digging. "And I can't find Dad's."

"Damn right you can't. I made sure of that the day after you told me you were going to make a secret entrance out of that thing."

Joe stopped. "How'd you do that?"

"I borrowed it from your mom. She said to keep it as long as I want." His stare challenged Joe. "Reckon I will."

"How come?"

"Because knowing that steel-trap of a brain you got in there, after about a half hour of using small hand tools, you'd be saying to yourself 'there's got to be a better way,' and in another half hour, you'd be back here with the chainsaw, which you ain't big enough to handle the *right* way, let alone the way you'd have to use it to get the job done, and about a half minute after that, you'd have the same number of arms left as you have legs."

"Oh."

"You'll thank me when you're thirty or so and using both those arms to toss your kids up in the air."

"I'm not having kids," Joe said. "They're too sneaky."

"You don't say?"

Joe crossed his arms. "I can do it without the chainsaw."

"Knock yourself out. Call me if after a week or two, you're only three inches into it." Fred seemed genuine. "I don't mind helping out, you know."

"Thanks." Joe turned back to his digging. *Now I have to hollow it out myself.*

Fred lowered his voice. "Joe … about yesterday … on the phone …"

Joe picked the earth with his shovel.

"I was just celebrating … someone's birthday, and had one beer too many."

"Okay."

"I didn't mean to scare you or anything."

"It was fine, really." But it wasn't.

"Sometimes grown-ups … we get all wound up with stress and everything, and once in a while we need to do some unwinding, and … well … sometimes we have a drink or two to help with that." He chuckled. "And sometimes we get a little too unwound."

Joe pitched his shovel into the ground and gave Fred an accusing stare.

"Did you get home all right?"

Fred seemed surprised.

"Yeah, sure Joe, no problem. Thanks for asking."

"I meant did you drive yourself home?"

Fred coughed. "Yeah, after I sobered up a bit."

They stared at each other in a wordless argument.

"Did you listen to my voice message yesterday?" Fred said. "The one I left before we talked?"

Joe went back to poking the dirt with his shovel.

"Didn't know you left one."

Fred sighed. "I'd better get going. You be careful now." He gave Joe an impassive wave and left.

Joe waited until he was gone before climbing up to the backhoe, where he picked up the phone and sat down. In a few seconds, he was listening to the message Fred left yesterday.

"Hey Joe." Fred let out a heavy breath. It sounded like he was in his truck—there was the ding like that of an open door with the key left in the ignition.

"It's about … uh … three o' clock, and I was just calling to see if—cuz today's my son's birthday and, well, I can't be with Phelps since he's in California with the b—with his mother. So, I was thinking, if you and your mom didn't think it was too weird, that we could go out for ice cream tonight and y'all could help me celebrate Phelps's birthday. Give me a call."

Joe put down the phone. He didn't think it was weird at all.

He picked up the phone again. "Hey, Fred … do you still want to do ice cream sometime?"

20

Fred-Extra

MOST PEOPLE DON'T OWN a pair of one-legged jeans, but Joe did. One might think that the one-legged-jeans of a person missing their right leg would have the right side cut off, but Joe's one-legged jeans had the left leg removed and vent holes cut in the thigh portion of the right leg, which let his natural leg *and* his stump breathe while his prosthetic stayed covered. He'd learned early on that a sweaty stump is an itchy stump, and an itch you can't get to without pulling off your pants is a nuisance. So on Saturday before he began the day's work, Joe changed into his one-legged jeans at the condo.

He felt guilty for not working at the library today, but promised himself he'd put in extra hours once the condo was hidden.

Joe was looking forward to hollowing out the stump, but before he could start that, he'd need to finish the entrance walls, because shaking the stump could make the dirt in that area cave in. While a side cave-in would be disastrous, dirt dropping from directly *above* was inevitable, and not an issue; replacing it later, when the roof was on, would be easy. Fortunately, the mighty oak stump's lateral roots branched out far enough to hold it in place while Joe worked under it.

Yesterday, he'd built the entrance floor and connected it to the main floor. He'd also begun the entrance walls, using the same double-wall construction as before. These walls, along with a beefed-up ceiling structure, would need to be strong enough to buttress the weight of the stump, in case its roots ever gave out. If the entrance caved in, the condo could become his tomb—just one more concern of Building Inspector Fred's.

Joe began cutting his lumber. He measured out the correct length and marked it on the wood. He then aligned the mark with the miter saw's laser line, grabbed the saw handle, and placed his finger on the trigger.

Suddenly, Joe jumped back from the saw. Up on the edge of the hole in front of him was a German shepherd, its head hunkered down below its shoulders, surveying the condo. From time to time it glanced at Joe, but seemed to think he was just one interesting object among many.

"What are you doing there, son?" a voice boomed out from above and behind.

Joe froze, afraid to turn and see who it was. Whoever it was up there was a big cloud that could rain an awful lot of trouble on him.

Joe swallowed hard. "Nothing much."

I was hired by an NIU professor to dig for Potawatomi Indian artifacts? How stupid that sounded now—he hadn't even thought to change the story once the digging was done.

"Doesn't look like nothing much to me," the voice said. "In fact, I'd say it looks quite like something." He had a way of articulating that reminded Joe of someone who narrated TV commercials.

"Just doing my job." *And now you'll ask me what that job is, won't you?*

"And a darned good one too."

Joe turned around to face his interrogator. The man was much older than he'd sounded. He wore a maroon apron with safety goggles stuffed in its pocket. He had a dust mask pulled up onto his forehead and red marks on either side of his nose from where the mask had rested. It was old Mr. Pruitt.

"You're the McKinnon boy, aren't you?" he said.

"Yes sir." Joe gulped. "I'm Joe."

"Man-o-live. I've seen many a fort built in these woods over the past fifty-odd years, but this one takes the cake."

Crap. He's got me pegged. "Thanks, Mr. Pruitt."

"I've been hearing sounds for the past month or so. I guess that was you, wasn't it?"

"Guess so, Mr. Pruitt." Joe stared at the man who now held his future in his hands.

"It sounded so much farther away. Did you put up all that carpeting just to absorb noise?"

"Yes sir."

"Incredible," he said. "You didn't do all this by yourself, did you? Digging the hole? Building these walls? Bringing in all this lumber and these tools?

"Yes sir, I did." *Don't mention Fred.*

Mr. Pruitt whistled. "Son, I'm impressed. Really, I am."

Joe blushed. He felt his blood pressure drop a notch or two. "Thanks Mr. Pruitt. You really like it?"

"Well, aside from being completely illegal, I'd say this is a fine example of what a boy can do when he puts his mind and his back into something. Kudos to you, young man."

Joe began breathing easier. "So you're not going to turn me in?"

Mr. Pruitt called to his dog. "Fred! Come here girl!" She'd evidently wandered too far into the woods for his comfort. The dog jumped over and around fallen branches, then trotted back to Mr. Pruitt's side. He caressed her ear for a moment, then commanded her to lie down. Fred lay down with her front paws crossed and hanging over the edge of the hole, panting rhythmically.

"A girl named Fred?" Joe stood up.

"Frederica—after the opera singer Frederica von Stade," Mr. Pruitt said. "You probably never heard of her. You never met her?"

"I've never met *any* opera singers."

The old man laughed. "No, I mean my dog." Joe could tell Mr. Pruitt liked him. "I've had her for … oh … four or five months now. She's a rescue dog."

"I don't think—no, wait—didn't you have another German shepherd before?"

"That was Johnny."

"Yeah, I remember him. Was he named after Johnny Depp?"

"Johnny who?" Mr. Pruitt squinted.

"You know, Captain Jack Sparrow—famous pirate?"

"Never heard of either one of them. No sir, I named him after Johnny Carson."

"Oh, I heard of him. He was on TV a long time ago."

"Seems like yesterday to me … but I guess it was pretty long ago, now that you mention it. Mr. Carson had outstanding character and manners, and he had something you don't always see these days—integrity."

Joe shuffled his feet. He couldn't help feeling that Mr. Pruitt was dissing his generation.

"My dog Johnny had all those traits too. But he got old and he died," Mr. Pruitt said, looking down. "That's when I got Fred here."

"Oh, I'm sorry to hear that—about Johnny. He was a good dog."

"Yes he was. Thank you for saying so, young man."

"So … are you going to tell on me for what I'm building?"

"Should I?" Mr. Pruitt said.

"Ummm …" He hated such questions—they were often a trap.

"I don't know why I should," Mr. Pruitt said when Joe didn't answer. "All kids ever do these days is play with their video games and cell phones. I must say it's a great relief to find someone your age with this kind of ambition. I'd be the last one to discourage you."

"Oh … thanks Mr. Pruitt."

"You don't need to thank me; I'm just saying what I think. And I'm no fan of the government either, so I won't be shedding tears over one little hole in all the land *they* own." Mr. Pruitt peered past Joe at the space under the stump. "You mind telling me what in particular you're doing there?"

Joe turned and eyed his own handiwork.

"That's the condo's entrance."

"Condo," Mr. Pruitt laughed. "I like it." Then he furrowed his brow. "But how's that going to be the entrance?"

"Well," Joe said. "I still have to cut the top off for the trap door. Then I have to make a hole in the stump. The door lifts up so I can climb down inside. Makes it so nobody but me knows how to get in."

"I see," Mr. Pruitt said, narrowing his eyes. "How're you going to make a hole in that stump?"

"I was just planning to do some drilling, cutting, and chiseling until I get all the way through." Then he remembered Fred's suggestion. "If that doesn't work, I'll use a chainsaw."

"Chainsaw? No, no, no, that's a bad idea. You'll cut your arm off," Mr. Pruitt said. "Please don't do that."

How come everyone thinks I'm going to cut my arm off? Do people just assume I'm prone to losing limbs?

"But I'll tell you," Mr. Pruitt said, "that you'll be old enough to vote, maybe even old enough to drink before you chisel and drill your way through that oak."

"Well, I was planning to use a reciprocating saw too."

"Won't work."

"Why not?"

"The tip of the blade needs to come out the other side, otherwise the sawdust just gets packed in there and your blade gets bound up," Mr. Pruitt said. "I think mostly you'd burn your blades and get shaken around a bunch."

"Then what *would* work?"

If anyone knew how to do it, it was Mr. Pruitt. Dad once told him that Clarence Pruitt cabinets and furniture were practically a legend in Chicago. Only the wealthiest home-owners could afford the time and degree of excellence he put into his craft.

"Well …" He scratched the back of his head. "The first thing that pops into my head is a stump grinder, but—nah, never mind—it would be a lousy tool for this application. But you need to use some method of grinding or boring."

Joe ascended the ladder and walked over to the stump opposite from Mr. Pruitt. The old man studied Joe's odd jeans.

"Let me think about it a bit and get back to you," Mr. Pruitt said. "There's got to be a good way to remove a lot of wood fast."

"Okay, thanks. But I'm still gonna try my way first and see how it goes."

"Of course you are, son. How else would you learn? Just be careful. You're all alone here and if you get hurt, who's going to know about it?"

"I have a cell phone."

"All right, but say you were unconscious? Or you were too hurt to reach your phone?"

Joe hadn't thought about that before, and the way Mr. Pruitt said it, those possibilities suddenly seemed a lot more real and kind of alarming.

The old man's expression darkened.

"Let me guess. Your mother doesn't know about this, does she?"

Joe looked away. "Uhh, not exactly?"

"Which means no. Does anyone know?"

"Just you." *Please don't make me stop.*

"I see." Mr. Pruitt let out a heavy sigh. "Well Joe, now we have a situation."

Mr. Pruitt gazed into the trees and stroked his chin. Joe never understood why men did this. Maybe there was some extension of the brain in the chin and rubbing it stimulated thought processes.

Joe knew that when he'd lost a leg and a father, he'd gained people's empathy—sometimes. And he knew if he were just another kid with two legs and two parents, Mr. Pruitt would be knocking on the McKinnons' front door in less than ten minutes. But so far, it appeared the old man liked Joe and wanted him to succeed.

So far.

"I'm sorry son," Mr. Pruitt said, "but I just can't let you continue to work out here alone like this. So stop what you're doing and stay put while I take care of something." And with that, Mr. Pruitt and Frederica left.

Joe began to pace. *I'm toast. He's going to tell Mom. She won't ground me, but the guilt she'll give me will be way worse.*

He sat on the stump. *Maybe I should just get on the phone right now and confess everything? He doesn't know she's at work ... maybe he doesn't even know where she works, so that would buy me some time.*

Joe stewed over it for another ten minutes when to his surprise, Mr. Pruitt returned. He was alone, but he had a pair of two-way radios.

"Here's what we'll do," he said. "Every time you come out here, stop by my house first. You know where I live, don't you?"

Joe nodded.

"Good," Mr. Pruitt said. "That way you can pick up one of *these* freshly charged and I'll know you're out here. Then, every fifteen minutes—no, that's too often—every twenty minutes, I'll call you, just to hear you say you're still alive. If you answer, that's all we need. But if you don't, I'll assume something's wrong, and I'll come out to check on you. At the end of the day you can bring the radio back to my house."

"Okay." It was way better than being ratted on, but every twenty minutes? *At least Fred only makes me call twice a day.*

The condo's four-star secrecy rating was now down to three and a half. But in the corner of Joe's mind, there was comfort in knowing that if he did slice off a finger, his trail of blood would be shorter to Mr. Pruitt's house than any other house in Palos Ranchos.

"If you stop by and I'm not home, just leave me a note and I'll bring the radio out to you when I get back. Mostly I'm home because that's where I work. But I do live it up from time to time, if you call going out to Denny's living it up.

Anyway, I guess that's enough banter. I know you're itching to get back to work, so have at it."

With that settled, Mr. Pruitt showed him how to use the radios. Then he bid Joe a good day and left.

***

Twenty minutes later, the radio squawked.

"Carson to Sparrow. Everything good? Over."

Joe quickly found the volume knob and turned it down before answering.

"Sparrow. Everything's good. Over."

21

Are We Having Fun Yet ... Over

FINALLY IT WAS SUNDAY and Joe was ready to hollow out the stump.

He made his check-in call to Fred, gathered his tools, and fired up the generator. Under the stump, he started by drilling half-inch-diameter holes inside its outer edge, about four inches in. Then he used the reciprocating saw to connect the holes, forming a cut-line inside the perimeter of the stump. He did get shaken around a little, as Mr. Pruitt predicted, but since the holes were just a few inches apart, there was relief before the blade started riding too far out of the cut. The oak wasn't easy to cut through; he'd have to change blades frequently.

On top of that, since he was cutting into wood above his head, sawdust snowed on his face and down his shirt, making him itch. Sometimes sawdust got into his eyes, and he had to use some eyelid-holding, eye-rolling techniques to remove the specks. It only made matters worse when he wiped his face and eyes with a sawdust-covered shirtsleeve!

After a fierce round of boy versus stump, the perimeter line was finished. Next, he drilled a single hole inside the perimeter and used a narrow chisel to knock out a chunk about half an inch square by an inch long.

Joe stepped back to look at his progress. After an hour and a half, he'd removed one piece of oak smaller than a clothes pin.

He decided to make another drilled-hole perimeter inside the last ring of holes, and after that, he was able to knock out a ring of chunks.

Total time: three and a half hours. Amount of wood removed: very little.

Joe sat down and surveyed the results so far. He was less than one percent through, and he had a blister in the crook of his right hand, multiple splinters, scratchy red eyes, itching under his shirt, arms that felt like lead, and a stiff neck from looking up. On top of that, he had to stop more than a half-dozen times to answer Mr. Pruitt on the radio. And this was just half a morning's work.

Maybe I should round up some termites and let them eat through the stump. It seemed Mr. Pruitt was right: this was going to take a while.

So Joe tried other methods. Capitalizing on the trench he'd already chiseled out, he used the reciprocating saw to cut off angled pieces. Then he tried using a circular saw, but it was way too cumbersome and dangerous to use upside down, not to mention the spray of sawdust it threw at him and the blade binding and smoking.

Next, he put a cutoff wheel on the drill, and created a stinking cloud of smoke as he burned his way a centimeter or less into the unrelenting wood. Then he decided deeper holes would be better, so he began drilling with a twelve-inch long bit. That experiment came to an unhappy end when the drill bit snapped off about five inches into the stump. In desperation, Joe outfitted his drill with a grinding wheel. All the grinding wheel did was make a smooth dark finish on the wood.

If the stump had a voice, it would've been snickering.

Joe threw down the drill and kicked the generator switch off. That was when he noticed Fred up above, chainsaw hanging from his hand.

"Need some help?"

Joe leaned against the wall and stared at the floor.

"Everybody needs help sometimes," Fred said. "No shame in that."

"I want to do this by myself."

Fred set the chainsaw down and crouched near the edge of the hole, then sat. Some dirt fell into the hole as he settled in.

"It's still your condo. Nobody's taking that away from you."

A small breeze stirred above. The silence was soothing, especially after all the noise he'd been making.

"You know, it took probably more than fifty different people to build my house," Fred said. He picked up a clump of dirt and flung it at the backhoe bucket. "Of course, I could've done it myself. I can do all the trades, you know."

There was a distant skidding of tires. Joe sat and braced his head between his hands with his elbows on his knees.

"But then it would have taken ten years to build it," Fred said. "Ten years, Joe. Do you know what ten years is?"

"A decade," Joe said with no interest.

"That's right … a decade. And in the great scheme of things—in the life of this planet—ten years is nothing. It's a hiccup. It's a fart in time. But in a man's life, ten years is what … ten, fifteen, maybe even twenty percent of his life? And I ain't no model of healthful living. I could die when I'm fifty. Do you think it would've been smart for me to spend twenty percent of my life living in some dumpy apartment, waiting for my home—my sanctuary from this whacked-out world— to be built?"

"No." Joe crossed his arms and rested them on his knees. He laid his head sideways on top of them.

"So whaddya say I help you get this thing done … so you can get on with living?"

A familiar scratchy sound startled Joe to his feet.

"Carson to Sparrow. How's it going out there? Over."

Fred jumped up and scanned the area.

"What the hell's that?"

Joe grabbed the radio and held it up for Fred to see.

"It's okay. It's just a guy who lives near the woods." Joe motioned to the east; Mr. Pruitt lived to the north. "I have to answer him right now or he'll come out to check on me."

"Wait!" Fred said. "*Who* is it?"

"He's just a nice guy, don't worry. I really need to answer before he comes out and sees you."

"Carson to Sparrow. Are you okay? Over." Mr. Pruitt enunciated more distinctly this time.

Fred waved him on. "Go ahead, say what you need to."

Joe pushed the radio's *talk* button. "Sparrow. I'm good. Over."

"Roger. Over."

Fred raised an eyebrow. "Carson and Sparrow? What's with the 1972 CB talk? Who was that guy?"

"He found me out yesterday. He's worried I'll cut myself to pieces too, so he gave me this radio and calls me every twenty minutes to make sure I'm not dead."

"Okay. But who is he? *Where* is he? What does he know?"

Joe had thought about this happening. He'd hoped to keep Fred and Mr. Pruitt in the dark about one another, even though they already knew each other. When Joe was just a baby, Fred and some of his crew had spent several weekends helping Joe's father expand Mr. Pruitt's workshop.

But regardless of their past acquaintance, Joe felt it was better to keep them apart, lest they start feeling the need to form a committee. That's how it was with grown-ups. One kid and one adult could talk to each other like equals. Add another grown-up to the mix, and suddenly the adults are the equals, and the kid becomes a flunky.

"He's over on the other side, in Crestview," Joe said. "I don't think you know him. Don't think you want to."

"Why wouldn't I want to?" Fred was growing agitated.

"Same reason you wouldn't want *him* to know *you*."

Fred opened his mouth to speak, then closed it again.

"He thinks he's the only one who knows about the condo," Joe said. "That's why he made me take this." He held up the radio, feeling now like he was in charge. "That's why we can't use the chainsaw—it'll be too loud. If he hears it, he'll think *I'm* using it, and when he comes out to stop me from cutting off my arm he'll see you."

"I want you to tell me who he is!" Fred said. "What if he's a pedophile … or a psychopath?"

"He's neither, Fred. I'm sure of it. If I tell *you* who *he* is, then I'll have to tell *him* who *you* are."

Fred digested this. "Sounds like extortion."

"No, it's just what's fair."

"No such thing as fair in this world, Joe." Fred shook his head. "No such thing."

Joe shrugged.

Fred picked up the chainsaw.

"I don't like it." And he trudged away like a dog that had just been shooed out of the house.

Joe sighed and sat back against the inner wall. This part of the project just wasn't as much fun as he'd thought it would be. And it was too bad Mr. Pruitt found him out. He'd been about to give in and let Fred cut that hole in the stump.

22

What Goes Around ...

ON MONDAY, JOE WAS ALMOST relieved to return to school. He'd worked so hard over the weekend that his muscles ached, and he had scratches on his hands and arms. There was a small bruise on the side of his head from bumping into a temporary wall support he'd nailed up. He looked like he'd been in a fight with an angry rose bush.

Joe loved riding his bike to and from school, especially in the spring. In suburban Chicago, nature boasted her colors to their fullest in May and June, and the shimmering dewed greens were a sharp contrast to the deadness and dirty snow patches that had been there not too long ago. Dandelions poked through the lawns of less attentive yard-keepers and willows swept their long limp cords along the ground with even the smallest breeze.

A few rich kids from Palos Estadas were also on their way to Halverson. One of them was Eric, from Joe's art class. Eric was lumped with the dumber kids in other classes.

According to Dad, even the not-so-smart could get somewhere in life—maybe not far, but somewhere. He'd said: *Money can take you places, but with brains you'll know what to do once you get there.*

"Hey," Joe said as he passed the four kids.

"Hey," they said with hardly a return glance. From their exchanges, he guessed they were playing games on their phones. Joe didn't get it—how could anyone spend so much of their lives in some make-believe world? What did they have to show for it in the end?

Work hard Joe, but make sure you have something worthwhile to show for it when you're done.

That could have been another topic for his persuasive speech—how video games were a waste of time—assuming he wanted ninety percent of the boys at HMS to hate him. Joe was happy with the subject he'd selected: how to get solar panels on every home in America. It wasn't his biggest passion in life, but his presentation would have visual aids, making it seem more like show-and-tell than speech. Even so, the thought of speaking in front of the class still gave him the willies.

I'll be scared—they'll see that I'm scared—then I'll get more scared.

The pressure intensified when Mr. Z declared that this persuasive speech was the final exam, and anyone who missed it for *any* reason would receive a failing grade. Mr. Z also made it known that, since it *was* a final exam, it commanded a significant portion of the semester grade. Skipping out on the speech was not an option.

Joe meandered through the grocery store parking lot, playing chicken with the light poles. There were only a few cars there this early. At the farmer's field, he checked in both directions before entering the packed trail over plowed earth. Rumor had it that the field's owner liked to chase people off with a pepper gun, so Joe always rode across it as fast as he could.

From there, it was a short jaunt through a patch of scrub, a plank ride over a ditch, a quiet roll through ten feet of grass, and up the school driveway to the bike racks. This week, Joe would have to play it safe and attend PE. He didn't want to risk Mr. Lomas calling home to talk to his mother about how too much absence could affect his grade.

After Joe chained up his bike, he began walking toward the courts to shoot some hoops with other kids, when a voice called out:

"Mr. McKinnon!"

Joe reeled around. It was Mr. Lomas.

"Mr. McKinnon, would you come here please," he said in a way that Joe and every other kid on Earth instinctively recognized as bad news.

Most of the kids nearby quieted down and stared at Joe, trying to glean some hint of what he'd done—some sign of his criminal side they hadn't noticed before.

Joe limped slowly toward his PE teacher. As he neared Mr. Lomas, he cast his eyes downward … giving away every bit of his guilt if it hadn't been discovered already.

"Let's go have a talk with Mrs. Killam."

The seventh- and eighth-grade administrators at HMS were known as "Torture 'em and Killam." Although Joe had never seen her smile, he knew deep down inside Mrs. Killam was probably okay and she may even have had a family of her own. But at school she was the essence of law and order.

Joe felt his mouth going dry. He hadn't planned what to do if he was caught. He hadn't planned on *being* caught. Denying it would be futile. He'd be dealing with experts in their field who'd probably been police-trained on how to sift clues and gather evidence. No, he needed to have a reason—a kid's reason—why it was necessary for him to leave school early all last week without permission. Not that any excuse a kid came up with would be good enough to warrant cutting class, but he didn't want to leave the impression that he'd been ditching just for the fun of it. That would make him a delinquent. With the right excuse, they'd see this as a one-time bad decision from a good kid.

"Have a seat right here, son." Mr. Lomas motioned to a chair by an office door. "Mrs. Killam will be with you in a moment."

"Okay." *Think! Think! Think!*

Then he remembered what his dad once said: *The truth will set you free.*

A couple minutes later, the door opened and Alex Hoffman walked out. His red eyes and sad face marked him as a broken man. A few seconds later, Mrs. Killam appeared.

"Joseph McKinnon."

"Yes ma'am."

"Come on in Mr. McKinnon," she said, with no sign of malice, compassion, or anger. She stood aside so Joe could enter first.

Joe's heart pounded hard and he felt his face going pale. The chair he sank into was comfortable, leather, surely not something purchased by the school district. On one wall was a poster of the solar system. It had a white line with an arrow pointed toward Earth and the words "You are here" printed at the other end of the line. Mrs. Killam also had the exact same Einstein poster Joe had in his bedroom, with Albert's quote "I never think of the future. It comes soon enough," only it'd been modified with a red marker to say "I always think of the future. It comes too soon."

"I have that poster," Joe said.

"*Do* you?" Mrs. Killam stared at Joe, not glancing even for a second at the poster.

"Uh, yeah." Joe locked his fingers together and started a circling thumb race.

"Mr. McKinnon, have you guessed why you're here yet?"

"Yes ma'am."

"Then why don't you tell me." Mrs. Killam leaned back in her chair.

"For cutting class last week." His eyes avoided hers.

"Mmmm-hmmm," she said. "For four days." Then she opened her drawer and pulled out a piece of paper with one of its corners torn off. "And is this your handiwork?"

"Yes ma'am."

"I *know* it is. See, I talked to your mom, and she doesn't remember writing any note excusing you from PE."

Joe pictured his mom's disappointment, which he'd see later in person. Mrs. Killam must have just talked to her, because Mom hadn't said a word about it before he left for school.

"Now for the big question," she said. "Why?"

"Why what?" Joe said, knowing it was a mistake to waffle with this woman, but wanting to delay the inevitable as long as possible.

Mrs. Killam leaned back and narrowed her eyes.

Joe gulped. "My prosthetic was really bothering me, and I needed a break from exercising, so … I wrote that note to get out of PE."

"Wouldn't your mom write the note for you?"

"Probably, but I didn't ask. I didn't want her to worry and waste money taking me back to the doctor."

Mrs. Killam raised her eyebrows.

"I figured if I didn't exercise for a while, maybe it would start feeling better all by itself." *Hey, this sounds pretty good.* He felt the color returning to his face.

"Mmmm-hmmm. So then Mr. Lomas told you to go to the media center for the rest of the week. Right?"

"Yeah, but I decided to go home and do my work there so I could take off my prosthetic—you know—so my leg could heal better."

"Uh-huh," Mrs. Killam said. "And how's your leg now?"

"It's all better. I can go back to PE now." Joe smiled and nodded with enthusiasm.

"Right." The administrator peered out the window. "See that bike rack over there?" She looked down the end of her finger as she pointed.

Joe followed her finger, and nodded. "Yeah?"

"That's where your bike is, right?"

"Yeah …" *What does that have to do with anything?*

"I know it is, Mr. McKinnon, because I watched you put your bike there this morning."

Joe gulped. *Not good.*

"And to be honest with you, when you walked away from your bike, if I hadn't known better, I'd have thought you had the two legs you were born with—same as any other boy at this school."

The blood that had just come back to Joe's face a minute ago did a U-turn.

"And then, Mr. Lomas called you and the darnedest thing happened. You started limping like a war veteran."

Joe said nothing. There was nothing he *could* say. The evidence may have only been circumstantial, but for kid prosecution that was good enough.

The first period bell rang.

"Now why don't you tell me why you really ditched seventh period last week?"

Joe's lip quivered. His eyes filled and spilled over. There were times when the truth was all that was needed—but now was not one of them.

"I'm just tired of being a freak," Joe said. "When I put my gym shorts on, everyone stares at my prosthetic. I don't like it anymore." He put his arm up to cover his eyes.

Mrs. Killam tapped Joe's arm with a box of tissues and he took it. She sighed, took a sip of her coffee, picked up a marker and began squeaking it across the whiteboard.

Joe wiped his eyes with the palms of his hands, and squinted to focus on what Mrs. Killam was writing.

"My artwork isn't that great, but it'll get the point across," she said as she drew some angled lines.

It was the word OVER arching over the vertical word LEAP, with angled lines coming from the word LEAP and converging on the horizon.

"This here's supposed to be a hurdle," she said, pointing to those angled lines. "And since you're in eighth grade, you've probably already read these words here. What does this say to you, Joe?"

"It says 'leap over,' and the word OVER is going over the word LEAP."

"That's right. But I need to tell you what the letters in these words stand for, because in this case, they're not just words, they're acronyms." She wrote the following words under her drawing:

Laziness
Excuses
Anger
Pity

Open-minded
Victims
Embrace
Responsibility

"Need I say more?" she said, plopping the marker on the whiteboard's tray.

"Uh, who's the victim?"

"You were—I was—everyone is, at some time in their life."

Joe took her word on that.

"I'm not lazy," he said pointing at the word.

"From your grades, I'd say that's true. But what about this word here?" She tapped the marker by the word Excuses. "You ever find yourself making any of these?"

The late bell rang for first period.

"No, not really," Joe said.

"I'd have to disagree with you there. You just laid a big fat one on me along with those puppy dog tears a minute ago. 'Kids are staring at my prosthetic'? You and I both know the kids in your PE class don't even notice anything different about you anymore. If you had two heads, they'd hold conversations with both heads at once, and not think twice about it, no pun intended."

Mrs. Killam was more than perceptive. She was a mind reader.

"I'm going to be blunt," she said. "You were a victim in an accident that took your leg. I was a victim of people who didn't like my skin color."

Joe suddenly became aware of their difference, and now that she'd pointed it out he felt uneasy.

"When I was in college, Joe, I had my bicycle locked up in a bike rack just like that one out there. When I went to get it, I found it was trashed, and the people who did it left a note saying they didn't want my kind at their college. I told a friend and she said I should find out who did it and get even with them. You know what I told her?"

"No ma'am."

I told her I didn't think violence was a good answer. So then she says we could go to the dean and demand he do something about it, and if he didn't, we'd refuse to go to class and we could walk around in front of classrooms carrying protest signs instead. You know what I said then?"

"No ma'am."

"I said 'No thank you, I'll just *leap over* this.'"

She stopped a moment and studied Joe's reaction.

"Yeah, she looked at me the same way. And now you're wondering—what does LEAP OVER have to do with anything? You see I could have stayed *angry* over my bike, and that nasty note they left. I could have used it as an *excuse* anytime I failed at anything. I could have become *lazy* and expected people to take care of me because I was mistreated. And I could have asked everyone to *pity* me. But *my* father told me NO! I had to leap over those hurdles, or I'd get stuck behind them, and all the other hurdlers would pass me by."

Joe wasn't sure what the connection was to ditching school, and waited to see if she'd clear it up.

"Joe, all I'm trying to say is don't use the tragic events of your past as an excuse for anything you do wrong—or don't do at all—in your life. You ditched school last week. Look me in the eye and *tell* me it was because of your prosthetic."

Joe looked Mrs. Killam in the eyes.

"No ma'am, it wasn't."

"Thank you." She pulled out a yellow pad, glanced at her watch, and filled out a pass for Joe. "I believe the bell has rung. You may go to your class now."

"Is that all?" He took the pass, feeling he might be pressing his luck asking, but needing a final word on all this.

"And the truth shall set you free. That's all Mr. McKinnon. First time, we talk. Second time, it gets a little uglier. Let's make sure there's no second time, all right?"

"Okay," he said, offering her a handshake.

Always offer your hand in greeting, thanking, and leaving someone. I guarantee you son, it makes a great first and last impression.

Mrs. Killam took his hand, and if Joe hadn't known better, he'd have thought she smiled.

23

Not Just Joe

AFTER SCHOOL, JOE DECIDED to take 127th Avenue. Although it was a faster way home, getting hit by a car might be better than facing Mom later.

There would be no more cutting school to work on the stump, which meant he'd have to let Fred bring out the chainsaw. While he was giving up on something he yearned to do on his own, he felt relieved giving the job to someone who knew how to do it right. Fred would get it done quickly and safely—that's all there was to it.

Joe survived 127th and was now loitering past Algonquin and Brain STEM.

Life was so much easier at Algonquin, when I was just a kid.

Although dispirited over the doom to come when Mom got home, he couldn't help looking for Jun among the kids exiting The Brain. He slowed as much as he could while coasting past. Everyone was eager to get home—to work on their math and science, no doubt.

But he didn't see her, so he resumed pedaling.

Suddenly she appeared ahead of him, walking along the road. Her thumb was hooked under the strap of her peace-sign peppered backpack. In her other hand she carried a flute case.

Joe gathered a fistful of courage and slowed as he passed her.

"Hi," he said.

"Hi Joey!"

She knows me! He rode another thirty feet before his inner voice kicked in. *Stop it—be a man!* He came around and coasted back, then made a U-turn and began to ride alongside her.

"You *know* me?" Joe said.

Jun smiled. "Of course," she said. "We went to Algonquin together, remember?"

Joe's heartrate shot up at least twenty-three percent.

"Right," Joe said. "But we weren't in the same class. You were like, one grade below me … I think."

"No," Jun said. "You were like, one grade above me."

Their eyes met in a momentary flicker of mirth.

She giggled. "My name's—"

"Jun," Joe said.

Jun faked surprise. "You *do* remember!"

"Well, yeah … of course I do."

Joe zig-zagged to keep his balance as he tried to match her pace. She seemed to be slowing down.

"So, uhhhh …" *What should I say?* "Don't you go to The Brain—I mean, duh, you obviously go to The Brain—how do you like it there?" *Great … of all the lame things to ask.*

"It's okay. It's school. How's your school, Joey?"

His heartrate went up another eleven percent.

"Same … it's school. By the way—no biggie—but it's just *Joe* now."

"Okay—*Just Joe.*" She giggled again. "That's a nice name too."

"Thanks," he said. "So's Jun."

"Thanks. I'm named after my nai nai."

"What's a nai nai?"

"That's my grandmother. My father's mother is nai nai—my mother's mother is lao lao."

"Oh," Joe said. "Then you can call me Joe-Joe." *Idiot!*

Jun laughed. "Can I maybe just call you … Joe?"

Right now, he wouldn't have cared if she called him Josephine.

"That works," he said.

She gave him another smile.

For too many seconds, there was only the sound of her feet crunching the road's gravel shoulder. Joe watched her from the corner of his eye. She didn't seem to want to get rid of him. It was *his* turn to say something.

"I see you play an instrument." He nodded toward her case.

"The flute. Do *you* play anything?"

At the moment, he wished he were a symphony maestro.

"Not really," he said. "I have an electric guitar. Haven't really learned to play it yet."

"Oh, too bad." She seemed a little disappointed.

"My dad used to play guitar," Joe said. "He was *really* good. I guess he thought I might be good too."

"I bet you *would* be if you tried." She sounded sincere, hopeful … and chastising.

"Maybe. Just don't have the time right now."

"Oh," she said. "What did your dad play on the guitar?"

"Rock, mostly. Older stuff. Like from the eighties and nineties. You ever listen to any of that?"

"Mmm, I know *some* rock music," she said. "My friends listen to it—but not the real old stuff."

"I guess the flute's not much of a rock-and-roll instrument, is it?"

Jun laughed. "Not so much. Did your father play in a band?"

Joe wished she wouldn't talk about his dad so much.

"Yeah, just a garage band," he said. "Where do you play?"

A wave of sadness seemed to wash over her. "I'm very sorry about your father."

He blinked. "Oh … thanks."

Women are mysterious creatures, son. One minute they're happy, the next they're spilling tears. Don't question it. Just act like you understand them … but not too much—that'll make 'em mad.

They continued along with Jun watching the ground, her eyes darting up to Joe occasionally. He could feel her sadness becoming his.

"Well, guess I should be going," he said. "See ya!"

He pulled away, and was a good distance ahead of her when Jun called out.

"Hey, Just Joe!"

Joe turned his bike around and coasted toward her.

Elegant beauty.

Then he brought himself alongside her again—her thumb was still hooked under the strap of her backpack. Her flute case still rocked to and fro.

"Yeah?" Joe said.

"We should talk again sometime," Jun said. "It was nice."

"Yeah, sure!" he said. "See ya!" And as Joe sped toward home, he lit up inside like a Christmas tree.

24

Presenting Mr. Joseph Houdini

MOM WAS ALREADY HOME waiting in the kitchen with crossed arms. So much for having a little quiet time to think about what to say to her.

"Hi Mom, how come—"

"Sit." She pointed to a dining room chair.

Joe obeyed, but put his prosthetic leg up on an adjacent chair.

She glared at it and he put it back down. So much for pity.

"Talk," Mom said.

Joe looked down. "PE's a waste of time."

"Oh, really?" she said. "I wasn't aware your time was in such short supply."

"Life is short."

"Yeah?" she pursed her lips. "Well, shorter for some than for others."

Joe looked up at her.

"You know I meant … I wasn't talking about your father."

He cast his eyes back down.

"Yeah Mom," he said. "I know."

Mom let out a sigh and softened her posture.

"Okay, so just tell me why you did it."

Joe shrugged. "I don't know. Just got antsy to work on more important stuff."

"Like what?"

"Like my report for my persuasive speech and all my other homework."

"Are you behind? I thought you rearranged your schedule so you could get ahead of the game."

"Yeah but finals are coming up. I have a lot of studying to do."

"So hold off on your landscaping work until school lets out. I'm sure your customers would understand."

"They've been too patient already. I can't make them wait any longer. Besides, I'm almost done."

"Give me their number. I'll call and explain it to them."

"No! Mom," he said. "You don't need to do that. I'm doing good with the studying now. Those days I cut PE really helped. In fact, I decided to stop cutting before they called me down to the office."

"What did they say to you—at school? What kind of trouble are you in?"

"As long as I don't do it again I'm okay. Mrs. Killam was pretty cool."

"Well she sure sounded serious on the phone this morning." Mom began to smile. "I was afraid you might not come home today."

"She taught me to leap over things."

"Huh?"

What did she call it? "It's an acronym, I think," he said. "I'll explain it sometime."

"Okay," Mom said. "But no more ditching, right? Or I'll *leap over* to your customer's house and tell them you're through."

Joe laughed. "Okay." *Another narrow escape!*

"By the way, Fred called."

"Yeah?"

"We're going out for ice cream tomorrow, to celebrate Phelps's birthday."

"Oh?" *Play dumb.*

"It's a little weird, I know. Phelps isn't even here. But Fred's sad that he wasn't with him on his birthday, and I think he needs someone to make him feel better about that."

"Works for me."

"Of course it does." She smiled. "When wouldn't ice cream work for you?"

***

In his room, Joe reviewed the day's events. Aside from a few uncomfortable moments with Mom and Mrs. Killam, it'd turned out pretty good. At least the ditching-school thing was one less looming hammer waiting to drop. Now his stress list was down to getting the condo covered and giving a speech without passing out at the podium.

He did have an idea for a speech prop that should work well to illustrate his point and help to soften the audience … but he'd need some help from his mom.

And Jun. *Call me Joe-Joe* … he didn't really say that, did he? Oh well, even if he wasn't Joe-cool, there was no mistaking it—she liked him!

25

One Jun Day in May

THE NEXT DAY, JOE ZIPPED out of school and rode his bike faster than usual toward The Brain. When he got close he noticed Jun standing by the doors of The Brain, not moving, just peering out to the street. Then—though he might have been wrong about this—she seemed to be in a hurry to get to the street *and by sheer coincidence* got there almost exactly when Joe did.

"Hi, Jun." Joe slowed up alongside her.

"Oh, hi!" She seemed surprised to see him. "How was school today?"

"Pretty okay. How 'bout for you?

"Same." There was that smile again.

"Can I ask you a question?" Joe said.

"Of course."

"Why do you always bring your flute to school?" he said. "I heard Brain Stem doesn't have any arts or music … or sports."

A couple of girls passed them. One gave Joe a suspicious glance.

Jun said, "So … do you have study hall at your school?"

"Yeah, sort of."

"So do we, but it's called *creative time*. Our academics are pretty intense, so they give us a half-hour break in the afternoon to 'free up our brains.' We can even take a nap if we want. I go into the *noisy room* and practice my flute."

"How can you practice if it's noisy?"

"It's not too bad. They have cubicles with soundproof foam on the walls."

"Crazy," Joe said. "I mean … crazy in a good way."

"It *is* crazy," she laughed. "But I like crazy."

"Me too!"

There was a silence—an okay silence.

"Do you like to dance?" Jun said.

Joe gave her a sidelong look. Was she joking?

"My dancing career kinda got cut short."

"Why?"

Does she really not understand? "I'm missing something important for dancing."

"If you love to dance, nothing can stop you."

Joe didn't answer.

"I'm not talking about break dancing or the tango or anything like that," she said.

"Good, 'cause I grew out of my tango clothes."

Jun laughed. "I like your jokes."

Joe felt himself blushing. "Actually, I wasn't a great dancer even before I lost my leg," he said. "No one ever taught me."

She looked at him and her dark eyes glistened.

"I can teach you."

Their eyes held for the longest moment yet. He took a deep breath and restrained himself from acting like a crazed lottery winner.

If something is meant to be, you won't have to ask ... you'll just know.

"Our school is nerdy, but we do have dances," she said. "There's one this week. Want to go with me?"

He wanted to, but he didn't want to be the gimpy kid at some other school's dance.

"Umm ... I'd like to. What day is it?"

"Friday night at six thirty."

"Friday? He shook his head. "I can't go. My mom won't let me go out on Fridays anymore."

"Why not?"

"Ummm ..." *Think fast!* "She's superstitious. The car accident with my dad happened on a Friday and some other bad things have happened on Fridays, so she makes me stay home on Fridays."

"Oh, I see." She was somewhere between ponderous and disappointed. "And you were riding your bike and almost got hit by that lady in the car on a Friday."

Her acuteness was impressive. "Yeah, that's right!"

"So why does she let you ride your bike on Fridays then?"

Shit. "It's … only Friday *nights* she's superstitious about."

"I see." She was trying not to smile—Joe could see that. Then she stopped walking. Joe halted late and had to back his bike up beside her.

"Some of our school dances were on *Saturday* nights this year," she said. "So maybe next year then? On a Saturday night?"

"Sure, why not?" Joe said. *That'll give me all summer to practice!*

She continued walking, and Joe followed.

"Can I ask *you* a question?" Jun said.

"Go for it."

"Is your mom still sad?" She did that female empathy head-tilt thing.

"You mean … about my dad?"

She nodded.

He looked away. "I guess, sometimes."

"I'm so sorry."

Joe shrugged. "It's not your fault." *Why does she like to talk about this?*

"Are *you* still sad?" she said.

"Sometimes."

She looked down. "I'm so sorry, Joe."

"That's not your fault either." He looked over at her. "Really, we're okay. You don't need to worry."

"If you ever want to talk … they say sometimes it's easier to talk to a stranger."

Joe stopped. So did Jun.

"You're not a stranger." He smiled, and so did she. "No offense, but can we change the subject?"

"Okay." Then she said, "When are you going to learn to play your guitar?"

"When are you going to play your flute for me?"

"Right now."

She walked into the grass next to a tree and put down her backpack and flute case. Joe laid down his bike and followed. She clicked open the case exposing three different lengths of silver tubes—two of them decked with keys and hinges. She assembled it, gave it a test toot, adjusted the head piece, and tooted it again.

"Awesome, know any other songs?" Joe said.

Jun laughed into the mouthpiece. "Be quiet." She reached into her backpack and pulled out a thin music book with the title *Madrigal*. Then she opened it and handed it to Joe.

"Here, hold this for me." She positioned his arms for how she wanted the music to be—leaning against his chest, just under his chin—and said, "Hold it steady."

"Yes ma'am."

"All right, Just Joe," she said. "*Please.*"

She lifted the flute and formed her lips above the mouthpiece. Joe savored this chance to really study her face—to absorb every detail of what made Jun … Jun.

She began to play. The flute was way louder than he'd expected, but *Madrigal* was slow and soothing, moving and intriguing. It reminded him of a painting he'd once seen of a small Italian village with cobblestone paths and people from some age past.

Longer notes quivered while Jun swayed with the ebb and flow of the music. Joe soon found himself swaying with her, though to a lesser degree. He became lost in the world her music created, and it seemed she was lost there too. Although her flute could only play individual notes, they implied a whole chorus of tones.

At a pause in the music, Joe started to let his arms down. Jun shook her head and he perked back up. When she resumed playing, her finger movements were rapid yet smooth—like the village had become busy and filled with chatter.

That passage gave way to a slower one, and the piece finally ended with a single impassioned long note tapering to a dreamy end as the last light dimmed and sleep befell the village.

Jun lowered her flute. It was a few seconds before she returned from that world and lifted her eyes to Joe's.

He was motionless. The quiet lingered.

Finally, he managed to speak.

"That was … so …" The word escaped him.

"Thank you," she said.

The word came.

"Elegant."

26

What We Have Here is a Failure to Communicate

ON TUESDAY EVENING, Joe and his mom met Fred at The Shivering Cow—an ice cream shop that combined delectable sweets with intestinal cleansing. You could order flavors such as orange oat bran sherbet, chocolate cranberry swirl, or peanut butter prune, to name a few. Grown-ups liked the reduced-guilt factor, but for Joe, it was one step too close to eating pine cones or crunchy vegan flakes with soy milk. Luckily they also offered plain old chocolate chip cookie dough ice cream. *Thank you Ben! Thank you Jerry!*

Fred ordered a grizzly-sized hot fudge sundae and Mom got a dish of peanut butter chocolate with granola sprinkles. Fred paid for everything, after pulling out a coupon to lighten his total.

Mom chuckled as he resolved which combination of bills to use and dug into his pocket for change. "You must be the last person in town to pay with cash," she said.

Fred grinned. "Nothing like real American dollars."

At the table, Mom ate her ice cream in dainty half spoonfuls, as if smaller bites somehow translated to fewer calories.

"How's business?" she said.

"Slowing down some," Fred said. "But could be worse. Some of the other guys are hurting more than we are." He didn't let conversation get in the way of his eating, pausing between words to gulp down casserole-spoon-sized mouthfuls. "I heard the Voorsman brothers are about to go bankrupt."

"Well that's just Darwinism in the construction industry, isn't it?" Mom said.

"It's a case of 'what goes around, comes around' is what it is. Those two have been building tornado-food homes for too long. People like to gripe about the recession, but it gives the business a good cleaning out it needs once in a while."

Joe liked Fred's tough talk when it wasn't directed at him. He had a way of clearly laying out right from wrong that made you want to break out the pom-poms and cheer for Team Fred.

"We really shouldn't talk this way," Mom said. "They may be lousy builders but they still have families to feed." She paused. "But I wonder sometimes how they don't get sued out of business. I mean, if a competent, conscientious builder like Mick could get sued …"

His dad's workers always called him Mr. McKinnon, but to everyone else he was Mick. His birth name was Alan Joseph McKinnon.

"So that lawsuit's all over now?" Fred said. "Weren't they going to try and keep collecting payments after … after the accident?"

Mom glanced at Joe out of the corner of her eye. She knew this topic made him uncomfortable, that it even gave him nightmares for a while—someone going after his dad like that.

"We settled it after the accident, when the business sold," she said. "I'm just glad it's over."

So was Joe. He knew his mom could get pretty riled up talking about the personal-injury lawsuit against Dad's business. He didn't understand all of it, but essentially, the insurance company's lawyers had said that some work injury wasn't covered because of negligence, and they'd walked away, leaving Dad responsible for paying damages.

And it happened again after the car accident. One day Mom's lawyer was promising she'd never have to worry about money again, and the next day her lawyer was gone and Mom was back to work at the library. Mom wouldn't talk about it in front of him. Joe never understood what happened, but it was pretty obvious something had gone terribly wrong.

"So Phelps is fifteen now?" Mom said.

"Yup, according to my calculations," Fred said.

"That would make him a freshman?"

"Gonna be a sophomore next year. He'll be driving too, Lord help us all."

"Yes, if he drives anything like you." Mom made the sign of the cross. "How's he doing?"

Fred's eyes darted to Joe for a moment.

"I guess—as well as can be expected."

"You mean he's being a teenager?"

"He seems to have acquired a taste for …" Fred tapped his fingers on the table. "… liquids of a brewed nature."

"He's drinking?"

Joe pretended to be studying the Shivering Cow menu behind the counter. He had Jun's flute song stuck in his head.

Fred cleared his throat. "Well, not as part of his daily dietary plan or anything, but yes, he's been caught more than once."

"Must have gotten that gene from his mother's side, huh?" Mom smiled.

Fred laughed. "Must have."

"Well I'm sure he'll be responsible about it." Mom seemed to sense Fred wanted to get off this topic. "How's he doing in school?"

"Let's just say that *unlike* his old man, he's a little genius." Fred shot a look at Joe.

This time, Mom caught the look.

"Just like my Joe, huh?"

"That's right."

Joe dug at his ice cream, feeling the stares.

"Well, guys, I thought in the spirit of celebrating Phelps's birthday, we'd have a little party here tonight," Mom said. "And what better way to celebrate than with gifts?"

With that, she reached into her purse and pulled out a small box covered in Spiderman wrap with a ribbon.

Joe thought this was strange. Not the Spiderman wrap—that was just Mom. But it was only yesterday he'd been in deep for ditching school, and now she wanted to celebrate someone else's birthday by giving *her* son a gift?

"Before I give you this, you have to promise not to abuse it," she said.

"Sure, Mom," Joe said as he struggled to break the ribbon. "What is it, a puppy?"

"In that small box?" Fred said.

"Could be." Joe continued to yank at the ribbon. "A really tiny puppy."

Mom laughed.

Fred pulled out a small hunting knife. "Let me give you a hand there, sport," he said as he sliced the ribbon.

As Joe's fingers tore off the wrapping, he and Fred exchanged puzzled looks. On the box was a picture of a stapler.

Joe looked at his mom, who rolled her eyes.

"Oh, I can't believe they did that." She reached back into her purse and fished out her phone. "I'm going to call those idiots right now and find out what the heck they were thinking." Her finger poked and slid across the screen. Just after she put the phone to her ear, the box started to ring—an old-fashioned ring like some phone from the fifties.

It startled Joe and Fred nearly spit out a mouthful of ice cream.

Joe opened the box, slid out a phone, and answered it.

"Hello?" His eyes darted from side to side.

Then he heard his mom's voice in stereo.

"Hello, is this Joseph McKinnon?"

He lowered the phone, and cast a look at his mom.

"Okay, okay." Mom laughed and hung up. "Oh, that look was priceless!" She laughed some more.

"What's it for?" Joe said. "Who'm I gonna call?"

"Well, me for starters," Mom said. "I just wanted … I think you need it right now, that's all. And you can use it to call Fred."

He and Fred looked at one another and busted out laughing.

"What's so funny about that?" Mom said.

"Nothing," Joe said. They looked at each other and laughed again.

"I thought you'd like a cell phone." Mom looked down at her ice cream. "Most kids your age would beg their parents for one."

Fred coughed and rolled his eyes toward her.

"I love it, Mom, and it's a cool color too."

She perked up. "I knew you'd like camouflage. Goes with how you painted the backhoe."

"Booyeah!" Joe avoided looking at Fred for fear of cracking up again. Suddenly he brightened. "And I can call my friends whenever I want, right?" *Like Jun—someday.*

"*Within reason*, young man." A mom had to be a mom. "I don't want you on it talking and texting all day. And you can't use it while you're in school. *And* you can't be on it after … let's say eight o'clock at night."

"Okay." It really was okay—he didn't plan to use it much anyway.

"And I want you to keep it on after school. You know, so you can let me know where you'll be hanging out and when you'll be home."

"Oh … okay." *I get it now. An army-colored leash. Now I have three leashes and three different people tugging them.* "Thanks, Mom."

***

Later that night, Joe realized something. He should've asked Fred about bringing the chainsaw to hollow out the stump—

he could've asked him while his mom was in the bathroom. *Too late now*. He'd give Fred a call tomorrow.

27

Stuff Happens

If one hand gets tied behind your back, keep working with the other. If the other hand gets tied, start walking toward where you'll be working once your hands are freed. If your feet get stuck, use your time to think about how you're going to get the job done once you're untied and unstuck—and pray that you'll be smart enough not to get into that situation again.

Joe decided to follow Dad's advice: he could go out to the condo and spend hours accomplishing nearly nothing on the stump, like he had on Sunday, or he could be smart and wait until Fred brought out the chainsaw, and until then he'd work on completing his persuasive report.

Giving in and letting Fred help was wounding to Joe's pride, but he had a higher purpose than *building* the condo—he wanted to *use* the condo. His pride would have to suffer.

Regardless, he still had to figure out how Fred could use the chainsaw without Mr. Pruitt hearing it. Joe's noise suppression tactics could muffle a lot, and using the chop saw at the bottom of the hole was quieter too, but chainsaws were really loud, and Fred would be using it both below and above the stump. The sound would travel, and though Mr. Pruitt might not hear it from inside his house, he would definitely hear it if he was outside.

During algebra, Joe pondered the problem. He considered building more sound muffling, but that would take up too much time. He could make decoy noises to draw attention elsewhere ... but that didn't seem very feasible.

In language arts Joe came up with a better idea. It was so obvious he couldn't believe he hadn't thought of it right away. They would just use the chainsaw when Mr. Pruitt wasn't home. But when was that? Joe and his parents used to see him during Sunday mass at St. Andrews, and sometimes they'd see him having breakfast at the IHOP afterward. But Mr. Pruitt was home last Sunday morning; he'd called Joe on the radio that day.

Crap!

Still, there had to be times when Mr. Pruitt left his house. All he needed to do was go over to Mr. Pruitt's and fish the information out of him. Heck, he could do it today, right after school.

***

Calisthenics: punishment for the lazy and the rebels … a walk in the park for the other five percent—like Joe. He could do almost anything a person with two God-given legs could do, though he had trouble with jumping jacks. So while everyone else's hair flopped up and down, Joe jogged in place. The boys did their exercising on the softball field, to the sounds of the district maintenance men mowing and edging the adjacent soccer field.

Joe loved softball; he could hit, field, and pitch. Even the direction of running the bases worked out, because it was easier for him to turn left than right. And even better, he'd been picked for the same team as Jack Kazden and Steve Sergenski, the two best athletes ever to set foot on HMS soil. Softball, dodgeball, floor hockey, basketball—whatever the sport, Jack and Steve made the rest of the boys look like lumbering neophytes.

The opposing team wore red shirts sporting the HMS Red Devil's logo, with a white rectangle where kids had written their last name. Joe's team flipped their shirts inside out, making them dark blue. It was a much cooler color in Joe's opinion, like being the Eagles versus the Mud Hens.

After fifteen minutes at bat, Joe's team was already around the batting order with only one out. Red team looked frazzled.

It wouldn't be long before Mr. Lomas run-ruled the blue team so the red team would get to bat. In the meantime, Jack Kazden was at the plate again—almost a guaranteed homer.

Suddenly, a scream came from the soccer field. Everyone turned to see one of the maintenance workers cupping his hands over his eye.

Mr. Lomas said, "Boys, stay here!" and sprinted over to the injured man. Joe had never seen him move so fast.

The other worker turned off the mower, and within seconds, he and Mr. Lomas were attending the writhing victim while the boys speculated about what had happened.

"I think he got stung by a wasp," Jack said.

"No, man," said another. "Something shot out of the mower and nailed him right in the eye. I heard it—like the mower hit a rock or something."

"Aw, dude! That happened to me once, only it hit me in the shin. I had a nasty cut," Tom Benson said. "Things shoot out of the mower at, like, a thousand miles an hour. His eyeball could be a goner!"

"Oooooo," everyone said together.

Then Mr. Lomas bellowed "Sergenski! Run to the office and have them call 9-1-1!"

Steve Sergenski didn't move. Instead, he pointed toward the school, the entrance of which Joe was already fast approaching.

"Wow, that was fast," Jack said. "I never even saw him go."

28

More Stuff Happens

JOE RODE HOME IN A DAZE. He didn't take the express route past The Brain; even Jun couldn't cheer him up today. How could he smile and laugh when the mowing accident was still fresh in his mind?

As the messenger, he'd had the privilege of leading Mrs. Killam and Mrs. Atkins (the school nurse) to the scene, where it took a moment for anyone to think to tell him to go back with the rest of the boys. In that moment, he'd seen Carlos—the man's name was sewn on an oval patch on his shirt—sobbing. Eventually, the nurse managed to pull Carlos's hand from his eye, exposing the bloody mess. Mrs. Killam turned her head and winced. Then, Mr. Lomas thanked Joe for his quick thinking, and asked him to lead the other boys back to the media center and explain to Mrs. Adams why they were there.

By then they could all hear the sirens closing in.

At home, Joe dropped off his backpack on the porch and pulled out his new phone.

He texted: "hi mom im home going to shoot sum hoops."

Today's accident left a disturbing image in Joe's mind. Something as simple as mowing the grass, and now a man might lose his eye or be brain damaged. How much more dangerous was the work Joe was doing? And if he got hurt like that, would he even be able to call for help?

He stopped at the end of his driveway. He didn't *have* to go out to the condo.

I could just stay home.

His breath quivered as he closed his eyes.

Don't be afraid son, there's nothing to fear but fear itself.

And maybe a nail in the eye.

He let go of the handles and sat up on his bike, letting gravity turn his front wheel.

There's one thing I fear more than getting hurt trying to do something, and that's going to my grave with the regret that I didn't try at all. Joe sped off.

At Mr. Pruitt's, he pushed the doorbell button, ringing an authentic set of deep chimes, not some cheesy electronic reproduction. Frederica came to the door and barked once.

But no one answered the door.

Joe peered through the rippled window next to the door but detected no movement inside except Fred trotting away.

Maybe he's in the shop?

As Joe walked around to the shop entrance, he looked down at the sidewalk—dark stains led all the way up to the door, and on its smooth white surface, they dripped down like some amateur's heavy-handed paint job.

Joe tapped at the door and backed up several steps until he was off the sidewalk. Darkness seeped through from the shop's window blinds. All was silent.

He stepped forward and touched one of the drips on the door. Under its darkened fragile skin, was a brighter wet redness.

Joe felt his face flush and his mouth go dry. He reached for the doorknob—locked. Making a wide circle around the house, he approached the front door again. He grabbed the handle and pressed down on the thumb latch—locked. Frederica revisited the side window with a low growl followed by a whimpering cry. Joe backed away until the whole house filled his field of vision.

This is way, way wrong.

Joe hoped that at any moment, Mr. Pruitt would open the door, or come whipping around the corner in his gold Town Car (Mr. Pruitt really hauled ass in that old car).

Maybe I should call the police ... or Mom. But if that was blood—if someone attacked Mr. Pruitt—why would it be outside the house?

He needed to get away, to think about what he should do.

***

Joe arrived at Ground Thirteen, stopped ... and stared.

The stump! A slice had been cut off the top, and the stump itself was hollowed out. Upon closer inspection, the hollowing wasn't quite finished, but it was close. One could push a hockey stick all the way through. Sawdust, dirt, and chunks of wood littered the surrounding area.

Joe's excitement strained against his vocal cords, as he raced toward the ladder, but when he got close, he stopped again. Random-shaped blocks of oak and sawdust were heaped on the floor beneath the stump, and on the floor, mixed in with the sawdust and sprayed all over the walls, was blood.

Oh my God! Mr. Pruitt!

Joe scooped up his bike and flew back to Mr. Pruitt's house. He circled the house, banging on all the doors and windows he could reach.

"Mr. Pruitt, are you in there? Mr. Pruitt, answer me!" But there was only Frederica—barking at first, then whining, and finally disappearing somewhere in the house.

"Mr. Pruitt!"

Joe stood back from the house, breathing like an asthmatic, wanting to cry. He pulled out his phone and stared at it.

Who do I call? Mom? No! 9-1-1? No—Fred!

He punched numbers, jumbled them, tried again, and put the phone to his ear. *Nothing!* He checked the number. *Damn! Forgot to push SEND!*

Long delay. Finally a ring. Another. Another.

"Hello?" But the voice wasn't Fred's.

"Sorry, wrong number."

As Joe pulled the phone away he heard "Wait, wait…don't hang up!"

"Who is this?" Joe said.

"This is Fred Fergussen's phone. I'm Clarence. I'm taking calls for Fred right now. Who am I speaking with?"

Joe's eyes darted in search of the right answer. It was Mr. Pruitt. He sounded different on the phone, but how many Clarences could there be in the world?

"Umm. Where's Fred? Is he okay?"

"He's had better days. Who is this, please?"

"This is Joe," he said, "Joe McKinnon."

Mr. Pruitt let out one long breath.

"Oh … hello Joe, this is Mr. Pruitt. You must not have heard." He paused. "Fred's had an awful accident."

Joe swallowed hard.

"But don't worry son, he'll pull through just fine." Despite his reassurance, there was doubt in his voice. "I've pieced some things together about … well, the situation with you and Fred. I think you and I should talk—very soon."

"Yeah, okay." Joe's face would make a ghost look tan.

"I'm at St. Jerome's Hospital, but I'll be home soon. How about when I get there I call you back at this same number? Can you come over to talk?

"Um … I think so. Mr. Pruitt?"

"Yes, Joe?"

"Is Fred going to … to die?" Joe's throat closed off on the last word.

"Not anytime soon he won't. He's in a good hospital with good doctors. I expect it's about the same with Fred as it was with you … when you lost your leg."

Joe nearly dropped the phone. "He's getting his leg amputated?"

"No, Joe, his arm," Mr. Pruitt said. "His left arm."

29

A Bloody Mess

"YOU LOOK A LITTLE GREEN, JOE." Mom twirled up spaghetti on her fork.

How do moms always know when something's wrong?

"Oh, just thinking about a thing that happened at school today."

Even crusty bread laden with butter wedges—one of his favorites—wasn't appetizing right now.

"What happened?"

"This guy was mowing the grass—Carlos." Joe stared at his plate. "He ran over a rock or something and it ricocheted and hit him in the eye. It was pretty bad … blood all over his face."

Mom winced. "Ooh, that's terrible. You saw it happen?"

"Yeah, everybody in PE saw it. I got an extra close look at it though."

"Oh, I'm so sorry Joey. You want to talk about it?"

"I'm all right. Can I save my dinner until later? I'm not really hungry right now."

"Sure, just put it on the counter and I'll cover it up for you. Why don't you go watch something funny on TV to help cheer you up?"

"Can I go ride my bike instead?"

"Of course honey, just don't go too far."

"Okay." Joe kissed his mom, leaving her a souvenir smudge of spaghetti sauce on her cheek.

Outside, it was breezy. The feel of the air told him spring's freshness was becoming summer's solid warmth.

While at home, Joe had kept his phone on vibrate in case Mr. Pruitt called. He decided he'd tell his mom about Fred's accident after he found out exactly what happened. But since Mr. Pruitt hadn't called, Joe rode his bike down to see if he'd come home yet.

Of course, Joe already knew what happened—any pinhead could piece *that* together. Blood at the condo, at Mr. Pruitt's, the stump hollowed out … Fred had cut off his arm with a chainsaw while working on Joe's secret entrance.

Joe felt awful. *I did this. If it wasn't for me, Fred would still have his arm!*

Just as he parked his bike near Mr. Pruitt's front door, the gold Town Car slung into the driveway. Mr. Pruitt was somber as he waved at Joe. Frederica sprang to the front-room window, whining and clicking her nails on the glass.

Mr. Pruitt opened his car door and sat there for a moment. He looked tired and worried.

Joe's hands slipped into his pockets and he slouched.

"Hi Mr. Pruitt."

"Hello Joe." He shook his head with a deep sigh, closing his eyes for a moment. "It's been one helluva day."

Joe slouched further.

"Come on inside and I'll fill you in. Then we'll see if we can sort things out."

Without a word, Joe followed Mr. Pruitt into the house.

Joe sat at the kitchen table, hands folded in his lap, while Mr. Pruitt picked through record albums in his living room. Then, the man went into the kitchen and gathered fixings for dinner, both his and Frederica's.

Suddenly, from inside a fancy, dresser-like structure came the sounds of an opera lady vocalizing her woes. The bass was loud and muddy. Occasional scratching sounds reminded him of the old turntable his dad had once brought out and demonstrated for Joe's amusement. He could still picture the needle coasting up and down on the record's warped surface.

"You hungry?" Mr. Pruitt said.

"No thanks. I just ate."

"How about dessert then? I have chocolate ice cream, ice cream sandwiches, coffee cake, apple pie. It's Mrs. Smith's—the neighbor, not the store brand."

"That's okay. I'm not really hungry."

"Well excuse my manners, but I haven't had anything since breakfast." He wasted no time diving into the subject. "I suppose I should tell you what happened to Fred today."

"I think I already know," Joe said. "He cut off his arm with a chainsaw out at the condo."

Mr. Pruitt paused. "That's part of the story."

Joe's phone vibrated but he ignored it.

"Yes, he was using the chainsaw to hollow out your stump," Mr. Pruitt said. "And best I can figure—from what little he told me and what I saw at the condo—the chainsaw slipped out of his hand as he was holding it upside down. It tore deep into the muscle and bone in the elbow area." He hesitated. "Maybe I shouldn't go into so much detail."

"No, I'm good." But Joe cringed at the thought of the chain's sharp teeth biting into Fred's arm. And those words—*your stump*—made his stomach sink further.

"Anyway, it was too torn up to repair. They had to remove his arm just above the elbow. Let's hope he isn't … wasn't left-handed."

Joe felt his face tingling.

"How …" He searched for the right question. "When can he go home?"

"Believe it or not, amputations are a fairly routine procedure these days. He could be home in as little as a week. But being completely healed and getting back to normal … well, that depends on Fred."

"He's strong." Joe's eyes pleaded with Mr. Pruitt for agreement. "He'll be back to normal really fast."

"Yes, he *is* strong."

Mr. Pruitt set Frederica's bowl on the floor, then placed his own dinner on the table across from Joe—a bologna sandwich, chips, and three sweet pickles. Most people would call it a lunch. *It must be nice to eat whatever you want whenever you want.*

Joe cupped his chin in the palm of one hand and ran a fingernail along the line separating the halves of the table. It was spotless, not a speck of food stuck there.

Mr. Pruitt pulled out a chair and sat.

"I haven't really had a chance to talk with Fred about the condo, but before the paramedics arrived, he did tell me to go get the chainsaw."

"How did … how did he know *you* knew where to look for it? I never told him about you."

"He just happened to show up at my shop door this morning—lucky he made it. Lucky I was there and lucky I had all my tools turned off and I heard him, for that matter. I guess he knew my house was the closest to the woods. After I called 9-1-1, he started to tell me where to find the chainsaw. He was very worried about it, as if he didn't have bigger problems right then. So I asked him 'Is it at the condo?' and he looked surprised—just before he lost consciousness. That's when the paramedics came. With all the medical attention he was getting, and his being knocked out after the surgery, I didn't get a chance to talk to him further."

"So you went out there and got the chainsaw?" Joe's phone vibrated again. *Must be Mom.*

"Right after the paramedics and police left. And I did something I never do, Joe—I lied." He looked upset. "I told the police I thought the chainsaw noise was coming from a different direction. When they went that way looking for it, I went out to the condo to get it—it was still idling—and I hid it further out in the woods, far enough that the police shouldn't find it. I still need to go out and get it before some kids run across it."

"Why did the cops come?" Joe's voice was trembling now.

"Police always come to accidents. They like to write reports, explain what happened—make sure there wasn't mischief. That's their job. And it gives lawyers something to chase after."

"Lawyers?" Joe's breathing was getting more rapid and shallow. "Is Fred going to get sued?"

Mr. Pruitt smiled. "Fred get sued? No, nobody's getting sued. But sometimes lawyers do encourage people to sue big companies for what they call 'wrongful injury due to defective products' or for lack of warning labels—as if someone wouldn't know that operating a chainsaw above your head to cut a hole in an oak stump is dangerous." He took another bite of his sandwich. "But still there could be trouble. That's why we need to talk. You *do* understand how this can open up a whole can of worms?"

"You mean the condo?"

"Exactly. For now, all work on the condo has to stop. Agreed?"

"Yeah, sure. I mean—of course." Yesterday Joe couldn't have imagined anything that would make him stop working on the condo. Today, he couldn't imagine wanting to finish it.

"I wish I could tell you when work can resume," Mr. Pruitt said. "But I can't. Today was a real eye-opener. If that had been *you* getting hurt so bad out there—well, I don't think I could live with myself."

Joe was silent.

I've ruined Fred's life and Mr. Pruitt could get arrested. He felt he should just go fire up the backhoe and fill the whole thing in.

Yes. That's exactly what I'm going to do—before anyone else gets hurt.

30

Responsible

BEFORE THEY PARTED COMPANY, Mr. Pruitt showed Joe where he hid a spare key to his house.

"What happened today reminded me that I'm an old man all alone," he said. "Mrs. Smith and the Wiersmas have keys to my house, but it can't hurt to have another responsible person able to get in. You never know what situations might arise these days."

Joe wondered what he'd done to earn the title of *responsible person*.

Before getting on his bike, he took the phone from his pocket to see who'd called—it was Mom. He put the phone in silent mode. Just before he turned the corner onto Oak Street, he saw something familiar out of the corner of his eye: Fred's pickup. He'd parked it farther down Woodside lane in an inconspicuous spot. It worked—Joe almost missed it.

He rode over and stood on the truck's side step to peer through the window. On the rearview mirror were wallet-sized photos: one of Fred's son, Phelps, decked out in graduation garb, and another of Fred and Phelps holding up a stringerful of rainbow trout. Joe didn't remember those pictures being there before. The cup holder held a coffee tumbler in one slot, and a binder-clipped stack of coupons and gift cards in the other. There was a newspaper on the passenger seat along with a clipboard and next to that was a new pair of work gloves still attached to a cardboard hanger.

Joe made sure the doors were locked, then pedaled home, fighting the urge to cry.

When he rounded the corner onto Oak Street, he saw his mom, standing at the end of his driveway, looking up the street in the opposite direction. When she turned around her hands went to her hips and her posture stiffened.

Uh-oh.

Joe put on his best innocent face, but that didn't change his mom's demeanor.

"Why didn't you answer your phone?"

"Uh, I didn't hear it."

"What do you mean you didn't hear it? Don't you have it turned on?"

"Yeah, it's on."

"Then how could you not hear it?"

"I don't know." Joe pulled out his phone and entered his swipe pattern. "Oh, the ringer was off. I see someone tried to call. Hey look, it was you!"

"Don't get cute with me! From now on you keep that phone in ring mode and you answer it when I call! Comprende?"

"Comprendo." If Joe had a tail, he'd tuck it between his legs right now.

She softened a bit. "There's something I need to tell you."

"What, Mom?" He put his phone back in ring mode and shoved it into his front pocket.

"We have to go to the hospital. Fred's been hurt."

"What happened?" Joe wanted to ask how *she* found out.

"He had an accident with a chainsaw. Joe …" She began to cry. "Fred had to have part of his arm … amputated."

"Oh God." Joe didn't have to try hard to seem shocked—seeing his mom crying made it hard not to burst into tears himself. "It's okay, Mom. Nothing can keep Fred down. He's real tough."

Mrs. McKinnon put her arms around her son. "I know he is, Joe." There seemed to be more she wanted to say, but she only kissed the side of his head. "C'mon. Let's put your bike away and go see Fred."

***

They drove to St. Jerome's Hospital in Mom's crimson Sequoia—the big SUV that had replaced her little red Honda. Although she never said so, Joe was sure that after seeing what happened to the Civic, she wanted something that wouldn't be crushed quite as easily. And the Sequoia had one other feature the Civic hadn't: a St. Christopher medal hanging from the rearview mirror.

"I'd like to know how it happened," Mom said.

"What do you mean?" This would be Joe's chance to see what people who weren't in the know were thinking.

"I mean … Fred's probably used every power tool there is, and I know he's used chainsaws plenty of times. Accidents happen, I know, but Fred and your dad used to yell at guys on the jobsite if they used tools dangerously or horsed around with those nomadic nailers."

"*Pneumatic*, Mom. *Pneumatic* nailers."

"Whatever. Mrs. Wislinski heard from Mrs. Smith that he was cutting a tree right here in the neighborhood when it happened. The police searched around, but they never did find where he was working. He just showed up at old Mr. Pruitt's house bleeding all over the place, and passed out before the ambulance arrived." She made the sign of the cross on herself. "Thank God Mr. Pruitt was home."

Joe kept quiet. Mom continued to speculate on why Fred was even in the neighborhood and who might have hired him, and why the police never found his chainsaw, which was probably *her* chainsaw that Fred had borrowed.

Mr. Pruitt was right. If this was any indication, there would be a lot of curiosity about where and how the accident happened. People were nosy and they gossiped and they'd keep in touch with the police about every little thing they saw or heard. Mr. Pruitt's advice—to stay away from the condo—would have to be followed.

31

(Not) Good to See Ya

JOE AND HIS MOM ARRIVED and found Fred asleep in his hospital bed. Other than numerous wires coming from his body, three IV bags dripping fluids into his right arm, an unmanly hospital gown, and a bandaged stump where his left arm had been, he looked just like Fred.

There were a few other visitors there too, talking quietly to each other. There was Wally, the plumber; "Tin Man" Tom, the roofer (an expert at bending and installing tin flashing on a roof); and some neatly groomed, smooth-faced guy in a spiffy dark-gray suit. He looked familiar, but Joe couldn't place him.

"Hi fellas," Joe's mom said as they entered through a propped-open door.

They all turned, and Wally and Tin Man lit up at the sight of Joe's mom.

"Hey-hey, Lori!" Tin Man came over and hugged her, then turned and gave Joe a strong handshake.

"I've been keeping my eye out for you, kid." He did his *I'm watching you* hand signal, pointing two split fingers at his own eyes, then pointing at Joe.

Wally was next. He cradled Joe's head in his sandpaper hands the way you'd hold up a melon to guess its weight.

"Man you've grown!" Joe started to reach out for a handshake, but Wally pulled him into a bear hug and gave him several pats on the back that rattled his ribs.

"What've you been up to, sport?" Tin Man said.

"Just hangin' around, I guess." It'd been a while since he'd dealt with the manhandle greetings so common with his father's friends: the shoulder punches, the oxygen-deprivation hugs, the knuckle-cruncher handshakes.

The well-dressed man reached out and firmly shook Joe's hand.

"Hello young man, my name's Francis." He smiled and Joe thought that made him look even more familiar. "How are you?"

"Hi, I'm Joe."

He studied Francis's attire: charcoal-gray suit with a gold American flag pinned to his lapel, a maroon tie with a smart-looking tie clasp, gold cuff links, and a gold band on his ring finger. His watch was black with gold numbers on a face encircled by tiny diamonds.

"Are you a doctor?" Joe said. *Doctors are rich, and this guy's definitely rich.*

The guys chuckled a bit.

"No, I'm an attorney."

Joe gasped.

"What's wrong?" Mom said.

"I … I … my throat's real dry. Think I'll go get a drink," he said, as he shuffled toward the door.

Once out of the room, he ran down the hall, passed the elevators, and slipped into the men's room where he closed himself into a stall—but the stall's frame was bent and the latch wouldn't catch. He let go of the door and it creaked back open a couple of inches.

Mr. Pruitt said there wouldn't be any lawyers. Fred lost his arm, and now a lawyer's here looking for somebody to sue, and it's my fault. And Mr. Pruitt—he could go to jail, or lose his house! Why did I ever dig that stupid hole for that stupid condo?

A moment later, the restroom door opened. Joe heard the ker-klunking of hard-soled shoes, steady and pronounced. They crossed just in front of Joe's stall before coming to a halt.

He pushed his door closed and looked through the crack. It was the lawyer, and he was looking down at the sink. He cleared his throat, then the clearing got louder and turned into coughing, which deepened until finally he turned around, went into the stall next to Joe, and spat.

He returned to the mirror where he combed his hair and primped himself.

Joe stayed motionless, holding the door closed with one hand. He hung his head down and stared at the floor.

The silence seemed unending.

"Hello?" the lawyer said. His voice reverberated throughout the restroom.

Joe froze, his eyes widened. How would he explain sitting there like this if the lawyer pushed his door open?

"I know you're there—answer!"

Joe started shaking. He could hear his own breathing— that shook too. The lawyer took a couple steps, then stopped.

There was no sound except the beeping from a distant piece of hospital equipment.

"C'mon, pick up the phone Stephanie," the lawyer said. "I know you're home."

Joe closed his eyes, then peeked through the crack again to see the lawyer half-sitting on the vanity, talking on his phone.

"All right then. I'm on the south side. I'll be home in less than an hour." Then he ker-klunked his way out of the restroom.

***

Joe waited a few minutes before going back to Fred's room. When he arrived, everyone was still there talking quietly, including the lawyer. Fred was still sleeping. Tin Man made his *I'm watching you* sign at Joe again.

Mom turned and smiled. "There you are … I was just about to call you. I thought you got lost."

"I did." Joe was relieved his phone hadn't rung. "How's Fred?"

"The doctor was in here before you and your mom got here," Wally said. "He said Fred's going to be just fine."

"That's a relief," Mom said. "Has he been awake yet?"

"Not really, just some mumbling," Tin Man said.

"Poor Fred," Mom said looking over at him. "As if life isn't tough enough already."

"He kept mumbling about a condo," Tin Man said. "At least that's what it sounded like he was saying, didn't it?" He turned to Wally.

"Yep, that's what it sounded like to me," Wally said. "He mentioned Phelps—and Joe—and a bunch of other nonsense."

"Pretty sure I heard him say something about Commissioner Gordon, too." Tin Man snickered. "Must have been dreaming he was Batman!"

Joe had an urge to run to the restroom again.

"Anybody else been here?" Mom said.

"Just the old guy—that neighbor of yours who brought him in," Wally said. "I think his name's Charlie. He's the one who called and told me about the accident."

"That must have been Mr. Pruitt," Mom said. "Clarence Pruitt. Why'd he call *you*?"

Joe was wondering the same thing.

"Well, that's kind of a funny story," Wally said. "He said he was looking through the contacts on Fred's phone for some next of kin—just in case—and he found *my* number under *mother* and gave me a ring."

"Should I ask?" Mom said with a grin.

"Evidently—and this goes way back—Fred here thought I complained to him too much about certain guys not doing their job right. I told him he should make them get their act together or get 'em outta there. So he says to me, *yes mother*. And after that, he called me mother whenever we talked business." He started to laugh. "I didn't know he put me into his phone that way, though."

"So then you called Tin Man—and you both dropped what you were doing to come here," Mom said. "That was sweet of you guys."

"That *was* very considerate of you," the lawyer said. "My brother has some loyal friends."

"His brother?" Joe stared at the lawyer. "I didn't know Fred had a brother!"

Mom turned to the lawyer. "He *did* keep you well hidden, Francis. Before today I think we've only met once."

"Some people don't want anyone to know they have an attorney in the family—especially if he's their twin brother."

Joe could see it now: the lawyer did look like Fred—a slicked-up, smooth-talking version of Fred—but a close copy nonetheless.

"I don't know why anyone would be ashamed of that," Mom said.

Joe gaped at her. *How can she say that after what they did to us?* He was surprised she didn't just spit on his shoes and stomp out of the room.

Out of nowhere Tin Man said, "Hey, how do you stop a lawyer from drowning in your pool?"

Wally gave him an elbow and a dirty look.

"Take your foot off his head," said a groggy, barely intelligible voice.

"What's that, Fred?" Mom went over to his side and laid her hand on his shoulder.

"How you stop a lawyer from drowning in a pool," he said. "Take your foot off his head." His breathing was labored, his eyes glassy.

Joe laughed. Fred looked over at him with a weak smile, then looked to the ceiling and closed his eyes. "Damn."

"Can I get you something?" Mom said. "Do you need the nurse?"

"Who's here?" Fred said.

"Well ..." She moved aside so Fred could see. Everyone else moved in closer. "There's your brother Francis, Wally, Tin Man, and Joe."

"Why'd you bring *him*," Fred said.

"Joe?" she said, looking baffled.

"No, the *lawyer*." He glared at Francis. "Better get to the emergency room—I think I just heard an ambulance pull up."

Francis pained a smile. "I came to see my brother. I'm here to help you in any way I can."

"Fsssssst."

"It's probably just the anesthesia," Mom said to Francis. "I'm sure he doesn't mean to—"

"It's *not* the anesthesia." If not for his current weakness, Fred surely would've rattled the windows. But his disdain for his brother shone in his eyes—what little of them could be seen. "Frank, get out!"

Everyone shrunk back. The lawyer turned to Joe's mom.

"It's probably best that I leave." Then he turned to Fred. "Call me if you need anything."

As Francis walked through the door, Fred said, "You know how to get a lawyer down from a tree?"

Frank hesitated, then kept clunking down the hall.

Fred yelled as loud as his scratchy, doped-up voice would allow: "Cut the rope!"

32

Dream on, Dream off

TO SOME DEGREE, WALLY and Tin Man were good at bringing Fred's bitter mood around. They teased him about being left alone with power tools, told him he could no longer scratch his butt and pick his nose at the same time, and tried to remember which hand he'd favored for nose-picking anyways. They said losing his arm might be the best thing that ever happened to his liver, since he wouldn't be able to open beer bottles anymore. When Tin Man started to make an unseemlier joke about Fred's stump, Wally cleared his throat and motioned toward Joe with his eyes.

Joe caught the gesture.

He said, "God thought for some of us, life would be too easy with all four limbs, so He wanted to make it more fair for the rest of you."

The guys thought that was pretty good.

Mom smiled. She probably didn't think Joe heard her when she'd said that to him on his thirteenth birthday.

After that, the guys gave their well wishes to Fred and made their exit.

Fred let out a deep sigh.

"Boy, I've done a lot of stupid things in my life, but this one …"

"Don't worry, I'm sure you'll surpass it someday," Mom said.

"Thanks," Fred said.

"Well, if you want some advice on how to adapt from someone who's been through it …" She put her arm around Joe.

"Maybe I could use some of that advice already," Fred said, still sounding slow. "Lori, you mind going to the gift shop and buying me a newspaper?" He turned his dopey eyes to Joe. "I'm sure there's one around here, but I want a fresh copy without germs."

Mom stepped over and patted Fred on the shoulder. "Sure. I'll take my time."

As soon as she was gone, Fred said, "We have to talk."

"I know," Joe said. "Mr. Pruitt told me."

"He talked to you already?"

Joe nodded.

"That old geezer saved my life, you know."

"I know."

"So he's the one. The ten-four CB radio talker."

"Uh-huh."

Fred worked to wet his tongue so he could talk better. "I don't have much steam left, so let's just set things straight."

Joe nodded. "Okay."

"Condo stops. Stops now."

"I know."

"Too dan … dangerous. You shouldn't be out there …" He nodded off for a second. "… alone."

"I know. I'm sorry, Fred. I'm so sorry. I'm gonna … Fred?"

Fred was sleeping.

A nurse came in. "And how's Mr.—"

Joe turned and snapped his finger to his lips.

"Shhhhh!"

33

Left Rites

ON THURSDAY AFTER SCHOOL, Joe found himself pulling up to the curb in front of The Brain. He'd decided that if he waited for his life to be perfect before he saw Jun, he might never see her again.

He was happy to see her waiting in the same spot where she was last Tuesday. Joe stopped and waved. She waved back, but remained standing there.

That's weird. Joe laid down his bike and walked up to her. She glanced at Joe then resumed looking up and down the street.

"Hi Joe," she said. "Try to not look like you're talking to me."

His heart sank, but he stood next to her without facing her.

"Are you that embarrassed to be seen with me?" he said. "I mean, are my clothes out of style or something?"

"Of course not." Jun giggled. "It's my mom. She's picking me up for my flute lesson and if she sees me talking to you, she'll ask about a million questions—she's so nosy about my life."

He relaxed. "She doesn't like you hanging out with handsome boys?"

She laughed again. "If that was it I wouldn't need to worry, would I?" She gave him a playful jab with her elbow.

"Probably not." He jabbed her back.

"Didn't see you yesterday."

Joe hesitated. "Yesterday wasn't a good day. Didn't think I'd be much fun to be around."

"I'm sorry," she said. "People don't always have to be fun to be with a friend, you know." Joe could almost sense her slight head-tilt. "You know the saying, for better or for worse?"

He smiled, but his stomach felt like it was doing somersaults.

"I didn't know we were getting married!"

"You *are* kind of cute … oh rats, there's my mom." She scooped up her backpack. "I gotta go. See ya!"

She ran down to the curb as a car turned into the entrance and up to where Jun was waiting. The passenger window was rolled down and Jun's mom began chattering in Chinese. While Jun put her backpack and flute in the back of the car, her mom gazed at Joe. He turned his head and brought his hand up, combing it through his hair.

Joe watched as they pulled away. Jun's arm was hanging out the window giving him a secret wave.

He waved low too. "See ya … friend."

***

A short while later, Joe found himself under the stump, looking up. Light shone through.

A tree stump for an entrance, huh? And a secret push button hidden in that tree over there to open it, I'm sure.

There was nothing funny about it now.

Using a shovel, Joe scooped up some bloody sawdust and poured it into a five-gallon bucket. Tears began to flow. When the bucket was full, he went up the ladder and found a patch of ground about twenty feet from the condo. He wanted a spot among the trees, but one with plenty of sunlight.

He found the perfect place, dug a hole, and poured the sawdust into it.

Last night he'd asked the nurse—the one he shushed—if he could have Fred's left arm. After a momentary look of shock and dismay, she'd said that even if the arm hadn't been bagged and sent away for incineration, hospital policy forbade them from giving away surgically removed body parts—

unless a hospital administrator gave permission prior to surgery.

After he thought about it, he was a little relieved not to have Fred's arm. He might have had nightmares about it crawling up the steps to his room, or knocking on his window and calling out *Joe! Joe!* in sign language. Yep, it was a good thing hospitals had those body parts burned.

After burying the sawdust, Joe erected a cross using scrap wood and a single screw. Then he made the sign of the cross on himself—something he hadn't done since before the accident—and closed his eyes in prayer. They remained closed even when he heard the panting of Frederica drawing near.

Mr. Pruitt stopped about a car length away. Joe finished his prayer and made the sign of the cross again.

"Very nice, son," Mr. Pruitt said. "Not that it's any of my business, but who've you got buried there?"

"A little part of Fred." Joe petted Frederica.

"Good Lord! That isn't his arm buried there, is it?"

"Nah, they wouldn't give it to me." He was still kneeling in front of the grave. "It's just some of his blood. Thought I should do something to … to … I don't know."

"I understand. I didn't mean to intrude on your ceremony—just came to look at the scene of the crime."

His heart skipped. "Crime?"

"Figure of speech. What're you going to do now?"

Joe looked down. "Fill it in."

Mr. Pruitt seemed caught off guard.

"Now?"

"As good a time as any," Joe said.

"Don't be too hasty, now. Why don't you leave it sit, and see what happens?"

"Why, so someone can fall into it and break their neck?"

"If it hasn't happened before now … look, I think it'll be safe for another few days. Just let it sit. Trust me, it's not a good idea to make big decisions right after an event like this.

The mind needs time to sort through it all while the emotions settle down."

Joe stood up. He tossed the bucket and shovel into the condo.

"I just want it all to go away."

He mounted his bike and rode off.

34

Get a Grip

JOE SAT WHILE THE DOCTOR finished talking with his patient.

"Don't give me that crap." Fred pointed a finger at the doctor. "I've seen pictures where someone's had a chunk of their leg bitten off by a shark, and *they* kept all their limbs."

"I assure you that if this person you speak of had the kind of bone and nerve damage you had, they would not have kept their limb," the doctor said. "We very carefully assessed your situation and studied the images—the scans—from every angle. If there was any hope at all for saving your arm and elbow, we would have attempted to do so."

"Even if it meant sending me to another hospital? Even if it meant *them* making money off of this instead of *you*?"

The young doctor looked at Joe and his mom, who quickly looked away.

"Mr. Fergussen, I assure you—"

"Assure this!" He made a gesture Joe was pretty sure he wasn't supposed to see. "Go remove a healthy organ and make yourself fifty grand." Fred turned his head toward the window.

Without another word, the doctor spun on his heels and left. He first went up the hall one way, then down the other, looking away from Fred's room as he passed.

"I take it you're not happy," Mom said.

"Ahhh, what does he know? Punk kid with a stethoscope and some fancy half-million-dollar diploma. Just turned old enough to drink last week, and he's making decisions that affect people for the rest of their lives."

"Better he didn't start drinking until *after* he got his diploma, don't you think?" Mom said. Joe chuckled.

"A good buzz every now and then might have made him a little more human," Fred said. "*I assure you Mr. Fergussen ...* Ivy League momma's boy."

"Would you like us to come back another time? Maybe after they give you a fresh dose of meds?"

Fred's expression quickly changed. He reached over and took her hand.

"No, please don't go," he said. "I was just blowin' off some steam. You know how I am."

"That I do. Would you like another germ-free newspaper or anything else?"

"Actually, I could use a cup of coffee. But be sneaky about it—the nurses around here will cut your arm off if they catch you." He held up his stump but there was no trace of humor on his face.

"Of course. Is it safe to leave my son alone with you for a few minutes? If you don't kill him, he might just cheer you up."

Fred looked over at Joe, still sitting quietly in the guest seat.

"Cheer would be a pretty tall order right now." Fred forced a minimal laugh making himself cough. "But I suppose it's safe enough."

She gave Fred's hand a final squeeze before departing.

"Your mom's a good woman," Fred said. Joe stared at the floor.

"You ever feel like your left leg is still there?"

Joe looked down at his left leg, then back at Fred.

"Yeah, because it is."

"I meant your missing leg."

"Yeah, sometimes. They call it phantom limb. It hurt at first, but the pain went away after a while."

"Mmm." Fred moved his stump, and Joe stared at it like it was a freak-show attraction. He wasn't sure why it bothered him since he had one of his own. "You never did tell me ..."

"Tell you what?"

150

"Why you were building the condo."

"Doesn't matter now," Joe said with equal measures of sorrow, self-pity, and indifference.

"Course it does, chief. You were pretty hopped up on doin' this thing. Whatever good reason you had in the first place didn't just disappear with my arm."

"Yes it did." Joe sighed. "I never could've done what I wanted to do anyway. It was a stupid dream."

"All right, then …" Fred thought for a second. "Why are you so far away? Come over here. I don't bite … much."

Joe went over and stood next to the bed—miles closer to Fred's stump.

"So what do you wanna do when you grow up, anyway? Be a scientist or something?"

"Sort of a scientist, yeah."

"What sort? Chemist? Physicist? Unabomber?"

Joe gave Fred a dirty look. "Why do you always think I'm going to make bombs or something?"

"Ahhh, I'm just teasin' ya." Fred tapped Joe's arm with his fist. "Come on, what kind of scientist do you want to be?"

"Inventor," Joe said.

"Inventor?" Fred said.

"Yeah, inventor."

"*Inventor.*"

Joe gave him the stink eye.

"What's wrong with that?"

"Mad scientist sounds more exciting." His stump moved as he attempted to gesture with his missing hand. "What are you going to invent?"

"I have some ideas," Joe said. "But I'm not at liberty to discuss them."

"Oh, you're not, huh? Sounds like you've been talking to my brother the lawyer." He stared up at the wall-mounted television. "When you feel like you can trust me, I'm all ears, Joe."

"All right, I'll tell you."

"Don't strain yourself, kid."

Joe grimaced. "It has to do with cars …"

"Go on."

"I want to get rid of them."

"You know there's billions of them, don't you?"

"So? People are always willing to replace what they have with newer or better stuff."

"What would you replace them with?"

"I have this idea for an automated transportation system. Kind of like trains or monorails, but ones that go from inside your house to anywhere you want to go. Even people who can't drive could go wherever they needed to go. It would be the greatest improvement in transportation the world has ever seen! It would eliminate accidents, get rid of most of our need for gas, nobody would ever have to buy car insurance again, no more traffic jams, and police wouldn't have to spend time worrying about how people drive cuz they wouldn't be driving anymore!"

"Mmmm."

He glanced down at Joe's leg. Joe noticed. Then Fred looked up, not quite looking into Joe's eyes, and patted him on the arm.

"Nice idea … but not as easy as inventing a newfangled vegetable chopper."

"I know."

"Or an electric nose-picker. The guys say I'm gonna need one now."

Joe laughed a little.

"What does this have to do with the condo?"

"It was going to be my research lab."

"Why not use your dad's workshop? More convenient … lots of tools."

"That's where I'll build it, but I wanted a getaway to do all my planning and thinking. And to test some ideas."

Fred shook his head. "I don't get it."

"What's to get?"

"Seems to me you have all the solitude you need at home. You worried your mom's going to interfere? You *know* she would have interfered with your condo at some point, anyway. I mean, hell, if you're gone for hours at a time, don't you think after a while she would've gotten just a little bit suspicious?"

"I was going to tell her—after it was built."

"Why after?"

"Because I didn't think she'd let me do it. I figured once it was done, she'd ground me for a week or two for lying, then say *Oh well, I guess it's already done—he might as well use it.* You know—cut the gimpy kid some slack."

"Gimpy kid, huh? Is that how you see yourself?"

Joe shrugged. "Don't you?"

"What, think you're gimpy?" Fred gave the first genuine laugh Joe had heard since before he lost his arm. "Far from it, my friend. An' if you're gimpy, what does that make me? I ain't no gimp—but call me stumpy if you'd like."

Joe half-laughed. "No thanks, I'll stick with calling you Fred."

"I know it's a little late to be pressing on this *why build a condo* issue—could've saved us all a lot of trouble if we'd talked about it more up front—but I'm still trying to wrap my stumpy arm around the whole idea of needing an underground fortress in the middle of the woods to invent something. Can you clear that up for me? C'mon, Joe, talk to the phantom." He held up his stump like it had an ear attached to it.

Behold, the freak!

"I'm so sorry about your arm," Joe said. "I never meant for anyone to get hurt."

Fred patted Joe's arm. "I wasn't blaming you."

Joe's eyes became glassy. "You've done everything for me, and look what I did to you." A tear spilled.

Fred grabbed Joe's arm with a forceful grip.

"You've done nothing to me, you understand? This was my mistake!" His look was so intense, Joe felt it more than the iron grip on his arm. "If you start taking blame for other people's mistakes, you'll be a whipping boy for everything that goes wrong around you for the rest of your life. Take responsibility for your own mistakes and that's all. Got it?"

"But if I didn't start this project—"

"Did you ask me to hollow out that stump?"

"That hurts!" He tried peeling Fred's thumb off his arm.

"Did you?"

"No …"

Fred loosened his grip a little.

"Correct. Did you blackmail me, twist my arm, put a gun to my head?"

Joe gave a wet-nosed snort.

"No."

"Right again. My choice. My mistake. My responsibility. When *you* cut *your* arm off, then you can take the blame …" He let go of Joe and pointed to his stumpy arm. "But for this foul-up, let me enjoy my own self-punishment."

Just then, there was a knock at the door.

"Come in," Fred said.

"You any happier?" Mom said. She entered carrying a tray with three covered drinks.

"Immensely," Fred said. He gave Joe a pat on the arm. "Immensely."

35

Do the Math

IT WAS FIVE FIFTEEN A.M., AND JOE WAS at the kitchen counter setting a brushed-nickel measuring cup on a postal scale. On a notepad he wrote: *cup = 7.2 ounces.*

Next, he shoved the cup into a bag of sugar, heaped it full and leveled it off with a steak knife. Then he placed the cup of sugar on the scale and wrote above the previous measurement: *cup with sugar = 14.0 ounces.* He drew a line under the two measurements and wrote: *1 cup of sugar = 6.8 ounces.*

Next, Joe found the smallest teaspoon in the kitchen drawer: *1/8 tsp.* He hopped back to the calculator, punched in *100 ÷ 8* and wrote down the result: *12.5.* He scooped out one-eighth teaspoon of sugar and leveled it off. Now he needed a dark, flat surface to pour it on, but nothing jumped out at him. Their plates were white … aha—the construction paper in his bedroom closet! But as he started to get up, he noticed the countertop. It was dark green.

"Duh."

He poured the sugar on the counter. The color contrast was perfect, but the sugar heap was too tall for dissection, so Joe banged his fist on the granite trying to flatten it out. At first he banged softly, but soon he was beating the counter like an angry politician. The pile didn't move.

If only we had a flimsy tract-home counter.

Mom's voice yawned from behind.

"Honey, what are you so mad about?"

Joe's roving eyes found junk mail.

"Nothing Mom, just doing my project."

He pivoted the envelope on top of the tiny sugar pile until the sugar settled into a flat circle on the counter.

"I'm afraid to ask." She eyed his sugar pile as she shuffled into the kitchen.

Joe carefully lifted the envelope, then picked up the knife and, like a pizza chef, cut his sugar into twelve wedges. Using the knife, he scraped away all but one wedge of the white crystals, disposing the unneeded eleven-twelfths back into the bag of sugar.

Mom winced. "Well I certainly hope the counter and your hands were clean. Are you trying to limit your sugar intake or something?"

"It's for my report on solar power."

"Oh, I see." Mom poured some bran flakes into a bowl.

Joe hopped over to where his crutch was propped against the corner and with it, disappeared into his bedroom. A few seconds later, he reappeared holding an empty pill bottle; he'd saved some of these after his amputation surgery. Back at the counter, he swept the remaining bit of sugar—about one-hundredth of a teaspoon—into his waiting hand under the countertop, then poured it into the container.

"Mom, next time you go to the store can you buy me five bags of sugar?"

"So much for limiting your sugar intake," she said. "What on earth do you need five bags of sugar for?"

"It's for my report."

"Five five-pound bags?"

"Yep."

"Of granulated sugar?"

"Yep."

"I thought your report was on solar power."

"It is." Joe was already back at the table waking up his computer.

Mom dug into her bran flakes while studying him.

"They won't write 'most likely to filibuster' next to *your* picture in the yearbook."

"Huh?" Joe wondered how she could eat that tasteless cereal without any sugar.

"Promise someday you'll tell me what your report was really about?"

"I told you, it's about solar power."

Joe was now glued to the computer. Last week he'd asked his mom to share her expertise as a reference librarian and not only did she impress him with her knowledge of information sources, but he'd walked away knowing a government website to find statistics on just about anything. From that website, he'd found links that helped him gather the information needed for his persuasive speech.

There were about 130 million homes in the US—a lot of homes and a lot of power consumption. Joe decided he'd make the class see the enormity of this number by using sugar to represent homes: one-hundredth of a teaspoon for five hundred homes and one teaspoon for fifty thousand homes. Then by converting teaspoons to cups to pounds, he knew that 130 million homes could be represented by twenty-three pounds of sugar—or roughly four and three-fifths five-pound bags of sugar.

But this was just the start of the math. He was going to show that with an initial donation of one billion dollars split among a group of wealthy, environment-minded philanthropists, solar power could eventually find its way to *every* home in America.

Of course, he wouldn't show them all the actual numbers; his class would hate him if he walked them through that much math. This was where the sugar came in.

He still wasn't thrilled about it—the sugar was cool, but not *that* cool. Hopefully they wouldn't laugh him out of the room.

36

The Chase

AFTER SCHOOL, JOE RODE SO FAST he arrived at The Brain a few seconds before the bell. He sat on his bicycle near the curb facing the entrance. He no longer felt so bashful about coming by to see Jun. The way he saw it, their friendship was established when he acted as her personal music stand, and was further cemented by yesterday's brief encounter.

Next door, the jubilant Algonquinites squealed with delight as they raced off to start their three-day weekend. The Brainers seemed happy too, but showed a little more dignity, as befitting their academic supremacy.

Over the next few minutes, a wave of kids flooded out of The Brain—just not Jun.

At last, someone approached Joe. He thought she might be one of the girls who'd given him a weird look on Tuesday.

"Hey boyfriend!" she said.

Joe looked around to see who she was talking to.

"Yeah, you," she said. "Your girlfriend got picked up early by her mom today."

Is Jun telling people I'm her boyfriend? The possibility made him almost giddy.

"Okay, thanks." He started to ride away.

"She really missed you on Wednesday," she called after him. "You'd better send her some flowers or something."

Joe blushed, but he laughed and kept riding.

***

Although he'd missed seeing Jun today, his heart was dancing.

But his exhilaration faded when he turned onto Oak Street and saw the car parked across from his house. As he neared the gold-trimmed metallic-blue sedan, Joe could see a man with dark sunglasses in the driver's seat. *No way does that car belong in this neighborhood.* When Joe turned into his driveway, the man in the Lexus got out and started walking toward him. It was Fred's brother, Francis—the lawyer.

"Joe," the lawyer said. "I need to speak with you."

No you don't!

Joe dropped his backpack, cut straight through his lawn, blazed through the Evans' yard, and biked over twelve feet of their driveway. Once on Oak, he sped toward the woods as fast as he could pedal.

Meanwhile, Francis hopped back into the Lexus and flipped it around. He was heading toward Joe—fast.

With his lead, Joe could've gone straight through the field and into the woods for an easy escape, but instead he swerved right across the Anderson's lawn and onto Woodside Lane, heading for the other trail entrance. It was farther and riskier, but Joe didn't want the lawyer to see him heading toward the condo—he might come out there looking for him.

Despite his shortcuts and furious pedaling, the Lexus was closing in on him. Joe was almost at the trail, but he was on the wrong side of the street. If he crossed over now, the lawyer could speed past and use the ditch to wedge him in.

C'mon fake leg, stay with me!

Joe's left leg was burning when a car came around the corner from Birch Street. Joe lurched left in front of it. The driver braked, veered to Joe's right and laid on her horn. Even with her windows up and horn blaring, Joe could hear her yell, "Stupid-ass kid!"

The lawyer was forced to brake and swerve right onto the road's shoulder, which bought Joe the margin he needed to launch his bike off the edge of the road, over the ditch's dirt bridge, and onto the trail. But his momentum kept him going, out of control and off the trail into the weeds, and finally into the soft clumpy dirt of the freshly plowed firebreak. He soon came to a standing halt.

So did the Lexus.

The lawyer jumped out. "Joe, wait up! I just want to talk to you!" He headed toward the dirt bridge.

No you don't. You want to destroy what's left of me and my mom's life.

Joe was breathing hard, but his adrenaline wasn't spent yet. With a single heave, he lifted the bike's front tire out of its rut and back onto the packed-down trail.

"Joe, wait!" The lawyer sounded frustrated. "Come back!"

He baby-stepped down to the dirt bridge, a descent too steep for his slick-soled oxfords. By the time he made it across the ditch and through the weed berm to the firebreak, Joe was on the main straightaway trail that paralleled Woodside Lane and headed toward the golf course.

Once Joe passed the first strip of trees perpendicular to the trail, he took a left on another trail, which led to still another trail, which headed back towards Spooky Acres and Ground Thirteen. All these turns were out of sight from Woodside Lane, and well out of reach of ill-intentioned lawyers.

37

The Opposite of Intelligent Is …

JOE SAT IN THE SEAT of the backhoe facing the front bucket, which was full and poised above the hole. His hand rested on the joystick, ready to dump.

Time to end this thing.

He dropped the first scoop into the condo. He could hear the dull thud of the dirt and hollow sound of the rocks hitting the floor below, but couldn't see it. He was glad of that. He backed away and went to the pile for another bucketful.

It would go quickly until he ran out of dirt, at which point he'd have to go back to Spooky Acres for every bucketful—that would be tedious. But the way he felt now, he'd carry dirt from that ghost-infested hellhole one handful at a time if he had to. If Francis was looking for evidence, he'd have better luck searching for Elvis.

The second bucket was a little quieter, and Joe didn't hesitate dumping it. At some point he'd have to use the back bucket to pack the dirt, otherwise the resulting sinkhole might give away the former condo's location. He was going back for another load when his phone rang.

He pulled it from his pocket and hesitated.

"Hello?" Joe said.

"What's up, Joe?"

"Hi Fred, nothing much. How's it going?"

"Take a guess." Fred was grumpy.

"Sorry, dumb question."

"I'm still in the hospital, but I may be planning a jailbreak. Can I count on you?"

"Ummm … sure, I guess," Joe said. "When?"

"I'll let you know when the plan's solidified," Fred said. "What are you doing right now?"

"Filling in the condo."

"What! Why are you doing that?"

"Because it's through."

"Says who?" Fred said.

"Says me."

"Well …" It was unlike Fred to struggle for words. "Don't do it."

"Why not? You were right: it's illegal, it's dangerous, it's stupid."

"But it's your *dream*, man."

"It's stupid."

"Nobody's dream is stupid." Joe had to pull the phone away from his ear a little. "And no man has the right to tell another man not to pursue his dreams, even if they are … stupid—which yours isn't—aren't—whatever. I hate grammar. Especially with these brain meds—I mean pain meds."

"My dream cut off your arm!"

"Now *that's* stupid!" Fred said. "It was my own stinkin' stupidity that cut off my arm, not your dream … stupid!"

"Don't call me stupid!"

"I'm gonna reach right through this phone and wring your neck if you don't get it through your thick skull, McKinnon— *I'm* to blame for losing my arm! Nobody else!"

Joe remained perched in the seat of his backhoe with his eyes roving around Ground Thirteen as if trying to find a counterargument.

"Didn't mean to call you stupid, Joe." But Fred still sounded upset. "I just need you to understand once and for all, this was an accident that could've happened to me at any time. A guy working with big power tools who gets to feeling too comfortable with those tools is bound to have an accident some time. I've seen it happen too many times. Start to not respect the tools you're working with and they give you a little reminder of what they can do to you. Mine was a pretty big reminder. Coulda happened anywhere, anytime—so stop kicking yourself, because it wasn't your fault!"

"Okay …" Joe fidgeted. "But what about all the trouble me and you and Mr. Pruitt can get in? And what about your brother?"

"Frank? What about him?" From the sound of his voice, Joe could almost picture Fred on all fours in his hospital bed baring his teeth and growling. "Has he been talking to you?"

"He tried to. Just a little while ago he chased me into the woods."

"He—what? He literally ran after you?"

"No, I was on my bike and he was in his car. He nearly had me, too."

"You sure *you're* not on pain meds, kid?"

"I'm serious! I got home and he was waiting for me so I tried to get away and he chased me with his car!"

A moment strolled away in silence. Through the phone, Joe could hear what sounded like a home-improvement program on the hospital TV.

"Don't worry," Fred said at last. "It won't happen again."

More silence.

"Joe?"

"Yeah?"

"Dreams go on—despite anything that's happened, despite anything that's happening right now," he said. "And if that condo is important for your dream—then the condo goes on. How much did you fill in so far?"

"Two buckets."

"Peanuts. Scoop it back out."

More silence.

"Joe?"

"Yeah?"

"Have I ever lied to you?"

"How would I know?"

"Joe." Fred sounded serious.

"No … I guess not."

"Then know that I'm speaking the truth when I say this: Mick McKinnon would have wanted you to finish this."

Joe drew a deep breath and closed his eyes.

"Your father loved the woods," Fred said. "Some guys go to the bar or go fishing. Your dad walked out the door and down the street … and he went into the woods. He told me that's where he always went when he needed to reboot, or just to think things through." The background noise ended; Fred had shut off the TV. "And I've figured it out … you're the same way. That's why you're building the condo."

Joe moved the phone's mouthpiece away so Fred wouldn't hear his shaky breathing as the tears fell.

Fred gave him space to recover before continuing.

"And Joe?"

"Yeah?" He dug deep for composure.

Fred raised his voice. "To hell with my arm … and screw Frank! All dreams have speed bumps … now step on the gas and go!" Fred hung up. He'd surely woken up half the hospital.

Joe set his phone down. He was laughing … or crying … or both. A moment later, the phone rang again—Fred.

"Yeah?"

"Just be safe. Don't be stupid … like me."

And with that, Fred hung up again. He seemed to have forgotten how to end a phone call with "goodbye."

38

It's Thru

JOE DROVE THE BACKHOE to the condo's edge, lowered the rear bucket into the hole near the floor, and turned it upward. Then he descended the ladder carrying a square shovel and began filling the bucket with the dirt he'd poured inside just minutes ago. Within a half hour, the floor was clear, with only a scattering of dirt and stains on the plywood.

Next, after a quick peek from under the stump, Joe decided which method was best for finishing the job. He put on a pair of safety goggles—a bright new idea—fired up the generator, and plugged in his reciprocating saw. Then he centered a small stepladder under the stump—something Fred must have brought with him.

He lifted the saw. With a pull of the trigger, work resumed at Ground Thirteen.

As the saw shook in Joe's hands, sawdust rained down, powdering his face and falling down his shirt. Chunks of wood bounced off his arms. Before Fred got to the stump, it was an impregnable fortress of solid oak. Now it was a bloodless artery encrusted with cholesterol and Joe was a doctor, removing plaque to make a smooth vessel through which he, a large one-legged blood cell, could easily pass.

Joe felt a surge of satisfaction as the opening got bigger, letting in more light and making it easier to see what he was doing. The stump was giving up—it seemed Joe was going to win.

"What're you doing, Joe?"

He let the saw down and peered out. It was Mr. Pruitt. And the tone of his voice sounded less like "what are you doing" and more like "What do you *think* you're doing?"

"Finishing the stump," Joe said.

"Well, I can *see* that," Mr. Pruitt said with his hands on his hips. "What I mean is who gave you permission to start working on the fort again?"

"It's not a fort. It's a condo."

"That doesn't answer the question, son. Have you forgotten what just happened? Have you thought about what could happen to you out here all alone, using tools like that, without even telling me you're out here?"

"I have," Joe said.

"Regardless, *you* need to stop—right now—until *we* make a decision regarding *if* and when you can start again."

He'd never seen Mr. Pruitt angry before. But this wasn't Mr. Pruitt's dream, it was Joe's. And if Fred was okay with him going ahead, that was all the approval Joe needed.

Joe climbed the ladder, pulled out his phone and called Fred.

"Mr. Pruitt wants to talk to you." He handed his phone to the flustered old man.

Mr. Pruitt stared at Joe. "Who is this?"

"This is Fred." His voice boomed through the receiver as clearly as if it were on speakerphone.

"Fred, I came out to the *condo* ..." he glared at Joe. "And found our friend working on the stump with a saw."

"Good," Fred said.

"Good?" Mr. Pruitt said. "Why don't you take a good look at your left arm and say that again."

"Calm down, Clarence."

"Calm down?" Mr. Pruitt started pacing around. "I just spent over an hour today lying to the police on yours and Joe's behalf, and *yesterday* I had to go ... conjure up a crime scene to show to the police *and* your brother, who, by the way, just showed up and invited himself into the situation. Do you know how much trouble I can get in if they find out what I did? And you're telling me to calm down?"

"I'm hearin' ya."

166

"And that brother of yours isn't buying it," Mr. Pruitt said. "He's already onto Joe somehow—did you say something?"

"No, I didn't." He still hadn't lowered his voice, and Joe could hear every word. "What'd he say?"

"He didn't divulge anything—typical lawyer—just asked me what I knew about Joe, and whether I thought he knew anything about your accident."

"Don't worry about Frank."

"Is that all you have to say?"

"No," Fred said. "I also want you to leave Joe alone. He's doing what he needs to do."

"Are you kidding me?"

"I recently downgraded from two arms to one, so I'm not in the mood for kidding."

"I see. And you want me to leave Joe alone to end up the same way?"

"Do you work alone in your woodshop?"

"Yes, but I'm not a child and I—"

"Neither is Joe. He's a young man. Let him *be* one."

"But the danger is real. I can't watch while—"

"Then don't!" Fred said.

Off to the side, Joe grinned.

"I can't believe you would just let a youngster—"

"Oh, fer cryin' out loud, give it up already!" Even through the phone, Fred came across louder than Mr. Pruitt. "Stop being an old woman. If you can't stand behind Joe, then go back to your shop and let the man get back to work."

Mr. Pruitt dropped the phone from his ear, and after a second, handed it back to Joe. He then walked off, dismissing them both with a flick of his wrist and mumbling, "Go ahead, cut off *your* arm too."

Joe put the phone to his ear. "He left. I don't think he's very happy."

"Hated to do that," Fred said. "He *did* save my life. But things had to be straightened out."

Suddenly, Mr. Pruitt turned around and pointed his finger at Joe.

"You better hope your mother doesn't hear about this!" Then he turned and continued toward home.

"Did you hear that?" Joe said.

"No, was it worth repeating?

"He said *I better hope my mom doesn't hear about this*."

"She won't," Fred said.

"How do you know?"

"Because he's not a rat—and he knows I can still make a fist with my right hand."

39

Blip

AFTER FINISHING UP THE HOLE in the stump, Joe went home—with little daylight left to spare. Mom had called, worrying about where he was, but Joe was able to lay a nice cover story on her. Mom also said they wouldn't be going to see Fred tonight; he'd called and said he needed rest.

Approaching his driveway, Joe suddenly remembered being chased by the lawyer. Funny how that had been over-shadowed by even bigger drama. But it made him realize: his backpack was gone. He scoped the area where he'd dropped it, but it wasn't there. So he went inside.

"Hey Mom, did you see my backpack?"

"Well it's good to see you too, Joseph, my long-lost son."

"Sorry Mom, how are you?" He went over to the dining room table where she sat reading through mail and gave her a hug.

"Good, how are you?"

"Good. Have you seen my backpack? I left it outside when I came home from school and now I can't find it."

"Oh great. Don't tell me someone stole it and now we'll have to replace all your books."

"I'm sure it's around somewhere," he said. "I'll go look for it again."

Joe returned to the front yard.

I know lawyers are bad, but why would he want my backpack?

Joe scanned the yard in a circle, and there it was—up on the front porch near the door, the entrance nobody ever used.

As he approached it, he noticed something stuck inside the pack's top loop. It was a business card for the law firm of Shaffer, Fergussen & White. A note written on the back said:

Joe,

My number is on my card. Please call me.
There's something I need to discuss with you.

Francis Fergussen

Joe shoved the card into his pocket and went back inside. Mom was still going through papers at the table.

"I see you found it," she said. "Where was it?"

"On the front porch—forgot I left it there."

"You know what would happen to your head if it wasn't attached?"

"Yep. I'd lose it."

"That's right."

Joe picked up an envelope that didn't look like the usual junk mail. Mom glanced up at it.

"Oh, that's an invitation from Ramesh's family," she said. "They're having a party on Monday. That's Memorial Day in case you forgot. We're going, so keep your calendar open."

Joe snorted. *Like I keep a calendar?*

"A Memorial Day barbeque?"

"Not so much," she said. "It's Ramesh's graduation—he just finished his master's degree. So make sure you get your homework done before then."

Joe liked Ramesh—a lot. If the party was for anyone else, he might bellyache about it, but a party for Ramesh was worth going to.

"You know, I never formally RSVP'd," Mom said. "Why don't you call and tell them to count us in."

Joe let out a long sigh.

"All right," he said.

Mom gave him a look. "Don't strain yourself, now."

Joe called the number on the invitation and asked to speak with Ramesh, then sat at the counter and waited.

"You probably could've just told whoever answered that we're coming to the party," Mom said. "By the way, tell them we're going to the ceremony too. It's before the party."

Ceremony?

Before he could question her, Ramesh came to the phone. "Hello?"

"Hey Ramesh, this is Joe McKinnon."

"Hey, Joe. How are you?"

"Pretty okay. Just calling to say we're coming to your party."

"And the puja!" Mom said as she tossed more mail in the trash.

"And the puja, whatever that is." Joe left the room to avoid being used as Mom's telephone puppet.

"Yes, the puja," Ramesh said. "It's how we celebrate and receive blessings on special occasions."

"Would we have to wear anything special? Like a puja robe, or a hat or something?"

Ramesh chuckled. "You and your mom can dress as you usually do. You will only be observing."

"Okay. I guess we'll be there then."

"That's great!"

"Awesome. Oh—when does it start?"

"You're welcome to come over after twelve. The puja starts at two, we'll have a meal—the party will be later. Of course I hope you can stay for both."

"I'll tell my mom. Thanks Ramesh."

Joe went back to the dining area and returned the phone to its charger.

"I told Ramesh we're going to both things. He says *I* can wear whatever, but *you* have to wear one of those Indian robes and put a dot on your forehead."

"Perfect. Speaking of Ramesh, are you coming to the library tomorrow? He asks about you all the time."

"Can't, I'm still trying to finish up the Doersmas' yard. I'll see him at the party. And maybe next Saturday." *Soon I won't have to lie to her anymore.*

* * *

Lying in his bed that night, Joe checked his phone. There was a text message from Fred.

It said, *"Don't worry about Pruitt just keep the dream going."*

Joe plugged his phone into its charger and lay back in bed. The brightness of his alarm clock's LED display was obnoxious—he always kept it pointed away from him while he slept—and it illuminated his Einstein poster. Joe studied Albert's face as he waited for sleep to come.

What were you like when you were my age? Did you ever do anything you weren't supposed to?

The scientist's eyes twinkled with mischief.

Did anyone ever get hurt because of the things you did?

The wrinkles on his forehead showed worry.

What should I do tomorrow?

Albert said, *I never think of the future. It comes soon enough!*

40

Look Both Ways ... or Not

ON SATURDAY MORNING, on his way to the condo, the dewy grass and weeds overhanging the trail left Joe soaked from the knees down. It was now the end of May, and a lot brighter at this time of the morning than it was when he'd started the project over a month ago.

As he turned off the main trail toward Ground Thirteen, Joe remembered that April day when he'd fallen off his bike and cried.

Big baby.

Spooky Acres was just behind him now. He had half a mind to turn around and ride straight into it and yell "Bring it on, Spooky Acres!"—but the other half of his mind convinced him to do that later, when he wasn't so busy.

Once at the hole, Joe stopped and stared. In spite of all the recent interference, the condo had progressed to its most rewarding stage: roof construction.

Walls are nice for defining the space, but the roof—that's what makes the difference between being in a home and standing in an open field.

But as much as he wanted to start hanging trusses right now, he knew he needed to get the drywall down inside while it was still open.

Joe started by dragging a sheet of plywood until it hung over the edge of the hole, then laid a sheet of drywall on top of it. He went down the ladder and looked up at the sheets. Getting the floor plywood down hadn't been so bad— plywood doesn't get banged up as easily as drywall. Plus, he'd bunched up some towels at the bottom to help absorb the impact. But the drywall would break if he dropped it down that way.

He stroked his chin and pondered.

Up above, something shuffled in the leaves. Joe backed into a corner—should he hide? Then he heard heavy panting.

Frederica!

"Hiya Fred!" Joe said.

The dog stretched a happy yawn and wagged hello. A moment later, more leaf movement announced the arrival of Fred's owner.

"Morning Joe," Mr. Pruitt said.

"Morning Mr. Pruitt."

He sighed. "Joe, I need to apologize for yesterday. I didn't need to be so rude to you."

No, you didn't. "That's okay," Joe said. "No big deal."

"It *was* a big deal, Joe. That wasn't the usual me. I guess I was getting a little nervous in the service."

"Huh?"

"You know, nervous in the service? Hysterics in the barracks?"

Joe squinted.

"I'm just very concerned for your safety," Mr. Pruitt said.

"I understand."

"I spoke with Fred again last night."

Joe tensed. Fred wouldn't have changed his mind ... would he?

"It was a good conversation ... and we reached an agreement concerning the condo."

Joe noted his use of the word *condo* instead of *fort*.

"We decided construction can continue—but with a few stipulations. Those stipulations are as follows ... are you ready?"

Here we go. Here's where I lose control of it all.

"I hope so," Joe said.

"*One,*" Mr. Pruitt said. "I'm here when you're here, and that's for your safety. *Two*: you still make all decisions concerning the design and construction of the condo—unless there's a safety issue with something you're wanting to do. *Three*: we have someone help us with the roof, since that's the most important structural element of the project. That person is Tom something-or-other. He's one of Fred's associates."

"Tin Man?" Joe said.

"Yes, that's what he called him."

At least it's someone cool. "When's he coming? I wanted to start the roof today."

"I'll get to that. *Four*: if the need arises, your mom *will* be told about this."

Joe's eyes narrowed. "What need?"

"Well, I'm sure it won't happen, Joe, but if things go awry—if something doesn't go according to plan …" Mr. Pruitt got one of those squinty faces like you get when you're scratching a really itchy mosquito bite. "Okay, let's just cut to the chase. If you decide not to work within our guidelines—for instance, coming out here to work on your own—we'll need to tell your mom about the whole thing."

"You mean *you'll* tell my mom."

"All right, *I'll* tell your mom." Mr. Pruitt didn't seem to mind the clarification.

Joe kicked a chunk of oak. This wasn't Joseph McKinnon's personal enterprise anymore—it was a community project.

Hear ye, hear ye! Anyone who wants to build a condo in the woods, come on down! Just push the one-legged kid aside.

"You mind if I come down there, Joe?"

"Okay." There was a notable lack of enthusiasm in his voice.

Mr. Pruitt descended the ladder and put his hand on Joe's shoulder.

"Son, I know how you feel about this. Everybody's sticking their fingers in your pie. So let me help you see this from our point of view." He started to pace back and forth.

"Suppose you come to a busy intersection and see a four-year-old boy all by himself and he's about to cross the street. Maybe he's bright enough to know when to cross, maybe he isn't. All you know for sure is there's nobody else around to help him cross. You have three choices." He counted them out with his fingers. "You could walk away and mind your own business, you could stop him from crossing and try to find his parents, or you could help him cross … which would you do?"

Joe thought for a second.

"I'd call him over and test him to see how smart he was. If he passed the test, I'd leave him alone. Cuz you never know—he could be a four-year-old genius or a Harvard graduate with some kind of a gland-growth disorder. I saw something about those people on TV. Sometimes it makes you grow really big, other times it makes—"

"I think you're missing the point, Joe—"

"Besides, there's four-year-olds all over the world crossing streets and doing other dangerous things. I can't be there to save them all."

"Aha! But that's the point," Mr. Pruitt held up his index finger. "You're there for that *one*. If you *hadn't* been there, that would be a different story, but you *were* there. And you knew that if this little boy crossed the busy street and you didn't intervene, he might die."

"He's got to learn to cross the street sometime," Joe said. "Can't have his hand held his whole life."

"True," Mr. Pruitt said. "But the stakes are high, Joe, very high. If he's not savvy enough to cross a street yet, he may get killed. That's a tough education, don't you think?"

"I suppose."

"*Now* imagine he got hurt or killed, and *you* have to tell his parents later that you did nothing while their little boy ventured across the street all by himself."

Why do grown-ups have to be so right all the time?

"I get it," Joe said. "But pretty soon, everyone's going to know about my condo, and then I might as well put up a sign telling everyone in Palos to come and use it."

"Do you think me, Fred, and … Tin Man are going to go around telling people about being involved in something illegal?"

Good point.

"And once it's done, we're out of the picture. You can do whatever you want with this place, and we won't bother you one bit."

"I guess that's okay." Joe wasn't thrilled about it, but part of him was glad to have the help. After all the delays, there was no way he'd get this done by himself before school let out.

***

Mr. Pruitt and Frederica left and returned just a few minutes later with Tin Man. Frederica dropped to her belly at the edge of the hole, with her paws and snout hanging over.

"Hey, Tin Man," Joe said.

"Hey, Joe." Tin Man made his way down the ladder and surveyed the condo with wide eyes. "Holy mackerel! Did you do all this by yourself?"

"Pretty much," Joe said. "Except for the hole in the stump … Fred did that."

Tin Man approached the stump with his mouth hanging open. He peered through the opening and let out a dramatic whistle.

"So this is what did him in … Jeez, what was he thinking?"

Frederica whined, not happy they were down there without her.

Tin Man felt the stump's inner surface.

"He's gutsy, I'll give him that. And you can see his blood all over the—"

"We should probably get down to business here," Mr. Pruitt said, turning to Joe. "I have a proposal for you that might change how you look at this situation."

"What's that?"

"You be the foreman," Mr. Pruitt said. "Tin Man and I will be the hired help. That way you're still in charge and make all the decisions."

"Makes sense to me," Tin Man said. He walked over and faced Joe. "You've done a great job so far, why change management now? Just tell us what to do."

"Thanks," Joe said. The sincerity in Tin Man's voice was a relief. "But I've never been anybody's boss before. Makes me a little … nervous in the service."

Tin Man laughed. "Then this'll be a good experience for you. Your old man was good at it so it's probably in your blood."

Joe smiled. *I hope so.*

Mr. Pruitt crossed his arms.

"So then, foreman—tell us what you want us to do first."

41

Just Lying Around

IN NO TIME, THE DRYWALL was stacked neatly inside the condo, and the three sat down to discuss roof construction. Joe had a plan, and since he was in charge, Tin Man and Mr. Pruitt listened. He laid it all out: the reason for the low pitch, the use of two-by-eights spaced a foot apart, the extra anchoring to strengthen the walls, the waterproofing, the cargo hatch to get big things inside later.

Tin Man and Mr. Pruitt asked a few questions and made a few suggestions, but in the end, they decided Joe's roof design would be as strong as Fort Knox. It would easily hold up the wettest dirt, and it would take a direct meteor strike or a close-proximity nuclear detonation to make the roof cave in. And for the roof, overkill was a good thing.

By late morning, they'd already started building the trusses. It seemed like the three of them working together could do five times the work Joe could do alone, especially with Tin Man there; he'd built hundreds of roofs and didn't have to stop and think about what he was doing. From experience, he suggested using just enough screws to keep the trusses from falling over until they got further along.

"You don't want to go putting a dozen screws in each beam right away," he said, "because you might need to move them around later."

And he was right: the beams did need to be re-aligned after they discovered that one of the walls was bowed.

And to make the morning even sweeter, Mr. Pruitt lived up to his word: he let Joe be completely in charge.

***

At 11:30, Joe's phone rang. He held up his hand signaling for everyone to be quiet. Tin Man sat on top of the wall while Mr. Pruitt paid a visit to Frederica.

Joe answered. "Hi Mom."

"Hi Joe, how's the job coming?"

"Good."

"What're you working on now?"

"Uhh, I'm putting in a rock retaining wall."

Mr. Pruitt and Tin Man exchanged glances.

"Really?" Mom said. "I didn't know they had any slopes in Palos Crest."

"Mr. Doersma's having me build a slope with a retaining wall," he said. "You know … a feature. Said it would make his yard look more fancy."

A somewhat amused Mr. Pruitt shook his head while he stroked Frederica's throat.

"Oh, I see," Mom said. "Well I'm sure it'll look beautiful when it's done. You'll have to give me the guided tour someday."

"Sure thing, Mom."

"I was just calling to see if you wanted to go to lunch with me. Thought I'd pick you up and take you to Burger King or something."

"No, thanks—I packed a lunch. I just want to eat fast so I can get back to work. Maybe some other time?"

"Okay," she sighed. "Just thought you might want to spend some time with dear old Mom … and maybe I could meet the Doersmas. They must think I'm the world's worst mom for sending her kid off to work on somebody's yard without checking them out first."

Ooh, that's a tough one. "Actually, they said you must be a really special mom to trust her kid to take care of his own business … and that you did a great job of raising me. They said someday they'd stop over and introduce themselves." *Hope I didn't lay it on too thick.*

Mr. Pruitt shook his head again and Tin Man chuckled.

"They sound like nice people," Mom said. "Tell them I look forward to meeting them."

"Okay, I will Mom."

"I guess I'll see you at home for dinner then. I get off at three today—maybe we can swing by the hospital and visit Fred tonight."

"Sounds good. I'll be home by about five or five-thirty, okay?"

"Okay, love you Joe."

"Love you Mom. Bye."

Joe didn't look up. He didn't want to see the looks from Mr. Pruitt and Tin Man.

"I don't imagine that feels too good, does it?" Mr. Pruitt said.

"What's that?" Joe knew what.

"Lying to your mother."

Joe continued to look down. "No, but I have to—she'd never let me do this."

Mr. Pruitt exhaled a heavy breath. "Well, a man's gotta do what a man's gotta do. You think she really buys your story?"

"Sure." Joe looked from one man to the other. "Why wouldn't she?"

"Moms aren't as dumb as you think," Mr. Pruitt said. Tin Man nodded in agreement.

"Why don't you call her back and take her up on that lunch offer?" Mr. Pruitt said. "The condo can wait another hour."

"I'd kinda like to keep working on this."

"I don't know about Clarence," Tin Man said, "but I'm not as young as I used to be. Can't keep the same pace as you whippersnappers. And one thing bosses need to know is when to give their workers a break." He gave Joe a pleading look. "How 'bout it?"

Joe relented. "Okay. Let's break for an hour then."

"Thanks boss," Tin Man said. "You're a pretty decent foreman—no matter what the other guys say." He winked at Mr. Pruitt.

"I know how you feel about having to lie," Mr. Pruitt said. "I had to do that with the police the other day. I hated it, just hated it."

Joe lifted his bicycle.

You get used to it after a while.

<h1 style="text-align:center">42</h1>

A Mom's Intuition

"EVERYTHING OKAY?" MOM SQUEEZED the last drops from the dressing packet onto her salad—she was probably the only one in the restaurant not having a burger or sandwich with fries. "You seem a little quiet."

Joe shrugged.

"You don't want to confirm or deny that statement?" Mom had a knack for getting to the bottom of things.

"I'm just a busy guy, Mom." *Watch out!*

She leaned forward.

"I know what it is," she said.

Joe froze, then tried to look cool.

"I'm your mother. I can always tell when something's up."

"Well, I'm your son and nothing's up." *Poker face.*

Mom kept her eyes fixed on him while she took a bite of her salad.

"What's her name?"

"Who are you talking about?" But Joe couldn't hold back a smile.

Mom smiled too. "Is it Julie?"

"No."

"Ashley?"

Joe laughed. "No-ho! You don't even know her, Mom."

"Aha!" She pointed her fork at him. "I was right! Who is she? Who's put a spell on my son?"

Joe laughed again. "Nobody put a spell on me."

"Come on, tell me all about her. What's her name?"

Joe sighed. "Jun."

"Jun—oh, that's a beautiful name. Is she in one of your classes?"

Joe couldn't believe he was telling his mom about Jun—it was like she could just open him up and pull out information with a pair of tongs—but at least she didn't know about the condo.

"We both went to Algonquin, but now she goes to The Brain."

Mom paused.

"So she's younger than you?"

"Just a year younger."

"Is it official? Did you get down on one knee with a bouquet of flowers and ask her to be your steady?"

Joe nearly spit out his burger.

"Jeez, Mom! We just talk."

Mom studied Joe with x-ray vision. Joe tried to keep a straight face, but knowing what she was thinking made him crack a smile.

"We're just friends, I swear."

"You *are* a busy guy, aren't you? How'd you two start talking anyway?"

"I don't know. Just riding my bike past The Brain one day, and there she was walking along and we were like 'hey, what's up?' and just started talking."

"What a coincidence. That's just how your father and I met."

"Right!" Joe said. He thought she was just kidding, but she didn't smile.

"Is she cute? Do you have a picture of her?"

"Yeah she's cute," Joe said. "She has a tattoo that says *death squad* and some really cool piercings on her nose and lips."

"How sweet! And a purple Mohawk too, I hope?"

"Yep, like the daughter you always wanted!"

"You know how to make your mom happy, don't you?" She chuckled. "Come on, what does she look like?"

"I don't know, just your average seventh grader—except no braces. She has dark hair, brown eyes, two ears, one nose." *She's anything but average.*

"No picture, huh?"

"Sorry."

"That's what the camera on your phone is for," Mom said, "…but if she's not too photogenic, that's okay—looks aren't everything. As long as she rocks your world."

"She's not ugly."

"I'm sure she's lovely." Mom raised her eyebrows. "Will I get to meet her someday?"

"Sure, Mom. Someday."

"I bet she's sweet." Mom gave Joe a big smile. "And speaking of sweets, do you still need those bags of sugar? Because I'm going shopping today."

His stomach sank. The persuasive speech was fast approaching and he hadn't even practiced what he planned to say.

"Yeah," he said. "I still need them."

"If it's all coming back home, I'll be baking for years. Do you mind telling me why you need so much?"

He felt a stab of guilt. "I can give you some money to pay for it."

"No, honey—sugar's not *that* expensive. Guess I'm just nosy what you're doing with it."

"I'm using it to represent all the homes in America," he said. "And then I'm gonna show the class one one-hundredth of a teaspoon of sugar so they can see what five-hundred homes looks like in comparison."

"Oh … very clever."

"I'll pay for it, Mom. I wasn't thinking."

"Don't be silly—it's for school," Mom said. "New subject: how do you think Fred's going to be?"

"I think he'll get an arm with a detachable hook," Joe said. "Or a robotic arm like The Terminator."

Mom laughed. "That would fit. But I was more worried about him adapting to life with only one arm. His type of work requires a lot of … well, arm stuff."

"*I'm* doing fine with just one leg."

"Yes, but you didn't live with two legs for as long as Fred lived with two arms. I'm sure he was quite attached to the arm he lost."

They stopped eating. Their eyes met and they busted out laughing.

"Oh, we're so terrible!" Mom covered her eyes with both hands. "Let's change the subject again, shall we? What do you want to be when you grow up?"

Why is everyone asking me that all of a sudden? "Scientist-slash-inventor."

"What would you science-slash-invent? A faster computer?"

"Computers are fast enough," he said. "I want to make something that would really make a difference in everybody's lives."

"That's a very noble ambition. Were you thinking of anything in particular?"

"Maybe. Still thinking about it though. *Please don't pry, Mom. I promise I'll tell you when I'm ready—and I'll tell you about the condo too.*

"Well if anyone can invent something worthwhile, it's my son, Joseph McKinnon, the scientist-slash-inventor." She reached out her hand and laid it on his. "Joe?"

"Yeah?"

"I'm very proud of you working so hard." She squeezed his hand. "But I worry about you working *too* hard. You're so much like your father; he didn't take enough time to enjoy the rewards of his labor."

Joe leaned back. It wasn't like Mom to say anything critical of Dad, especially now.

"Hard work puts food on the table and buys you the things you need. But it won't buy you happiness … unless it's work you truly love."

"I know Mom," Joe said. "I get it."

"I'm just saying … you'll have your whole life to work. Enjoy being a kid, because once you're grown up, there's no going back—for most people."

"Okay, Mom—I will."

"And I think you should invent the smell phone."

Joe raised an eyebrow. "What's that?"

"That's the phone that lets you know you need a shower so your mom doesn't have to tell you. But since you haven't invented it yet … make sure you take a shower when you get home."

"Guess I sweated a lot today," Joe said. "Maybe because I'm nervous in the service."

Mom chuckled. "I think you look more hysterics in the barracks."

43

I Now Pronounce You …

JOE WATCHED AS MOM and Fred joked up a storm. Mom was laughing more than she had since before the accident, and her brown eyes sparkled. Joe liked seeing his mom happy, but he wasn't sure he liked seeing her so happy because of another man, even Fred—especially Fred. There was something wrong with that.

They tried to pull Joe into the conversation, but he kept his distance, laughing every now and then and giving answers just long enough to say *you two go ahead, I'll listen*. He was tired and worried about his big speech on Tuesday—only three days away.

His eyes glazed over as he drifted.

After about twenty minutes, the conversation hit a lull. Mom asked if Fred would like her to go down and get a newspaper. Fred said he would, and a few seconds later he and Joe were alone.

Joe found himself standing there below the TV, shuffling his feet, waiting for Fred to lead the discussion.

"You must be taking good care of your mom," Fred said. "She seems like her old self again."

"Yeah, seems like it."

"Why are you all the way over there? Come closer."

Joe stepped to the foot of the bed. Up close he could see that life had returned to Fred's eyes.

Fred lowered his voice. "Remember what I said about a breakout?"

Joe perked up and lowered his voice too. "Yeah?"

"It's gonna happen … soon."

"But you're still hooked up to a drippy bag—whatever that stuff is."

"Eh, that's just salt water and antibiotics. Probably charging me a thousand dollars a bag for it." Fred waved his stump at it. "Look, Joe, I need to get out of here. This place smells funny, the nurses talk to me like I'm an infant, and the doctors all think they're better than me. So I'm gonna vacate this bed and let 'em give it to someone who's good enough."

Joe smirked. "Don't the doctors have to say it's okay for you to leave?"

"You know what happens when you sit around waiting for people's permission to do things?

"What?"

"Nothing, that's what. And that's what I like about *you*, Joe."

"What do you mean?"

"Did you ask anyone's permission before you went and dug that big hole?"

"No …"

"Well, there you go. I'm not waiting for permission either."

Joe hoped Mom would come back and overhear Fred's talk. She'd make sure they chained him down or something.

"Don't you have to pay them before you leave?" Joe said. "Won't they send the cops after you?"

"Let *me* worry about the details."

But Joe *was* worried. He didn't want his friend going to jail. Couldn't Fred just wait another week or so until they let him go? Why did he always have to fight everybody?

Fred must have read his face well. With a curl of his finger, he motioned for Joe to come closer.

"Don't worry." Fred chuckled. "I'm just kidding you about breaking out."

"Really?"

"Hey! What did you get done today? I heard you had some extra help."

"Yeah, we got a lot done." Joe felt wide awake now. "We'll finish up the roof tomorrow."

"No kidding?"

"Yep. It's going really fast with three people."

"Wish I could be there to help." Fred sighed.

"I do too …" He searched for words. "And I bet if you were there, the whole thing would be done by now."

"Yeah, I bet." Fred seemed to sink at that.

Joe looked up at the TV to see one of those awkward commercials—a couple sitting in two adjacent bathtubs on the beach. It was even worse when he was watching TV with Mom—usually he'd leave the room to get a snack or something.

"So are you keeping the two of them in line?" Fred said.

"Yep." Joe nodded. "That's what the boss is for."

"Good." Fred's gaze drifted toward the window. "Glad to hear it."

Just then a nurse came in carrying a metal tray. She seemed aware of the recent smile shortage and was doing her part to conserve.

"Okay Mr. Fergussen, time to change your bandages. We'll need to have your visitor step into the hall while we do this."

"He stays." And just like that, the full force of Fred's personality was back.

The nurse shifted the tray to one hand and put the other on her hip.

"Now Mr. Fergussen …"

"Now nurse Goldie." Her hospital badge said Goldamere.

"I don't want to give him any nightmares from seeing your wound." She motioned Joe toward the door.

Fred snagged Joe's arm with his death grip.

"Pull up your pant leg—show her."

Joe obeyed.

The nurse didn't even raise an eyebrow.

"That's a shame, but he still needs to go."

190

"You think you're tough, don't you, nurse Coldie? Well you may have *seen* some ugly things, but this boy's *lived* through them. He's been to hell and back, and in my book, he's a whole lot tougher and a much better person than you. I'd rather have *him* change my bandages."

The nurse stiffened her lips. "Fine!" She slammed her tray onto the table and stormed out of the room and up the hall. "Aaaahh! They don't *pay* me enough!"

Fred winked at Joe. "I might have to marry her."

Joe laughed. "I think she pretty much hates you."

"Yeah, but she'll be back." He dropped his head to the pillow. All the gruffness was gone, leaving his face bleak. "I meant what I said, you know."

"About what?" Joe said.

"That you're a tough man."

"Oh … thanks."

"Fathers hope their sons turn out like you."

Joe shuffled his feet and looked up at the TV. An old episode of *Friends* was on. Phoebe played her guitar and sang "Smelly Cat." He could feel Fred still looking at him. He'd never been good with conversations like this.

I should say something ... what?

"You don't have to change my bandages, you know."

Joe chuckled. "I know." He stayed focused on the TV, hoping Fred would give up on a heart-to-heart and just go back to being a tough guy.

You're my friend, but you're not my dad.

Fred was silent. "Smelly Cat" ended, and the standard chatter-laughter-chatter-laughter rhythm of the sitcom filled the room. Joe kept his eyes on the TV, hoping Mom would come back soon.

He heard a funny noise and turned around. Fred had his hand over his eyes. He was shaking—and he was crying.

To see Fred like this—it was weird, unsettling, but more than anything it just hurt. Joe felt a wave of remorse, and suddenly remembered something Jun told him.

***

Mom returned with a newspaper and a tray of drinks and stopped at the door, no doubt caught off guard by what she saw: Fred sitting up in bed sobbing … and Joe hugging him.

44

The Boss

ON SUNDAY, JOE WAS NERVOUS. It was one day closer to D-day at school. He was beginning to doubt the cleverness of his plan to use props—the sugar—to distract his classmates. They might have bought Mr. Z's excuse last time, but they'd hardly be dumb enough to fall for it twice.

Joe awoke with these thoughts and carried them all the way to Mr. Pruitt's house, where the three planned to meet prior to going out to the condo.

Upon entering the house, Joe was greeted by the opera lady belting out punchy notes to a staccato piano accompaniment on Mr. Pruitt's 1964 Magnavox Astro-Sonic stereo console. He didn't know who the singer was, but the music was far too peppy for *this* early in the day.

"You feeling all right, Joe?" Mr. Pruitt said. "You're looking a bit peaked."

"I'm good, just a little tired I think."

"Maybe you should go back to bed. Wouldn't be a sin if you slept in once in a while."

But Joe insisted he was fine—that working on the condo would wake him up. So after declining all of Mr. Pruitt's offers—sleep, breakfast, coffee, juice—they headed out, with Frederica taking the lead. Tin Man had already phoned to let them know he was on his way. He said they should go ahead and start without him.

It didn't take long for Joe to shake off his thoughts of impending doom. Bad as it might be on Tuesday, today could be the most exciting time since the day he broke ground. Today—if things went well—the condo would be sealed up. But first, the trusses had to be finished.

Tin Man arrived carrying a circular saw, a cordless drill, and a carpenter's toolbox full of his own tools.

"Did you park in my driveway this time?" Mr. Pruitt said. "And did you look around to make sure nobody was around before you headed out here?"

"Yep, coast was clear," Tin Man said. "We're good to go."

Tin Man greeted a joyful Frederica and petted her … until she growled and bared her teeth at him.

Tin Man pulled back his hand.

"Hey, what's up with that?"

"Did you pet her near her tail?" Mr. Pruitt said.

"Yeah, doesn't she like that?"

"No—forgot to tell you. She's funny about anyone touching her back end, even me."

"I'll make a note of it. Can't say that I blame her, though."

The trusses went fast. Yesterday they'd spent a lot of time talking through the plan, but today was purely work. Together they were a well-oiled machine. Tin Man marked the pieces to be cut, Joe did the cutting, and Tin Man screwed them into place. Mr. Pruitt delivered the pieces between Joe and Tin Man so the two of them could stay put.

When the last truss was in place, they stepped back and beheld the awesome array of two-by-eights that defined the roof. Joe could hardly believe it was so far along. It might just be possible to cover the condo before the school year ended.

There was just one last thing to be done before they could start laying plywood on top: the cargo hatch. Joe had planned a hatch for getting the things in and out of the condo that wouldn't fit through the stump entrance. Tin Man had said it would be easier to truss the whole thing, then cut out and frame the hatch opening. And now that all the trussing was in, Joe pointed out where he wanted the hatch located, and how big it needed to be—four feet by four feet.

"To make it exactly four feet, we'd need to cut out part of four trusses," said Tin Man. "That's a lot of structural support to cut away. So why don't we just cut out three? That way, you'll end up with … let's see …" He pulled out a tape measure from his belt. "Forty-six inches, minus three inches for door stop … so forty-three inches straight across. If you have to get anything in that's four feet wide, like a sheet of plywood, you can get it in diagonally."

"What about furniture?" Joe said.

"Most furniture fits through a standard-sized door entrance, which is usually under thirty-six inches," Mr. Pruitt said. "Think about it: a furniture maker will go out of business if he builds furniture that people can't get into their houses!"

"That makes sense," Joe said.

"Just make sure whatever you want to put in here is under forty-three inches and you'll have no problem," Tin Man said.

"What about getting *to* the door?" Mr. Pruitt said. "You'll have to move the dirt aside and put it back every time you want to bring in something big."

Both men looked at Joe.

"Can't think of another way to keep it hidden," Joe said.

"Maybe it doesn't need to be hidden," Mr. Pruitt said.

Joe stared. "If it isn't hidden, people will find it." *How could you be so silly?*

"Sometimes you can hide things by putting them in plain view." Mr. Pruitt pointed to the stump. "Case in point."

Joe looked at the stump, then at Mr. Pruitt.

"Yeah, but there's no tree stump around here big enough. I mean, holy cow, the entrance is nearly four feet by four feet! I'd have to go to California with a dump truck and bring back a giant redwood tree or something."

Tin Man laughed, but Mr. Pruitt just smiled.

"I'm talking about a rock."

"I don't get it," Joe said.

Tin Man seemed content to listen, sitting on the stump with a Gatorade and petting Frederica while Joe and Mr. Pruitt squabbled.

"A big rock—one that looks like a run-of-the-mill Illinois rock, only bigger. No one would think twice about seeing a rock out here. There's lots of other rocks around these woods. Maybe not that big, but so what? I doubt many geologists come out here."

"I still don't get it," Joe said. "For one, where would we get a big rock like that? For two, how would I even *move* a rock that big out to this spot, and for three, how would I lift it? Oh, and four, the roof would cave in with a rock that big on top of it!" That last one might not be true—this roof could possibly be strong enough to support an army tank.

"For one, we'd make it ourselves," Mr. Pruitt said. "For two, three, and four, it'd be light enough to lift, or at least for two people to lift. How often do you think you'll need to go through there anyways?"

"*Make* a rock?" Joe said. He didn't like the sound of "two people" either—that meant someone would see everything he brought into the condo. This was supposed to be his place alone. He didn't want someone asking him a hundred questions: "So Joe, why are you bringing this inside?" or "What's that you got going on down there?" If he wanted that kind of nosiness, he could just use his dad's workshop.

"Haven't you ever seen fake rocks before? People use them in their yards to cover up their ugly stuff like water valves or electric boxes. They're made with foam, chicken wire, and a thin layer of concrete, so they're cheap to build—and from diagrams I've seen, pretty easy to build too."

"Oh," Joe studied the hatch. "But what if someone sits on it or starts smacking it with a stick or something? Won't it break?"

"We can make it as strong as we need to. And if we make it somewhat rounded on the sides and pointy at the top, it'll be hard for someone to sit on it."

"Won't the paint chip off it easy?" Joe said.

"You mix the colors into the concrete."

"What if they try to move it?"

"It'll be attached to your cargo door, and we can make it so you can only disconnect it from inside the condo."

"Don't see how you'd keep dirt from falling in when you open it."

Mr. Pruitt gave an agitated sigh. "Son, if you'd rather dig for an hour *every time* you want to get things into your condo, *then* spend another hour replacing dirt and disguising the ground, we'll do it your way."

Joe didn't want to dig every time he needed to open the cargo hatch, but he didn't want Mr. Pruitt calling the shots either.

"We'll do it my way." There was authority in Joe's voice. "No rock."

A locust ceased its call for a mate. Frederica's eyes shifted back and forth between her owner and Joe. Tin Man chugged the remainder of his Gatorade.

Mr. Pruitt sighed again. "Like I said. You're the boss."

45

Oh Sheath!

ONCE THE TRUSSING AND CARGO-HATCH framing were complete, the guys screwed down sheets of plywood. Driving in screws was quieter than nailing, and screws would hold better over time. After laying the full sheets, they started cutting the end pieces. As the sheathing filled in, the condo seemed more real, and after a while, Joe climbed below to feel the effect.

I can't believe it's really happening! I'm going to have my own place and nobody—well, almost nobody—will know it's here!

As Joe was climbing back out, some movement caught his eye out past the carpet perimeter. Someone was coming their way.

The trespasser was being cautious in his approach, but it didn't take more than a few seconds for Joe to figure out who it was: Nick, his old friend and neighbor.

"It's okay, I know him," Joe said in a low voice. "I'll go talk to him." He turned to Tin Man. "When I wave to you, do that *I'm watching you* hand signal thing. You know the one."

"Yup," Tin Man said with a smile.

Joe turned to Mr. Pruitt. "Can you make Fred growl when I snap my fingers?"

"At your service," Mr. Pruitt said.

Joe hurried toward Nick and motioned for him to stop.

"Nick, didn't you see the signs?" He put his arm on Nick's shoulder and steered him back the other direction.

"Yeah, but I figured—"

"Dude, you can get in such *huge* trouble for going past the signs." They were just approaching the back side of one of those signs.

"But *you're* here."

Joe stopped. "That's because I'm working for these guys."

"Yeah, right," Nick said.

"No, *really*. They needed someone who knew the woods really well, so they did some checking and found *me*."

"Why would they need a kid to show them the woods?"

"I can't tell you what they're doing or who they are." Joe used his most serious voice. "If I did, they'd take us both away and we'd never see our families again."

Nick laughed. "You're shitting me."

Joe didn't laugh. He turned them both around to face Mr. Pruitt and Tin Man.

"Do they look like they're kidding?" Joe waved from behind Nick. Tin Man did his *I'm watching you* hand gesture.

Joe turned Nick back around again.

"You don't *even* want to know where they're from."

"Where? Palos Crest?"

"Let's just say this is a matter of national security."

"Get out!" Nick said, sneering. "Then why's old man Pruitt there?"

"Mr. Pruitt's not who you think he is, Nick. And you need to keep your suspicions to yourself. All he has to do is snap his fingers and that German shepherd will tear you to pieces." Joe snapped his fingers.

Nick looked back to see Frederica growling and baring her teeth—Mr. Pruitt was scratching her back end. Then, looking dead serious, Tin Man pulled out a knife and began examining the blade.

Nick turned away with wide eyes.

"What are they doing here?"

"Criminals are everywhere," Joe said. "Even in Palos. And when they get caught … well, that little underground fort you see being built? That'll be the most unpleasant place they've ever been to."

Nick seemed to be falling for it, but Joe needed to be sure he'd stay quiet.

"And trust me Nick, you don't want these guys mad at you. They know how to find out *anything*. Now that they've seen you, by tomorrow they'll know *everything* about you: where you go, what you eat, what you've stolen …"

Although Nick had supposedly turned over a new leaf, Joe happened to know that over the years, he'd done more than his share of shoplifting—and with that bit of blackmail hanging over him, it really didn't matter whether or not Nick bought the *underground torture facility* story.

"What about you?" Nick's voice was a little shaky and although he was a ginger who'd recently emerged from winter hibernation, his face was getting paler.

"It's too late for me," Joe said, looking down. He wondered how much longer he could keep a straight face. "Whatever happens, at least I'll know I did something good for my country."

Nick shook his head. "Why don't you just call the police?"

"Nick …" Joe paused. "These guys *own* the police."

Nick glanced back one more time. As he did, Mr. Pruitt made Frederica growl again.

"So … what should I do now?" Nick said.

"Go home and I'll cover for you," Joe said. "And don't say a word about what you saw to *anyone*!"

And before Joe could say "See ya!" Nick was running.

***

Naturally, Tin Man and Mr. Pruitt wanted to know what Joe had said to make Nick turn tail and run. When he told them, Tin Man laughed so hard he had to hold onto his sides. Mr. Pruitt chuckled and pointed a sideways thumb at Tin Man.

"Now that's what you call *hysterics in the barracks*!"

46

Dark

IT WAS EARLY—VERY EARLY, and it was Memorial Day. Since Joe would be at Ramesh's for the latter part of the day, he wanted to get as much done as he could this morning.

He could almost taste completion. Only the cargo door and waterproofing remained before he could cover the condo with dirt. Of course, there was still the issue of running the power cable out to the streetlight. One end of the cable was already connected to the condo's breaker box, but the rest was coiled up waiting.

As they stood at the edge of the condo—Mr. Pruitt and Tin Man drinking their coffee—Joe stared at the cable. Mr. Pruitt took notice.

"What do you plan to do with that?"

"Nothing until the rest is done," Joe said.

"You don't have wiring for outlets or lights yet. It's going to be awful dark, working down there without electricity."

"Darker than dark," Tin Man said.

"I was just thinking about that," Joe said. "I can always use lanterns for light."

"Bad for two reasons." Mr. Pruitt listed them out with his fingers. "Fire hazard and fumes. You'll still have that generator won't you? And that reminds me—we have to get everything that won't fit through the stump out of there before you backfill—unless you want it to stay until you dig your hatch open again. Anyway, you can use the generator outside to power some lights until you get hooked up to the grid. Fred told me you were planning on tapping into a streetlight for power. Is that right?"

Suddenly Joe felt overwhelmed. How could he have finished so much, and yet still have so much left to do? And all it would take is one power line sticking out of the ground, one piece of construction debris, one passerby overhearing the generator, and it was game-over. He doubted others would be as gullible as Nick.

Mr. Pruitt must have read the worry on Joe's face.

"We're down to the finish Joe. All it takes now is a few minutes of planning to make sure we get the order right. The bulk of the work is done—and done well, I might add—but the finishing details are often what make the difference between success and failure."

"Yeah." He knew Mr. Pruitt was only trying to help, but he just wanted time alone to ruminate. That was just his way.

Tin Man stood up. "While you two figure it out, I'm going to make a quick trip back to the truck. Forgot my phone."

Joe and Mr. Pruitt gave him a wave goodbye.

Then they sat there like two NASA scientists trying to figure out how to get their battered spacecraft home. Power line, temporary lighting, backfill, all that leftover construction debris, wiring, drywall, stump-lid hinging, connecting to the street light, taking down the carpet sound barrier around the perimeter ... Mr. Pruitt threw out some ideas, but Joe didn't hear them.

I can't fail now. What would Dad and Jun think? He wished his father were here—he'd have the answer.

What should I do Dad? And tomorrow he still had to give his speech. Joe wanted to crawl into his bed and go back to sleep—or better yet, crawl under the bed and stay there until the end of the week.

... when all seems dark and you're hungry for daylight— stop. Breathe. Look around, choose a direction ...

Joe closed his eyes. He pictured his condo in its present state. Then he saw the problem with power and listed in his mind the different facets of the problem. An idea came to mind—just a rough idea at first, but his mind tried it, changed it, tried it again, changed it again … a few times, until it became a solution.

Mr. Pruitt was speaking loud, trying to get Joe's attention. "Joe? You want to hear—"

"I've got it!" Joe jumped up so fast he lost his balance and nearly fell over. "I'll dig a hole over there—maybe four feet deep, not very wide. I'll put the generator in it. Then I'll cover it with leftover plywood and dirt. Then I'll run a trench from the hole to the condo for an extension cord. I'll run the power line in the same trench, and put the coil down in the hole with the generator for now. Then I'll have light to work inside, but the generator will be covered and quiet. After power is hooked up I can use that hole to throw all the leftover construction garbage into and fill it back in! It's perfect!"

"Whoa, hold on there. That's pretty ambitious. Do you think it's really necessary to dig—?"

"Yes," Joe said. That'll buy me as much time as I need. In fact, I can put the construction debris down there now and even store some of the stuff I'm still using … no, I'll put that inside the condo—"

"All right, all right …" Mr. Pruitt laughed. "You've convinced me. Let's get to work."

47

The Boss?

MR. PRUITT GAWKED with disbelief as he witnessed Joe's excavating skills. Tin Man smiled—it wasn't the first time he'd seen Joe operate a backhoe.

"Just like his old man," he told Mr. Pruitt. "Born to build."

Within a short time, the generator pit was done, complete with walk-in ramp. Meanwhile, Mr. Pruitt and Tin Man had dug a trench between the condo and the generator pit. Then they placed the generator in the hole and covered it with plywood and a thin layer of dirt.

Once started, the generator was inaudible from outside the carpet perimeter. Joe pulled out his phone and dialed.

"Hey Fred, guess what?"

"Who's this?"

Joe paused. Fred's voice sounded like it was emerging from the depths of some miserable bog.

"It's, uh, Joe."

"Oh … Joe."

The moment hung. They were two creatures from different planets accidentally bumping into each other on the same asteroid.

"Did I wake you up?"

"No Joe, you're fine." But *he* didn't sound fine.

"Guess what?" Joe said.

"What?"

"The roof is almost done!"

"Oh, good, good, great … that's great, Joe," Fred said. "That's good news." He turned away from the phone and coughed.

"Fred?"

"Is that Captain Hook?" Tin Man said. "Tell him to stop lollygagging and get his butt over here to help out!"

"Tin Man says *hi*." Joe lowered his voice a little. "Are you okay?"

"That depends on your definition of okay ..." He sighed. "I'm fine. Just a little tired, that's all. Probably from doing all those one-armed push-ups."

Joe forced a laugh. "Yeah, probably."

In the battle of hot air balloon versus anchor, the anchor was winning.

"Listen, Joe, I don't want to keep you—you still have a lot of work to do."

"All right."

"Be good, and take whatever help comes your way—don't be too proud to do that," Fred said. "Because when you get older, you'll want the help and it won't be there."

"Okay ... well ... take care and um ... get some sleep."

"Yep." Fred breathed a heavy sigh. "Joe?"

"Yeah?"

They were leaving the asteroid. Little had been said ... and yet something was understood.

"Goodbye," Fred said.

"Bye." Joe sat motionless, staring at the phone in his hand.

"Something wrong?" Mr. Pruitt said.

"No ... I'm good."

But Fred's not.

***

They continued with the roof: a layer of heavy felt paper, a layer of ten-mil plastic, more heavy felt. They built a cargo door with two-by-sixes and two layers of the same plywood used on the roof and then covered it with a piece of quarter-inch acrylic to repel water and make a smooth surface to easily shovel dirt off of. Joe had found the acrylic in his dad's workshop—it wasn't easy to carry to the condo! Finally, they attached the cargo door using three security hinges.

The sky had grayed up. A few drops hit the tarp over the condo.

I hope Fred's okay.

"I do believe we're in for some spring showers," Tin Man said.

Mr. Pruitt went back to his house and returned a short while later with two utility lights and a bag of Chips Ahoy!s.

The inside of the condo was now dim and dismal. The only outside light came from the hatch and the stump—and pretty soon only the stump would provide natural light, which wouldn't be much. The utility lights weren't much to battle the darkness, but they showed that the condo would eventually need a lot of lighting fixtures.

Mr. Pruitt came down the stump ladder, briefly dimming the light from above.

"Kind of stuffy in here now isn't it?"

"Yeah, it is," Joe said. *What's wrong Fred?*

"Two things just occurred to me. You're not going to like hearing this, but you can't ignore either one of them. In fact, I'm surprised Fred didn't say something."

Mr. Pruitt was getting to be a real bummer, but Joe tried to put on a good face. If it weren't for him and Tin Man, he never would've gotten the roof up so fast.

"What's that?"

"Well, first off, you're going to need air circulation. Being completely sealed, you'll get no fresh air down here … and you'll suffocate."

Joe groaned—he couldn't believe he hadn't thought of this. "How do I fix that?"

"We'll get to that. Second—and the rain reminded me of this—you're a sitting duck for getting flooded out … no pun intended."

"But the whole condo is wrapped up. How could it flood?"

"Trust me, water always finds a way to get in."

"Don't see how it can get through plastic."

There was a thump from above as Tin Man sat on the roof with his legs dangling through the cargo hatch—no doubt devouring the Chips Ahoy!s.

"Well, think about it," Mr. Pruitt said. "What happens when it rains? The water goes through the soil, gets to the roof, then runs down the sides. You've got water coming from all around the walls as well—you know, where the rain hits the ground outside the roof perimeter. Where does it go?"

"Down," Joe said.

"It goes down all right, but then at least some of it seeps beneath the fort—condo—under your floor. What do you have under here?"

"About eight inches of gravel."

"Good! That's real good—gives you some distance between wet dirt and wood. Unfortunately, the water can still rise through the gravel up to the floor."

"I thought water could only go down?"

"Water tends to level itself out," Mr. Pruitt said. "If the water level *outside* the condo is three feet above the floor, it would try to be that high *inside* the condo too. The only thing that would prevent water from rising inside the condo would be if it was so perfectly airtight, the pressure of the inside air pushed against the water and kept it down. But we already know it won't be airtight, because if it were, you'd suffocate."

Joe struggled with this. He tried to picture water pushing up under the floor, but he just couldn't.

Mr. Pruitt said, "Did you ever take a cup into the bathtub with you, turn it upside down and push it down in the water?"

"Yeah?"

"And what happens?"

"It wants to float. When you push down on it, it pushes back up by itself."

"Exactly. That would be an airtight condo. Now imagine drilling a hole in the bottom of the cup and then pushing the cup into the water. What would happen?"

"Oh, I get it. It wouldn't float because the air would come out of the hole."

"Right. That would be a non-airtight condo. Get it?"

"Sort of. So what should I do?"

"Do you have scuba gear?" Mr. Pruitt said.

Joe gave him a sour look.

"Just kidding. You'll need to put in a sump pump."

"Oh, like we have in our basement."

"Yessir. Everyone with a basement has one. You ever notice that your sump pump turns on a lot when it's raining outside?"

He hadn't, but he took Mr. Pruitt's word for it.

"Okay, so how do we put one in *here*?"

"Shouldn't be too difficult." Mr. Pruitt studied the floor, then pointed out a spot—a corner close to the breaker box. He pulled a pencil out of his tool belt and drew a circle on the floor.

"How about right here?" Mr. Pruitt said.

Joe shrugged. He felt his mood becoming just like Fred's. Mr. Pruitt had the knowledge and now it seemed that Mr. Pruitt was the boss.

48

Standoff at Ground Thirteen

PRESSURE WAS STARTING to build again. Now Joe had to worry about it raining hard and flooding the condo before he could install the sump pump. But even if he got the pump in, there still wasn't power from the streetlight. If it rained hard, he'd have to get out there to turn on the generator—which meant he needed to temporarily wire the generator to the sump pump.

And there was still the issue of air circulation.

"We have to cut holes in the roof for vent pipe," Mr. Pruitt said. "Regular houses do the same."

"Not a big deal if we seal them up good," Tin Man said.

"Once through the roof, we'll run the pipe underground far enough away—it can come up out of the ground over there." Mr. Pruitt pointed.

"What if someone comes across it sticking out?" Joe said. "Won't that give me away?"

"We'll cover it with a fake rock with ventilation holes; intake on one side, exhaust on the other. We can anchor it down good."

It seemed Mr. Pruitt would get his fake rock after all.

"And we could run drain pipe inside the vent pipe to the same place," Tin Man said. "We dig a pit under the rock and fill it with gravel—that's where the sump pump would drain the water. That'd save us one hole in the roof, and make one less trench to dig. Just need to put the pit far enough away so the same water doesn't keep coming back to the condo."

"I like that idea," Mr. Pruitt said.

But Joe didn't. Running pipes through the roof meant sealing the gaps and letting them dry, and *that* meant they couldn't completely cover the condo right away.

"C'mon, Mr. Pruitt," he said. "Let's at least bury part of it! We'll just leave it open around the pipe holes."

"Let's not rush to fill it in," Mr. Pruitt said. "We need to be absolutely sure we're done with everything on the outside walls first."

"What's to check? The roof's done, the sides are wrapped."

Mr. Pruitt frowned. "Do you want to find out you forgot something and then have to dig it back out again? If that happens, you'll risk damaging all that hard work you put into the walls, and maybe slice into your roof seal."

"Oh." Joe looked down. "Guess not."

After walking around and inspecting everything, Tin Man and Mr. Pruitt listed the places that needed more sealing: the electric service entrance, the staples in the vapor barrier, and where the wall met the stump.

Mr. Pruitt suggested he and Joe go shopping right away for the sump pump, exhaust fan, and the other supplies they needed.

"How about I stay and do the digging for the pipe?" Joe said. "I have to leave in an hour anyway."

"How about you come with me for that hour?" Mr. Pruitt said. "Tom can stay or go with us—your choice, Tom."

"I'll stay," Tin Man said. "I need to take care of some business." He held up his phone.

"I'll stay too," Joe said. "I can have the digging for the ventilation line done by the time you get back."

"Don't you want to help me shop for supplies? It's *your* condo."

Doesn't feel like it anymore. "No, I trust you."

Mr. Pruitt laughed. "I certainly hope you trust me. There is a question of money, though. How are we paying for this?

In fact, I've been wondering how you paid for everything else so far?"

"I gave money to Fred, and he bought everything for me. I still have some. I'll go home and get you whatever you need. How much should I get?"

"How about you come with me, I'll pay for everything, and you can pay me back later."

"I'd rather stay and dig."

"It'd do you some good to get a change of scenery," Mr. Pruitt sighed. "I tell you what. We can stop and get a sub, my treat. Tom, would you like a sub?"

Tin Man, who was already listening to voice messages, shook his head and pointed to his tool box where a silver lunch pail was nestled.

Mr. Pruitt looked back to Joe.

"I'll eat later," Joe said. "I really want to get this done."

"It'll still be here when you get back," Mr. Pruitt motioned for Joe to go with him as he turned and walked a few steps away. "Come on."

Joe didn't budge.

Mr. Pruitt stopped and looked back at Joe. Frederica stopped and looked back at Mr. Pruitt. Leaves stirred in a small breeze. A Harley sputtered off in the distance. Joe's face was solemn, undeterred.

"Well then, I'll see you when I see you," Mr. Pruitt said. "Let's go, Fred!"

49

Praveen

SO MANY CARS LINED Ramesh's street Mom had to park a block away. Fortunately, it was a beautiful old neighborhood to stroll through. Joe's neighborhood was nice too, but this one had a certain opulence that Palos Ranchos lacked, from the massive trees to the pattern-cut lawns to the flower and hedge-lined paths.

"For being in the city … it's nice," Mom said. "What do you think?"

"*I'll* say it's nice." Technically it wasn't Ramesh's house, it was his parents'. Still, Ramesh never mentioned they were rich.

"Well, go to college, get a good job, and then you can live in a neighborhood like this."

"There's nothing wrong with where we live," Joe said. *And there's nowhere to build an underground condo around here!*

Mom gave Joe a side hug. "You're right. Nothing wrong with where we live."

They rang the doorbell and Mrs. Sunwari answered. Joe had pictured Ramesh's mom wearing a sari, but nothing like this: maroon, adorned with gold-leaf patterns, and a cream-and-gold border. The way it draped over her left shoulder and arm gave her an air of royalty. And though he'd imagined her with straight dark hair and a glossy red dot centered on her forehead, *her* hair was salon-done, wavy with reddish-brown highlights—and her forehead was dot-free.

"Hello, welcome!" Mrs. Sunwari's face was Ramesh's face. "I'm Sanya."

"Nice to meet you, Sanya. I'm Lori McKinnon, and this is my son Joe."

"Hi," Joe said. "Nice to meet you."

They all shook hands.

Sanya smiled at Joe. "So you are Ramesh's boss at the library?" Her accent was thicker than Ramesh's, but still discernable.

"Well … I'm not … but Mom is." Joe gestured to his mother.

Sanya laughed. "But I'm sure you'll be the boss someday, no?" She stepped aside and motioned to where there were rows of shoes neatly arranged in the foyer. "Please come in, and if you don't mind, you can leave your shoes here during the puja."

Joe and his mom removed their shoes.

Hope they don't serve that super-hot Indian food!

"Please make yourself at home," Sanya said. "I'll go find Ramesh. He'll be very happy to see you." She scurried off. "Ramesh!"

Most of the guests were Indian, and many were older. Groups of them chatted, some sitting, some standing. Everyone was gussied up. Joe was glad his mom had made him wear something nice.

There was soft jazz playing: a female vocalist sang in some Indian dialect. Joe wondered if this was an American piece translated into Hindi, or if India had its own jazz scene.

Jun would probably know.

The mocha-maple floor beneath them was partly covered with exquisite rugs. Tasteful art hung on walls while spaces were smartly punctuated with elegant couches and chairs. It reminded Joe of photos he'd seen in a home-décor magazine.

Mom spotted Mr. Sunwari and led the way over. Mr. Sunwari wore a maroon kurta and cream-colored scarf, and his squared black-framed glasses and sharp haircut made Joe think he must be a successful businessman.

"Hello, Mr. Sunwari," Mom said. "I don't know if you remember me—I'm Lori McKinnon? And this is my son Joe."

"Yes, of course, Mrs. McKinnon," he said, adding a slight nod toward Joe. "It is very nice to see you again. And we appreciate you coming to celebrate with us." His voice was deep and confident. He spoke with precision.

"I wouldn't have missed it for the world. Ramesh is such a nice young man, and a hard worker too."

"Thank you. We are quite proud of him." Mr. Sunwari scarcely looked at Joe, who took this to mean that he hadn't yet earned his place in adult conversation. "And we appreciate you giving him the opportunity to work at your library while he finished his degree."

"Well, we're all crazy about Ramesh—we'll be so sorry to see him go. I don't know *how* we'll replace him." She used the sad-regretful head-tilt women were so good at—the one Jun liked to use.

"Every new beginning comes from some other beginning's end," he said. "You've helped instill him with a good work ethic and that was just as important as his college education."

"I know I've heard that somewhere," Mom said. "'Every new beginning ...?'"

"The words of the Roman philosopher, Seneca the Younger."

So that's where Ramesh gets it from.

Ramesh approached. "Hello, Mrs. McKinnon. Hello, Joe." He hugged Joe's mom, then offered Joe a handshake. He wore a shin-length kurta like his father's, but his was off-white with gold embroidery and matching kurta pants underneath. A long maroon scarf was slung over his shoulders, reaching the bottom of his kurta.

"Congratulations, and here's a little something." Mom handed him a card from her purse.

"Thank you—that's very kind!" Ramesh said with a broad smile.

214

"Yeah, congrats," Joe said.

"Thank you, Joe."

Mom said, "With your smarts, I'm sure you'll be very successful. *Any* company will be lucky to get you."

"I appreciate your kind words, Mrs. McKinnon."

Joe wished this *Mrs. McKinnon* thing would stop. If they were at the library, Ramesh would just call her Lori.

Finally, Mr. Sunwari turned to Joe. "Young man, thank you for coming. After the puja we'll be having dinner. For now, I'm sure you will find it more comfortable with those your age. Ramesh, why don't you take your friend to where the other boys are playing?"

"Yes, Appa." Ramesh turned to Joe. "Come—I'll show you where the others are." When they were a little farther away, Ramesh said in a low tone, "I'm sorry—my father is from the old school."

"It's okay," Joe said. *I hope I'm not stuck with a bunch of strangers all afternoon.*

They descended to the basement where the younger crowd was shooting pool, playing Monopoly, and watching soccer on TV. Joe looked around—he was the only white kid.

"Everyone," Ramesh said. "This is my good friend Joe."

A few glanced up and said hello.

Ramesh turned to Joe. "Feel free to join in. I'm afraid I should return upstairs for a while." Then he turned to one of the boys shooting pool—he was maybe a year or two older than Joe. His hair flopped over his eyes and ears. "Praveen, can Joe play with you?"

"When this game is through," Praveen said. Although he looked Indian, Praveen had almost no accent.

Ramesh pointed to the adjacent room. "There are drinks and snacks on the bar. Please help yourself. I'll see you soon." Then he left the basement.

Joe sat in a folding chair near the pool table.

"Not there," Praveen said. "You'll be in the way." The other player cast his eyes drearily at Joe.

Joe moved his chair back into a corner.

"How's this?"

Praveen—poised for a shot—glanced over his shoulder. "Uh-huh."

Praveen's shot knocked in the three ball.

"Nice," Joe said.

Praveen said nothing, but did something that made the other kid turn away and chuckle.

His next shot missed. On the TV, the announcer let out an annoying "Goooooooooooooooooooal!!" which must have stretched for at least ten seconds. The kids watching hissed and yelled at the screen.

"Crap," Praveen said. He was looking at the TV too. Then he turned and stared at Joe.

"You watch football?"

"Uh, soccer?" Joe said.

"Never mind." He turned to his friend. "Your shot, Giri."

Joe wished Ramesh hadn't left.

Giri pointed. "Eight ball, right corner pocket."

"No way, man—you can't make that shot without touching my number two!" Praveen said.

"Watch me." Giri chalked the tip of his cue stick and positioned himself to shoot. After several practice strokes, a smooth, gentle tap sent the cue ball toward the eight ball. The two balls kissed, then the eight ball squeezed past Praveen's two ball and just nicked the cushion before dropping into the pocket.

A couple other kids had drifted over to watch.

"Whoa!" said a girl who'd been watching the soccer match.

"Awesome!"

"Great shot!" Joe said.

Praveen snapped his head toward Joe.

"Who asked *you*?"

Joe felt his heart rate picking up. Praveen kept glaring at him until Giri coughed.

216

"Never make it?" Giri said.

"Lucky."

Joe headed over to the wall to grab a cue from the rack. He hoped he'd be playing Giri.

"Winner racks," Praveen said.

"Loser racks," Giri said. "Winner breaks."

"Whatever." Praveen dropped the triangle onto the table and began pulling balls from the pockets.

Joe paused, set the cue back in the rack, and hobbled to the steps. He could feel the eyes upon him as he ascended. At the top, he closed the door, then limped down a hall away from the gathering.

There has to be a bathroom around here somewhere.

He was right. After he locked the door behind him, Joe looked in the mirror and fought back the urge to cry.

I should have stayed at the condo.

He hung his head, while he got his breathing under control. Then he looked up and scowled at himself.

Just be a man and join the party.

50

Puja

RAMESH SPOTTED JOE RETURNING to the living room and approached him.

"Didn't you want to shoot pool?"

"It's not really my game," Joe said. "Besides, up here is where the real action is, right?"

Ramesh smiled. "Right. And we'll be having the ceremony soon anyway—you have never seen a puja?"

"Nope." Just talking to Ramesh helped him feel better. "Are you sure I'm allowed to watch?"

"Of course. Others will be watching along with you."

Joe stayed with Ramesh but before long, Mrs. Sunwari clapped her hands.

"Attention please everybody. It is time for the puja!"

She then went to the back of the living room and opened the doors of an antique armoire. From inside it, she pulled out a silver tray which contained a lamp, a cup, and a decorated object that looked like a miniature coconut. On the back panel were small paintings of what Joe assumed were Hindu gods.

Some guests scurried off to other rooms—evidently they had things to take care of before the ceremony.

Mr. Sunwari brought over a bunch of bananas, some apples, and a cup of rice. His wife placed the fruits on the tray along with a smattering of rice.

A man in a long white tunic with an orange sash stepped forward. He introduced himself as a Brahmin and spoke to the crowd.

"For those who wish to participate in the puja, please gather close. For those not of the Hindu faith, please feel free to stay and observe—or if you wish, you may go to another room and quietly continue your conversations."

The crowd segregated into participants and observers. Joe relaxed when he saw there were at least six observers besides him and his mom—half were Indian. They all stood against the walls of the room while worshippers gathered around the armoire, mostly seated on the floor. Ramesh sat at the front of the group with his legs crossed and his parents beside him, facing the deities.

The basement crowd had emerged too. Joe caught Praveen staring at him. The soccer-watching girl also looked at him for a moment, then turned to pray.

When everyone was ready, the ceremony began.

The Brahmin began by placing red *tika* marks on the foreheads of Ramesh and his parents. The ceremony was performed in Hindi, but the Brahmin occasionally explained things in English. Everything seemed to center on the *thali*— the tray containing the fruit and other items. The Brahmin explained how he was calling in the gods, bathing them, dressing them with turmeric and rice, and asking that their blessings be bestowed upon the fruit, making it a *prasad*, which the participants would consume.

Next was the *aarti*, where a lamp was lit, the flame from its cotton wick fueled by a special butter called *ghee*. Worshipers chanted, sang, and prayed as a bell was rung. Then Mrs. Sunwari lifted and circled the thali around the deities' images while worshippers took turns touching her arm or the tray.

Joe was captivated. There was something beautiful about it, something comforting. It made him wonder if Jun's family was religious.

Finally, participants took turns scooping heat from the lamp's flame toward themselves, while placing money on the tray. Two lady-friends of Mrs. Sunwari helped cut the prasad. After offering the first of it to the Brahmin, they placed the pieces in small bowls on the dining room table. The Brahmin then announced that everyone, including observers, were welcome to have some.

"That was beautiful," Mom said.

"Yeah," Joe said. "It was pretty cool."

Everyone went back to mingling, and a while later Mrs. Sunwari made an announcement that food would be served in just a half hour or so.

"Hey Mom," Joe said. "I'll be back—just need to use the bathroom."

On his way, he passed Praveen, who leaned toward him.

"Sorry whitey," he said. "No burgers tonight."

Joe pretended not to hear him and continued to the bathroom—but it was locked. Rather than go past Praveen again, he entered an adjacent room, closed the door, and sat on the edge of a bed. His breathing was heavy.

What did I do to him? I should punch him in the stomach. No, that would ruin Ramesh's party and make me *look like the bad guy.*

Suddenly he noticed the door open just a crack. Before it closed, Joe caught a glimpse of the soccer girl.

Great, now she's going to tell the Sunwaris I'm snooping around their house.

The bathroom door finally opened. Joe checked that the coast was clear and switched rooms—he needed a few more minutes to gather his wits.

***

Praveen was right—they weren't serving burgers or any other kind of meat. But still, there was lots of good food.

Joe stayed close to his mom and listened to her talk. He noted how easily she fell into conversation and how comfortable people seemed to feel when they talked to her. He hoped he could do that one day.

Suddenly, Joe noticed the soccer girl talking to Ramesh. She seemed upset. Ramesh didn't speak much, just shook his head while holding his chin in his hand. It dawned on Joe that a goatee might help Ramesh think.

When their conversation ended, Ramesh took the girl's hand in both of his, nodded, and thanked her. Then he approached Mr. Sunwari, who had his back to Joe. Ramesh's eyes flitted between his father and Joe.

I should just go back to the basement.

Now Mr. Sunwari was turning around, walking toward Joe.

Joe clutched up. What had the girl said to Ramesh?

… but Mr. Sunwari walked right past him to Mrs. Sunwari.

What the heck is going on?

After a moment, the Sunwaris disappeared into the backyard. A minute later, they were back inside with another couple and a heavier woman. None of them seemed ready to party.

This must be about the girl. Maybe Praveen was giving her a hard time too.

"… I can't believe I don't remember the name of it," Joe's mom said while talking to one of Ramesh's professors. "Joe, what's the name of that new school right next—"

"Brain STEM Academy," he said without taking his eyes off the Sunwaris.

"Yes, that's it. Thank you honey."

I wish Jun were here.

Joe watched as Mr. and Mrs. Sunwari, the young couple, and the heavier woman went to the basement.

Ramesh appeared at Joe's side.

"Hey Joe, would you mind helping me carry some things outside from my bedroom?"

"Yeah, sure."

To Joe's surprise, Ramesh's bedroom was loaded with musical instruments. He had an electronic drum set, a hand drum, a trumpet, a trombone, and a keyboard. He also had two electric guitars, an electric bass, and an acoustic guitar—all leaning on stands. There were three music stands and sheet music everywhere.

"Do you play *all* these instruments?"

"I do," Ramesh said. "Music has been my passion since I was very small."

"Are you in a band or something?"

"In high school I was. Now I just play for my own enjoyment."

Joe sat at the drum set and picked up a pair of drumsticks resting there.

"Can I try?"

Ramesh smiled, "Yes, of course."

Joe began striking the rubbery drums and cymbals. He found the bass and hi-hat pedals too. Everything made faint thumping sounds until Ramesh turned on the control unit and an amplifier—then it became a real drum set. It seemed weird to hit the rubber cymbal and hear a metallic crash when his eyes told him it should make a rubbery thumpy sound. Joe began beating the drums wildly—Ramesh turned down the amp's volume.

"Sorry," Joe smiled. "Always wanted to try the drums."

Suddenly there was a knock at the door. Mr. Sunwari entered, followed by Praveen and the heavier woman, probably his mother. Next came Giri and the young couple—Giri's parents? They were a dismal lot, and everyone stood quietly waiting for Mr. Sunwari to speak.

"Joe," Mr. Sunwari said. "These young men have something to say to you."

Praveen spoke first without hesitation.

"I'm sorry for being rude to you." He looked up at Joe, his eyes sad but unafraid. "It was wrong, you didn't deserve it … and I apologize."

Everyone's attention shifted to Giri. "I …" He coughed. "I'm sorry too." His eyes made fleeting contact with Joe's.

It was Joe's turn. "That's okay." They seemed to be expecting more. "I accept both of your apologies."

Praveen's mother approached Joe. "You seem like a nice boy. I am very sorry for my son's behavior toward you." She turned to her son. "This is not the Praveen I once knew." She then ushered him out of the room.

Mr. Sunwari said to Joe, "Young man, please also accept *my* apology—for sending you downstairs to be with people you didn't know."

Joe nodded. "Yes sir."

"Please stay and enjoy the party. I promise you the rest of the evening will be much more enjoyable. Right Ramesh?"

"Yes, Appa."

Mr. Sunwari gave a brief smile, then left.

Joe and Ramesh said nothing at first. Joe tapped the drumsticks on the snare drum's rim. Finally he spoke up.

"That was intense," he said. "I didn't mean to poop on your party—it really wasn't that big of a deal."

"My father doesn't tolerate such things—and I do not tolerate my friends being treated badly." Ramesh shook his head. "I'm sorry, Joe. I should not have trusted Praveen with you."

"What do you mean?"

Ramesh hesitated. "There is some reason for his behavior—not an excuse, but a reason."

Joe was intrigued.

"Like you, he lost his father. It was about a year ago."

Joe swallowed. "An accident?"

"It was the cancer."

His heart sank. "That's awful."

"He's still very angry—especially at … how can I say it nicely?"

"At white people?"

Ramesh sighed. "Yes."

"I could see that. But why?"

"Because they believe it was his father's change to the American diet that killed him."

"Is that true?"

"Who can tell? Regardless, Praveen is very sad."

Joe felt a lump in his throat.

"Maybe I should talk to him."

Ramesh sucked air through his teeth. "I think that would not be good right now. Besides, he is going home."

Joe jumped up and sped from the room. He searched the living area, catching a few stares in return. Then he saw Mrs. Sunwari near the front door, closing it behind her. He rushed toward her.

"Mrs. Sunwari, did Praveen leave?"

"Yes, he and his mother just got into the car."

"Excuse me!" Joe said. He brushed past her, scrambling through the door to the sidewalk. To his left, he spotted a silver car pulling away from the curb and accelerating past the Sunwaris' house. Praveen was in the passenger seat—looking at him. Joe started to wave, but Praveen's look stopped him.

I should have been nicer to him.

Mrs. Sunwari came to Joe's side. "He's a good boy," she said. "He's just had a rough year."

Joe watched the car until it disappeared around a corner.

He sighed. "I know."

51

A Shift in Perspective

JOE HELPED RAMESH CARRY a few instruments to a huge back patio where a parquet dance floor had been assembled. Behind it were amplifiers, a small mixing board, guitar pedals, and taped-down wires. There were two microphones on stands and colored lights for the stage and band area.

Afterward, Ramesh changed into regular clothes. He still looked dressy, just not so … Indian.

By now, people were arriving for the party. Some of them were Ramesh's age—college friends—but others were older, probably friends of the family. Ramesh kept busy socializing, accepting gifts and congratulations from everyone. Joe wanted to spend more time with him, but knew his friend had to mingle with the other guests.

Joe and his mom mingled too. She seemed to like talking to Ramesh's professor—they had a lot of similar opinions about this and that.

Soon people were gathering around Ramesh's band area. Joe and his mom joined them. Ramesh's setup was pretty impressive—like he'd done this before.

"I knew he had an interest in music," Mom said. "But didn't know he had *that* much interest."

"I hope he plays something good," Joe said. *And I hope he doesn't embarrass himself.* He couldn't help but think of those American Idol auditions where contestants who thought they were good were actually awful—it was tough to watch.

Ramesh had an iPad plugged into the mixing board. He fiddled with it and did a series of sound checks before finally speaking to the crowd.

"Hello, hello, hello." Ramesh's voice boomed through the monitors. "Hello everyone, are you ready for the entertainment?"

The crowd applauded. Some whooped and whistled.

"Thank you for coming. You are all very special to me."

Two young women yelled out, "We love you, Ramesh!"

The crowd laughed and cheered.

"Thank you, Katie and Lauren." Ramesh seemed a little embarrassed. "First, I will play two songs in honor of the city we live in. I hope you enjoy them."

He sat down at the keyboard and began to play.

The music was jazzy. To Joe, some of the chords sounded sour and the beat was hard to follow, but everyone else seemed fine with it and Ramesh appeared confident. The professor nodded.

"I think I know what this is," he said.

"I don't recognize it," Mom said. "What is it?"

"Chicago."

The piano came to a soft end, and a few began to applaud, when suddenly Ramesh stood, picked up his trumpet, and tapped his iPad. In a second, he started belting out the continuation of the song which many recognized.

Mom cocked her head. "Oh, of course. It's 'Does Anybody Really Know What Time It Is?'" She began to snap her fingers and sway with the beat.

Joe gave her space and soon realized his mistake—her swaying only increased. The song finished and the crowd began to applaud again when Ramesh immediately sat back at his keyboard, tapped his iPad, and began playing "Saturday in the Park." This time he sang as he played. Joe gaped.

Was that really Ramesh singing so strong, so loud, so ... good?

The audience was really getting into it. A group of women, including the ones who'd shouted their love to Ramesh earlier, gave him a big "Woo-hoo!" and began dancing among themselves.

Ramesh then switched to playing guitar. He played a variety of popular songs and ended by playing some snippets from video games that all the kids recognized. Joe didn't know a lot of them, but even he recognized the *Super Mario Bros.* theme.

After more than forty-five minutes, Ramesh declared an intermission for dinner. He had to work his way through a throng of admiring fans—Joe was one of them.

"Dude," Joe said. "You never told me you could play like that!"

"There was never a reason to," Ramesh said. "Do you play an instrument?"

"I have a guitar." Joe looked down. "Don't really know how to play it though."

A bubbly Katie and Lauren broadsided Ramesh with a hug. Joe backed away.

"Ramesh, you are *so* talented!" one said.

"Can you play any Nirvana?"

Joe listened to Ramesh chat with the girls. He was the same skinny Indian Joe had known for years, but tonight—without even trying to be—Ramesh was cool.

And I thought Ramesh sat in his room all day studying books!

Eventually, everybody headed into the house where yet another spread of tasty dishes awaited, courtesy of Mrs. Sunwari and friends.

Joe had nearly forgotten how horribly the evening started—now he didn't want it to end.

After dinner, Ramesh returned to his one-man-band area and invited his parents to come up. They made short speeches telling how proud they were of their son. Then they all sat down on large pillows: Mr. Sunwari in the middle with a sitar, Ramesh to his right with a two-sided hand drum, and Mrs. Sunwari to his left with a smaller drum. On stage, a young woman performed traditional Indian dances. The unity and confidence of this family was enviable. And there seemed no end to the talents of the Sunwaris—in Joe's mind, they were the bomb.

After the music and dancing, Ramesh played some music from the Sixties through the Eighties. Joe's mom danced—*really* danced—and so did the professor. At one point, Mom grabbed Joe's hands and got him dancing too.

Hey, maybe it won't be so bad going to the dance with Jun.

***

As Joe and his mom left the neighborhood, they passed a patch of forest.

There is *a place to build a condo here!*

"Mom?" Joe said.

"Yes, honey?"

"Will I ever see Ramesh again?"

"Of course you will. He's not leaving the library just yet. In fact, he's going to be there all this week working the evening shift if you want to go see him."

"I mean after that—after he leaves the library and gets a job somewhere else. Will we ever see him again?"

They stopped at a red light. Mom turned to Joe.

"People who mean something to each other always find their way back into each other's lives," she said. "Besides, with cell phones and social media, it's easy to stay in touch with people."

Joe looked down. "It's not the same though."

"There's such a thing as airplanes too, you know."

"Yeah, I guess." He found himself wishing he'd made more time to volunteer at the library—the condo would always be there, but Ramesh wouldn't.

"You're sad to see him go, huh?"

"Yeah."

Mom sighed. "Me too."

***

When they got home that night, Joe pulled a case out from under his bed and wiped the dust off it. He unbuckled the latches, flipped it open and lifted out a white electric guitar—a copy of a Fender Stratocaster.

He plugged into a small amp, turned it on, and began to strum. It was badly out of tune, and he'd forgotten how to tune it. So he got on his computer to search for a guitar-tuning video, but on a whim, he entered "tango dance beginner" instead. There were plenty of choices; he picked one showing the man's steps.

Maybe I can surprise Jun!

Joe watched for a moment. *That looks easy.* He tried it himself. Somehow his movements weren't the same as the guy's in the video—they felt unnatural, less graceful. He tried several times but couldn't seem to get it.

Then he searched for "teen dance beginner" and found one that seemed reasonable.

Step-clap-step-clap … *I can do that.*

Joe tried it. In no time he was step-clapping all over his room and adding turns too!

Mom called up the stairs.

"What are you doing up there?"

"Nothing. Just exercising."

"Getting kind of late. You should go to bed soon!"

"Okay, Mom." *Guess I can work my way up to the Tango.*

Next he found a video on tuning a guitar. Within ten minutes, the guitar was tuned—he hoped.

After sampling beginning guitar videos where they did nothing but talk a lot, he finally found one that got right into it. The guy in the video made it look so simple. But out of Joe's amp came thudding clunkery.

Joe stood the guitar in the corner and shut off the amp. Dad had said something to him on his twelfth birthday, the day he got the guitar.

Nobody becomes good at anything without practice, and nobody becomes great at anything without passion.

Joe got dressed for bed—meaning he took off everything but his undies. He lay back and stared at Einstein. Tomorrow was his solar power presentation.

The world needs solar power—but it's not my passion. And everyone would know that when they heard his speech.

Joe sighed and hugged his pillow. Tomorrow might be awful, but tonight he had new and everlasting memories of the Sunwaris: trumpeting, dancing, singing … happy.

52

Big Day

UNDER NORMAL CIRCUMSTANCES, Joe would have been amused when Tyrone, who had a nasty cold, laughed and launched a monstrous gob of gorilla snot onto his upper lip. And since no self-respecting middle-school-aged boy carries tissues with him, Tyrone had to use the old hand-cover-duck-out-of-the-room-while-saying, "excuse me I have to go to the restroom it's an emergency" routine with the teacher.

Today, though, Joe was too tense to laugh at anything. He wasn't even conscious of reciting "The Pledge." It seemed nothing could distract him from his mounting terror until his homeroom teacher, Mrs. Ember, called him to the front of the classroom during a pause in the announcements.

The voice of Mrs. Johnson, the principal, blared from the wall speaker.

"As many of you know, last week we had an accident occur in which one of our district grounds maintenance workers severely injured his eye. But thanks to the quick thinking of one of our students, within minutes, emergency help came to the aid of Mr. Martinez who, thankfully, is now doing well and recovering."

Joe felt everyone's eyes upon him. Some showed admiration; others looked skeptical. Mrs. Ember had taken one hand off his shoulder and pointed down at him, in case there was doubt as to who the principal might be talking about.

"One of our eighth graders, Joseph McKinnon, saw that Mr. Martinez was injured and without anyone telling him to do so, had the wherewithal to run and get the nurse and an administrator *and* instructed Miss Charlotte in the front office to call 9-1-1. This is a perfect example of the kind of character we seek to build here at HMS."

Some of Joe's classmates gave him a premature golf clap.

"So today, we are proud to present the Halverson Middle School Outstanding Citizen Award to Joseph McKinnon in the eighth grade."

Applause and cheers broke out in Joe's homeroom as Mrs. Ember handed him the paper which declared him "Outstanding Citizen."

I could get used to this.

Tyrone returned from the restroom just in time to take a bow behind Mrs. Ember's back. He held up his hands and mouthed, "No, no, really, it was nothing."

***

Joe had brought all five of his five-pound bags of sugar to school in a carry-on-sized rolling suitcase. After announcements, Mrs. Ember asked him to take it to the office until he needed it, saying it would just be too much for him to lug around all day. Joe got the impression it unnerved her seeing a student at school with a suitcase.

The people in the front office also seemed a bit alarmed. One of them said, "If you don't mind, we'll need to have a look inside to make sure it's safe."

Joe showed them the sugar, and explained how he was using it as a visual example of just how big of a project it was to put solar power on every home in the country.

Upon examining the sugar and hearing his explanation, all were satisfied and the suitcase was parked behind Miss Charlotte's reception desk.

***

All day long, he received compliments, like "Way to go, Joe!" and "Dude, you're a hero!" and "We're very proud of you,

Mr. McKinnon," but he also heard things like "I bet I could've run faster" and "My aunt got hit in the eye—my uncle accidentally shot her with a pellet gun."

All of this would've been fun if he'd not been so worried about his presentation. He was having doubts about the subject he'd chosen, and even worse, he'd become so preoccupied with the condo and stayed up so late last night that although he had the presentation written out on notecards, he hadn't practiced delivering it … not even once.

***

Mr. Z stood at the door and greeted his students with a smile as they poured into his room.

"Hello … good afternoon … how are you … hello …"

The responses were weak.

"Hey outstanding citizen, are you ready?" He spotted Joe's suitcase. "I see you're all set to go on vacation. Hi Julie …"

After the last student entered, he strolled to the front of the class.

"Isn't this beautiful weather we're having?"

Their reaction might have been the same if he'd said he was going to drill their molars.

"Oh, come on now," Mr. Z said, still smiling. "The year's almost over. Soon you'll be working on your summer tans and playing video games 'til your thumbs bleed."

Silence—he was working a tough crowd.

"Alrighty then, how about we put this in your past? Who wants to go first?"

Joe's arm sprang up.

"Our star student … the carpet is yours."

"Umm, the floor's tile," Jack Kazden said. Even with his cornier jokes he always managed to get a laugh.

Joe rolled his suitcase up to the front, set it upright, and pushed down the telescoping handle. He felt twenty-eight pairs of eyeballs staring at him as he pulled his notecards out of the front skinny compartment and placed them on the podium. He scanned the crowd. The room had never seemed so quiet.

His eyes stopped on Antonio, a lanky kid with wavy dark hair, who reminded him of Ramesh. Joe thought of Ramesh, trumpet in hand, with that big smile, talking into the mic, singing, engaging the crowd—with passion.

One desk over, he saw Julie Silverstein. Julie looked nothing like Jun, but Joe still imagined it was Jun sitting there. He pictured her anime bangs and nearly black eyes, her cheerful voice saying "Hi, Just Joe." He thought of Jun playing her flute with grace … and *passion.*

And there was Dad.

Don't waste any more time son, do it!

Joe grabbed his notecards, walked over to the trash can and dropped them in. The class stared as he returned to the podium.

"Cars suck!"

A few kids drew audible breaths. Mr. Z showed no reaction.

"They make noise, pollute the air, maim people—they kill people," Joe said with tight lips and a look that dared anyone to contradict him.

"People spend large amounts of money to buy them, fix them, and insure them." His voice resonated. "Cars cost us billions and billions of dollars for roads, freeways, bridges, and government agencies to manage them. And in spite of the freedom we think cars give us, they really make us their prisoners."

Joe walked to the other side of the room. Twenty-eight pairs of eyes followed him.

"Who in here plans to live without a car? Raise your hand."

All were still.

"That's right. Because we *have* to have a car—*have* to. Is that freedom?"

He moved on quickly, knowing that whenever you posed a question to a room full of eighth graders, there was bound to be a smart aleck who answered.

"And here's another thing: Can you walk or ride your bike to a friend's house just a few miles away without crossing pavement?"

Jack Kazden spoke up. "Yeah, I could tunnel under it."

A few kids laughed.

"Sure you could," Joe said. He looked Jack in the eye. "And it would take you two years and then it would cave in on you—let's get real here."

Lacking a comeback, Jack squirmed in his seat.

"We live in a society of rectangle-shaped prisons created by roads," Joe said. "Yeah, you're free to cross the road most of the time. But some roads are hard to cross safely, and you're only allowed to cross them in certain places. Some roads you're not allowed to cross at all, like freeways and toll roads. To me, that's not freedom—that's prison."

He walked back to the podium.

"So what's the answer?" Joe said. "I'll tell you what's *not* the answer: airplanes. With airplanes, you have to schedule your movement ahead of time, go through a great big hassle at the airport, and pay a lot of money for tickets. And even if airplane travel was made more simultaneous—" He swallowed. "I mean instantaneous—you'd still need some way to get from your home to the airport."

"Trains and busses? Same problems. You have to travel by *their* schedule. And busses take you too much extra time to get anywhere because of all the stops they make. So what's the answer?"

He paused. "I call it JAMrail. JAM is the initials of my name—Joseph Alan McKinnon. JAMrail is like a monorail—anyone ever ride on a monorail? Like the one they have at Disney World or some airports?"

Most of the class raised their hands.

Abby said, "I rode the one at Disney World."

Antonio said, "I rode one in Las Vegas with my mom and dad and sister."

"A lot of airports have them to get you from one terminal to another," Julie said.

Joe held up his hand and everyone quieted down.

"That's right," he said. "But here's what makes JAMrail different: it comes right to your home. It comes right *into* your home. Some of you have garages attached to your homes and you can go right from inside your home to your garage and into your car. JAMrail is even better. It can pull up right next to any part of your home, a sliding door opens, and you step inside."

"Cool!" Jordan said. "Like *Star Trek*."

"Yeah," Joe said. "Like *Star Trek*, but no whooshing sound when the doors slide shut."

The class laughed.

"And once you step inside, you tell the computer where to take you, and it takes you there—not to a parking lot close by, but *right there*."

"Imagine in the morning, instead of waiting for a bus or having your mom drive you to school, you just walk from your living room or kitchen into a JAMrail car, say the words *take me to HMS*, and go. On your way to school, you can sit down to study for a test, watch TV, or finish getting dressed. You can get here all by yourself. And where the car lets you off, there'd be enough room for a bunch of cars to drop off students at the same time, so there's almost no wait."

"And someone like me, who likes to ride his bike, won't ever have to cross any roads. I'll be able to ride on a network of bike paths that go *under* the JAMrail, which is something like twelve feet off the ground—and also quiet."

"But that's not all. You can take JAMrail anywhere in the world anytime you want. So you could walk into your JAMrail car and say to the computer *take me to Bogota, Columbia*, then

236

lie down and go to sleep, or read a book, or make yourself a pizza—JAMrail cars can have a fridge and a microwave—and while you do those things, it'll take you to Bogota. You don't even have to worry about how it gets you there."

Julie Silverstein raised her hand and Joe pointed to her.

"How about if you want to go to a country on the other side of the ocean?" she said.

"Take the JAMrail. A bridge across the ocean is possible. Hell, they made an island in the ocean in Dubai just so they could build a freakin' hotel on it!"

There was a group gasp. Joe stole a quick glance at Mr. Z—he was unfazed.

"There might have to be some new kind of bridge invented over really deep water—like a floating flexible bridge. But just think of the time that could be saved. People who spend an hour or two driving every weekday could now save time in two ways: one—shorter commute time because JAMrail can go faster and with no traffic lights, and two—while they ride, people can read, pay bills, eat, take a nap … anything!"

Mr. Z pointed to his watch and held up two fingers. Joe thought he looked pleased.

"Just a couple more things about JAMrail: You don't have to have a lot of money to ride it. You don't even have to own one—but you can if you want. You can rent one every day, like a taxi, but cheaper because there's no driver. But if you want a really fancy JAMrail car, you can buy one. And JAMrail cars would be cheaper to buy because the chassis— the part that rides on the track—would be the same across all cars, no matter who makes them. And if it needs service, you can send it to the mechanic by itself."

Out of character for Jack, he raised his hand.

"Yes, Jack."

"What if it's broken and *can't* go to the mechanic? Or what if it breaks down in the middle of the rail?" he said.

"Good question," Joe said. "There will be a tow car that a JAMrail car fits inside of that can lift a JAMrail car off the rail and take it to the mechanic. And there will be spider cars that ride over the JAMrail cars for emergency vehicles."

"And lastly, *anyone at all*—little kids, old folks, people in wheelchairs, even pets—will be able to travel anywhere they want at any time. But it *will* have parental controls so little kids and pets don't take trips without permission—like to Bogota."

The class chuckled.

"That's it," Joe said. "Any more questions?"

Antonio raised his hand.

"How fast will it go?"

"In neighborhoods, it would go slow—maybe thirty. Around local areas, it might go fifty. Going across town it could go a hundred. Going across country it would link onto a special kind of JAMrail where it would go maybe three hundred miles an hour, maybe more. It would have to hook up to a maglev car to go that fast."

The class *wowed* at that.

"Okay, very nice, Joe," Mr. Z said. "Everyone, let's give Joe a round of applause."

The room resounded with enthusiastic applause.

Mr. Z continued. "You certainly had command of your subject. You were authoritative, and your opening line was a real grabber—although I wouldn't recommend anyone else use *dicey* language in their presentation. And what made you decide to throw away your notecards and speak off the cuff?"

"Don't know," Joe said. "Just didn't need them, I guess."

"Well evidently you didn't because your delivery was smooth and it appeared that you didn't miss a beat."

"Thanks." Although he wanted to smile, Joe tried to remain professional.

"Some visual aids would have made good support for your talk. And hard facts—like numbers—would have been helpful too."

"Okay."

"One more thing, Joe," he said. "Wasn't your talk supposed to be about solar power?"

"Yes, but I decided my JAMrail presentation would be better."

"Not that you weren't successful, but I wish you would have told me. When did you decide to ditch solar for JAMrail?"

Joe couldn't help grinning.

"About ten seconds before I started my speech."

53

On a Dime

AS SOON AS SCHOOL WAS OUT, Joe called his mom to tell her all about his hot dog of a day at school. She decided they should celebrate with a pizza from Bella Magnifico.

It was no secret that Bella Magnifico had the best crust on the south side, which meant they usually had to wait an hour before picking it up. So Mom ordered it from the library, left work early, and came home with the pizza just before five o'clock.

While he waited, Joe spent time studying for his last two tests before finals, which were both tomorrow. He thought about going out to the condo, then changed his mind—he needed the break from Mr. Pruitt.

When Mom arrived, she turned on the local news and they sat down to eat their sausage pizza.

"Mmmm," Joe said. "I love BM's."

"Oh Joe, don't call it that. Call it Bella's, or Magnifico, but don't call it that."

"Sorry—I keep forgetting."

The newscast's introductory music faded and the anchors reported the day's top headlines: a suicide bomber struck somewhere on the other side of the world, the President talked about terrorism, some woman gave her opinion about the economy and interest rates, the World Health Organization was making predictions about the flu this coming winter, blah, blah, blah.

"That reminds me," Mom said. "We need to get shots this year."

The pizza's tiny triangular pieces were gone first. Mom and Joe both liked them because they had a lot of sauce and they were crispy. The remaining end-squares were next to disappear.

A commercial came on showing people eating droopy pizza wedges. Joe felt that pizza cut into squares tasted better, though he wasn't sure why.

When the news returned, it was to the scene of an accident.

"… a tragic end to an otherwise beautiful Memorial Day weekend for one family …" Their car was T-boned—so mashed up, you couldn't tell what model it was anymore. The reporter announced it was now known that the three deceased occupants of the smashed vehicle were two parents and their daughter: "the Song family from Palos Heights."

Joe's pizza fell to his plate.

"Such a shame," Mom said. "And from our town too."

The camera then switched to the vehicle that hit the car: a black Dodge Ram Quad Cab pickup.

"Mom—"

"Oh my God—"

The news anchor announced that the man driving the pickup was identified as a forty-two-year-old man who'd allegedly been drinking after just leaving a local hospital where authorities said he was recovering from an arm amputation surgery.

Mom stood up from the table.

"Oh my God, oh my God!" She was already halfway to the phone when it rang.

Joe ran up to his room and scanned the books on his shelf until he found his yearbook. He leafed through his fifth-grade class and slowed when he reached the fourth grade. His finger finally came to rest below a black-and-white photo.

It was Jun Song.

***

Joe sat on the edge of his bed, his yearbook on his lap. Tears journeyed to the corners of his lips.

He could hear his mom down in the kitchen, talking to someone on the phone. She sounded like she was crying.

Joe was angry. There was no one for *him* to call except Mr. Pruitt—but Joe didn't want to talk to him. He looked at his watch: 7:10.

Maybe I do know someone.

He hobbled down the steps. "I'm going out." He ran past his mother.

"Joey, where—" But the door had already slammed shut.

***

In twenty minutes, Joe's bike was parked in the library's bike rack. He found Liz at the checkout desk along with Henry—a guy Mom called *socially inept,* which was partly why his schedule didn't coincide much with Mom's.

Liz smiled, but it melted when she saw Joe's face.

"Are you all right, Joe?"

"Yeah, fine." He raced past her into the office area—empty.

He checked the storeroom and the reserve shelving area—no one. He went back through the office, feeling Liz's stare as he walked toward the far corner of fiction. Then he followed the wall like a cockroach, looking up every aisle. Finally, in the six hundreds of non-fiction, Joe found him.

Joe limped up the aisle to Ramesh's book cart and placed his trembling hands upon it. His lip quivered. Without a word, Ramesh stepped closer and put his arms around Joe, who collapsed to his knees, taking the skinny Indian down with him.

"I just heard the news," Ramesh said. "I am very sorry your friend was in that accident."

Joe sobbed on Ramesh's shoulder while Ramesh gestured to Liz, who'd been watching from the end of the aisle. She left and quickly returned with a box of tissues. She crouched down and patted Joe on the shoulder, but left when Ramesh shook his head.

After a few minutes and some curious looks from passing patrons, Joe recovered enough to speak.

"She sh-shouldn't have died." He cried harder at the sound of his own words.

Ramesh stopped patting Joe's back. "What *she* are you speaking of?"

"Jun," Joe said. He sat up and blew his nose. "Jun Song."

Ramesh looked confused. "I'm sorry, I don't know Jun Song."

"She's one of the people who died in the crash. I knew her. And Fred killed her!" He started sobbing again, so hard he had trouble breathing.

"Was she your classmate?"

"No, she's … she *was* one grade below me." Joe stood, wiping his eyes, his breathing still doing the herky-jerkies.

Ramesh led Joe to the office behind the circulation desk and closed the blinds. Joe looked up—almost 7:45 on the analog clock. Mom didn't like digital clocks. She said digital displays were fine for scientific instruments and nuclear-bomb timers in James Bond movies, but she liked to know how close it was to the next minute, and not be held there, hanging in suspense for that digit to flip. She didn't like clocks with ticking second hands either—like a warning that an alarm was about to ring, a reminder that life was ticking away. Only a clock with a smooth-turning second hand would do.

"I'm sorry you lost your friend," Ramesh said. "I see you were very close to her."

Joe laughed a stuffy-nose laugh.

Ramesh flinched.

"I just started talking to her." He looked through glassy eyes at Ramesh. "It's just … I mean …"

"You cared for her and you think you would have become close."

"Yeah, pretty much," Joe wrinkled his brow. "How'd you know?"

"I'm familiar with love."

Joe's face relaxed, then tightened up again. "She'd still be alive if that jerk didn't get drunk and kill her."

"You're angry with Fred?"

"Shouldn't I be?" Joe was surprised Ramesh didn't echo his sentiment.

"There is a Hindi saying: *Boils on one's own body are considered painful while those on others are deemed painless.*"

"What's that supposed to mean?"

"That one cannot know the pain of others."

Just then, Henry poked his head around the corner.

"Hey Ramo, I know you're a short-timer, but library? Books? Work?"

"Yes, yes, I will be there." It was rare to see Ramesh agitated. "I am with a friend right now."

Henry sported a sour face, then retreated from the doorway.

Ramesh turned back to Joe and rolled his eyes. Joe was still searching for the wisdom in what Ramesh had said.

"Nobody's pain makes it right to kill a family," Joe said. "I don't care if he had *all* his arms and legs amputated—at least then he wouldn't have been able to drive."

"Perhaps he had pain before he lost his arm—the kind that's here." Ramesh put his palm to his heart. "Perhaps being in the hospital he was not able to escape the pain inside."

Joe was ticked.

"Why are you sticking up for him?"

"You are wanting to fill your heart with hatred. If you do this, it will give you pain for a long time and it may cause *you* to create pain for someone else. Think about Praveen. If you hadn't learned where his hurting came from, his meanness might have caused you to be mean to someone else one day. How do you feel about Praveen now?"

Joe stared at the floor.

"Understand the cause of Fred's hurt and you will break the cycle."

"How?" Joe breathed normally again. There was something calming about Ramesh. *How could someone so young know so much about life?*

"Fill your heart with understanding," he said. "Then there will be no room for the hatred."

"But you just said I can't understand someone else's pain."

"You cannot understand how their pain feels. But you can understand that they *have* pain, and you can choose to believe them when they say it feels bad, even if it doesn't seem to you like it should."

Joe pondered this. Maybe he did know some of the suffering in Fred's life.

Henry came into the office again, this time more peeved than the last.

"Ramo, come on man, back to work."

A stern and motherly voice came from behind him. "No Henry, why don't *you* get back to work?"

As Henry looked down and slinked away, Joe's mom filled his void.

54

Swear to Tell the Truth, the Whole Truth …

ON WEDNESDAY AT SCHOOL, nobody said a thing about Jun Song, and that bothered Joe. Not that he wanted to talk about it, but didn't anyone care? He did overhear two of the sixth-grade teachers talking about that *drunken idiot who killed the family*, but they clammed up when they spotted Joe eavesdropping.

Joe took two tests that day. Even though he let his hand mark down the answers without paying much attention, he still knew he wouldn't get less than a B+ on either one.

It didn't matter. Nothing mattered.

On his way home, Joe took the express route and rode past Brain STEM Prep. Kids poured through the front doors—but all he could see was the one girl who was missing.

The sky began to cloud over and the wind picked up, nearly shoving him off the road. A cold front was moving in.

***

At home, from his bed, Joe stared at Albert on the wall. His mind told him he had to finish the condo. His body ignored it.

I never think of the future. It comes soon enough.

Yeah … and sometimes that future sucks.

The doorbell rang. Mom always said not to answer the door when she wasn't home. But today, who cared? He looked through the peephole: nobody. He peeked through the curtain of the window beside the door.

The lawyer was looking back at him.

"Joe, will you please speak with me?" he said.

"I'm not supposed to open the door," Joe said.

"That's fine," the lawyer said. "Why don't I go down to the end of the sidewalk to the steps, and you can just come out and stand by the door?" He started backing away. "You can keep the door open in case you feel the need to go back inside. You can talk to me from a distance—I just can't talk to you through a door."

The lawyer sat just where he said he would on the worn concrete steps.

Joe went outside, keeping the door open as the lawyer had suggested. He sat on a different set of steps near the door, a little further away.

The lawyer turned so he could see Joe. His hair flopped over his forehead. He still wore dress slacks, but no suit jacket. His tie was loosened and off to one side. He could stand to drag a razor across his face; the stubble made him look a lot like Fred.

Joe rested his chin on his thumbs and watched the lawyer warily. A cool spring wind whooshed up the leaves in the silver aspen and made branches on the willow squeak.

"Thank you," Francis said.

"For what?"

"For caring enough to come out and talk to me."

Joe stared off into the distance, but watched the lawyer out of the corner of his eye.

"A lot has happened, Joe … a *lot*." He sighed. "For one, I failed."

"Failed what?"

"Failed my brother … and my mother. She always told me 'when I'm gone, make sure you watch over your brother'—and I didn't. Not good enough, anyway."

Mrs. Wislinski drove by slowly. She eyed Joe and the stranger, giving the lawyer an extra dose of suspicion.

"Do you know what an alcoholic is?" the lawyer said.

"Yes."

The lawyer's eyes became glassy. His mouth opened twice to say something, then he turned away.

Joe stood up and walked down to Francis who scooched over, making room. Joe remained standing.

"Guess you're wondering why I wanted to talk with you?" Francis said.

"Yeah, sort of figured you'd be getting to that."

The lawyer smiled. "I see why Fred likes you."

A hefty gust flared up and rocked the willow. Nearby, a tin garbage can blew over, its lid rolling away and banging to a stop against a wall.

"Fred's in a world of trouble."

"I know."

The lawyer snapped off a dandelion flower by the bottom of its tubular stem.

"When I wanted to talk to you before—that day you ran away from me—I was trying to prevent something like this from happening. I wanted to get some dirt on Fred, get him in a little trouble … hopefully scare him before he found big trouble. I thought if I could show he'd been drinking when he cut off his arm, we could force him into rehab." He spun the dandelion between his thumb and index finger. "Now he's going into the toughest rehab program there is."

Joe remained silent, waiting for more.

"Being a lawyer, Joe, I sometimes represent people who, like Fred, have hurt others and are looking to avoid the consequences. So with Fred being my twin brother, and with my being quite good at my job, it's only natural that I step in and try to rescue him from the heavy hand of the law." He flicked away the dandelion and squinted up at Joe. "But I won't."

Joe frowned.

"Because believe it or not," Francis said, "brother or not—he's better off where he is right now."

"Then why are you here?"

"I saw Fred today. The only reason he was willing to see me is because of you. He wanted me to give you a message."

Joe felt a chill—and not from the wind. Two days ago, a message from Fred would have been no big deal. Now he was getting a message from a murderer.

"What is it?"

"Check your phone—the one *he* gave you."

"That's his message?"

"That's what he said. He also said for you and your mom not to come see him for a while. He doesn't want you to be part of his life right now. He meant that in a caring way, you know."

"Oh." Joe didn't want to feel grateful toward Fred. "I guess that's it then?"

"I guess so, except for one thing."

"Huh."

"I was hoping you could tell me … what was Fred up to when he had that accident—the one with the chainsaw?"

Joe stared off.

"You see it doesn't make much sense to me. Why would he come way out here, seven or eight miles from his own home to cut down a tree? There's forest preserves within two miles of his house. I know he wasn't drunk—they tested his blood at the hospital. There were no signs he was drinking at the site of the accident either. And that Mr. Pruitt—he's hiding something." He looked Joe in the eye. "I can always tell when decent people lie."

Joe shrugged. "Why don't you ask Fred?"

"He won't answer me. In case you haven't noticed, Fred doesn't answer to anyone. I thought maybe you could shed some light on things. I've heard you two were pretty close."

"He never told *me* what he was doing." Which wasn't a lie. Fred never did tell him he was going to the condo that day.

"But you and Fred *were* close, weren't you Joe? Surely he said something to you that may have hinted at what he was up to?"

Joe felt like he was on the witness stand—this guy was smooth, too smooth.

"Yeah, we were kind of close, I guess." Time to play the ace. "Fred was like a father to me after my dad died." He turned his head away.

The lawyer rose, the wind blowing his tie sideways.

"I'm sorry Joe, I know what it's like to lose your father." He put a hand on Joe's shoulder. "I lost mine when I was six."

He dropped his hand to his side and clacked down the sidewalk to his immaculate Lexus. At its door he stopped and turned.

"You still have my card?"

Joe nodded.

"Look Joe, I know you don't know me, but if you ever need grown-up advice—guy advice—about anything, don't hesitate to call me."

"Okay." Joe crossed his arms.

Grown-up advice—from one of the same people who ripped off my dad and cheated my mom—right.

55

Mystery at Drop-Point Charlie

JOE DUG UP THE PHONE AT GROUND THIRTEEN. There wasn't much charge left when he turned it on, but there was enough.

A message had been left yesterday. Fred's voice was monotone, somber and weak—like someone who'd been shouting at a football game all day.

"Joe, go to Drop-Point Charlie. At the place you found this phone, look for an envelope. Ignore what it says on the envelope, just open it. Memorize the following numbers and tell them to no one: 29-64-11. Be good Joe—keep the dream going."

And that was it.

He listened to the message again, hoping for some hint of remorse, but there was nothing—no emotion whatsoever.

He made his way to Drop-Point Charlie and went to the tree. Inside the hole was an envelope with the following words written on it:

> Warning: The white powder inside this
> envelope is not anthrax

Joe paused for a second, gave it a half smile and tore open the envelope. There was a note inside.

> Go to my house. There's a key stuck in
> Styrofoam inside a fake rock next to
> the shed. Use that to open the lock on
> the shed. Inside the shed is a yellow
> plastic flashlight with a handle. Search

for it. Inside that is a key to the
deadbolt. There's bicycle tires hanging
in there too. Inside one of them is
another key and a stubby Phillips
screwdriver. That key is for the handle
lock. Take the keys, the flashlight, and
the screwdriver and go to the back
door of the house. Get in. Go down to
the basement …

And on it continued.

Puzzled, Joe tucked the note in his pocket, hopped on his bike, and rode back toward home. Just as he turned onto Oak Street, Mr. Pruitt came toward him in the Town Car. He spotted Joe and pulled over as his passenger-side window rolled down.

Joe slowed to a stop at the open window.

"Hello Joe, how are you doing?" Mr. Pruitt said.

"Hi Mr. Pruitt," Joe said. "Doing okay … I guess."

"I know what you mean," he said. "I don't think Hollywood could write a better drama than we've seen here in Palos recently."

"You mean a worse drama."

"I suppose that's the proper way to put it," Mr. Pruitt said. "Never would've thought Fred would do such a thing."

"Me neither." Joe wanted to get off the subject.

There was an awkward silence.

"So where do we go from here?" Mr. Pruitt said.

"It keeps going, same as before."

Joe's resolve to finish the condo was greater than ever. Nothing could stop him now, and anyone who tried would have to drag him kicking and screaming, fingers clawing at the ground, away from what he knew now was his passion.

"Son, don't you think that's risky?" Mr. Pruitt said. "After this, they might re-open their investigation into what Fred was doing with the chainsaw in the woods. They might start poking around again."

Joe stiffened his lips. "Let them."

Mr. Pruitt cocked his head.

"Are you all right son?" he said. "Is there anything I can help you with?"

Joe thought about the note in his pocket.

"Actually … I could use a ride."

56

Is It Safe?

JOE HAD NEVER OPENED A FLOOR SAFE BEFORE, and being nervous about getting caught didn't make it any easier. He spun the dial to the left several times and stopped at twenty-nine. Then he turned it right past sixty-four twice before stopping on sixty-four. Then it was left again past eleven once before stopping on eleven. Finally, he turned the dial to the right expecting it to stop—but it didn't.

Mr. Pruitt was parked in front of the long stretch of Fred's backyard. Hopefully no one would call the cops on him. Joe was somewhat surprised Mr. Pruitt was willing to give him a ride so far from home without telling Mom. Then again, look what else Mr. Pruitt was doing for Joe behind Mom's back.

Finally, after three unsuccessful attempts, Joe slowed down, counting his turns out loud, coming to rest precisely on each number. One last turn to the right and—bam! The dial hit the stop. With a turn of the handle, the door pulled open.

He pulled out a baggie filled with papers, then one with keys—lots of them. Next were manila envelopes and a photo album. On the front of the album was a baby picture—probably Fred's son, Phelps. And that was it—there was nothing else.

Joe studied the pile, then flipped through the photo album. Tons of pictures of Phelps. He then looked through the papers and envelopes: legal documents, titles, birth certificates, Fred's social security card. He pulled the note from his pocket.

> … Leave the uninteresting stuff like the
> papers and photos, but the interesting
> stuff is yours …

What's he calling interesting?

Inside the empty safe, Joe noticed four screws near the corners on one wall. He pulled the screwdriver out of his other pocket. It was an awkward reach, but after a little wrestling, he was able to remove all four of the short screws. A thin plate fell toward him revealing … more metal.

What?

Joe panned the flashlight around the inside of the safe. Nothing, just gray padding on the bottom. He lifted the padding—nothing but more black metal.

"Crap."

He screwed the plate back on and gave the safe one last look-see. Maybe the bag of keys contained a key to another safe, or to another room of the house? Maybe, but there was no time to search—Mr. Pruitt was waiting, and the neighbors could be growing suspicious. He had to get out of there, regroup, and come back another time.

He put back the photo album, then the keys. The keys hit inside the safe with a hollow clank.

Hey, what's that?

Joe knocked on all the safe's walls and found that the one under him—the one he couldn't see—sounded hollow. Joe scooted forward until his head was up against the closet wall. With flashlight pointed and neck bent so his chin was into his chest, he could now see four more screws, just like the opposite side.

In no time, the screws and plate were off. Joe shined the flashlight inside, revealing a good-sized space directly under him. Something was there in the way back. He reached in and pulled out a sample of the contents for a closer look.

His eyes widened.

"Holy crap!"

***

There was way too much to carry. He needed a container, something strong because this stuff was heavy. Joe looked around for something he could use. In the master bedroom the bed was made, but with two large open suitcases sitting on top. They were partly filled with short stacks of clothes, and there was a framed photo of Fred and Phelps on top of one stack. In that photo, Phelps looked to be about seven years old.

Where was Fred going?

Joe noticed the pillows. *Pillowcases!* Then he thought again—nothing says burglar like walking out of a dark, empty house with a weighted-down pillowcase. *I might as well put on a striped shirt and ski mask.*

Next he looked in the bathroom. He found a garbage can, but it was too small for the task. He noticed it contained three empty beer bottles.

Last, Joe went to the garage in search of a box. Instead, he found something better—a stack of five-gallon buckets. He took two of them, grabbed two towels from the bathroom, then went back to the safe.

In minutes, Joe emerged from the house carrying the two buckets. He was balancing like a tightrope walker.

Man, I had no idea it would be so heavy.

Joe shuffled his way to the Town Car as fast as he could, then knocked on the trunk. Mr. Pruitt opened it from the comfort of his leather seat. Joe loaded the buckets into the trunk and hopped in the car. They sped off, and Joe peeked out the back window behind them—they'd made a clean getaway.

"What are those anyway—buckets of sand?" Mr. Pruitt said as he sped back toward Palos.

"Nah, just some stuff Fred wanted me to get from the house."

"Felt the back end of the car sink when you dropped them in."

"Yeah …" Joe thought for a second. "Guess I should tell you. He wanted me to take his coin collection. Said the house and everything else would get taken away, but he wanted to make sure his son got his coin collection."

There was some truth in this. The part about getting it for Phelps wasn't so true. But it *was* a coin collection—solid gold and silver.

57

Holy Crap!

JOE PUT THE BUCKETS IN THE GARAGE FOR NOW. Mom was home, and if she saw them, she'd want to know what was in them.

Dinner was a somber occasion, just like the first couple months after Dad's accident—before Mom finally decided her moping wasn't going to help their situation. He hoped this time she wouldn't take as long to snap out of it.

Whereas Mom was dismal, Joe was angry—except he wasn't even sure who to be angry with anymore. What Ramesh had said about Fred's pain was true. It was pretty clear that more than anything else, Fred was missing his son. And very likely, just before the accident, he was packing to go see Phelps in California.

Joe wanted to talk to Mom, maybe get some reassurance that he wasn't a bad person for not wanting to be a prosthetic son for Fred. He wanted to talk about Dad too, but it was such a hard conversation to start and he didn't want to upset her.

After dinner, as Mom sat at the table, he hugged her. She patted him on the arm in return.

"I love you, Joe."

"I love you too, Mom. I'm gonna go do some homework now."

***

Sitting on his bed, Joe opened his computer's browser and searched "gold coins." A few clicks later, he found it: a picture of the exact type of coin Fred had given him, the American Gold Eagle. It was one ounce of pure gold. Another search revealed that the current price of gold was around twelve hundred dollars per ounce.

"Holy crap!"

Next he looked up silver coins. American Silver Eagles weren't worth nearly as much—less than twenty dollars per ounce—but when he was loading the buckets, he'd seen a lot of them.

Joe was intrigued. He just had to go see how many coins were in those buckets. He scrambled down the stairs.

"Hey Mom," Joe said. She'd moved to the couch, and was staring at the TV—something she rarely did. "Gotta go make something in the workshop for a science experiment. Should be back in twenty minutes."

"Okay, hun." He didn't think she'd notice if he said he was driving the Sequoia to Shanghai.

***

In the workshop, Joe took the towels off the buckets and laid them flat on the work bench. Then he carefully poured the contents of both buckets onto them. The three-inch-long plastic tubes were just translucent enough to see that there was something inside them. Fred had written *1-½" lead washers* on two sides of each tube with a thick black marker.

Aren't most people smart enough to know you wouldn't store something worthless like lead washers in a safe? Didn't fool me!

Joe separated the gold from the silver. There were eight tubes of gold eagles, and twenty-five tubes of silver eagles. He opened a full tube and counted: twenty coins. One tube of gold had only nine coins, but all tubes of silver were full.

Joe grabbed a pencil and a pad of paper from the workbench. The pad had sketches with dimensions, drawn by Dad. He flipped to a blank page and wrote:

25 x 20 = 500 silver coins

7 x 20 + 9 = 140 + 9 = 149 gold coins

"Holy crap!!" His new favorite saying. And then ...
Why?

This thought entered the back door of Joe's mind like an estranged uncle showing up to ruin a perfectly good Christmas dinner. Why did Fred give him all this money? Why not give it to Phelps? He could have at least explained it in the note, instead of just writing, "follow these instructions and *the interesting stuff* is yours." Joe could lose sleep over this.

But right now, there was another issue to deal with—namely, that this kind of loot couldn't be left lying around. Joe searched for a safe place in the workshop, then suddenly remembered what Mr. Pruitt had said:

Sometimes the best place to hide something is in plain view.

He grabbed one of Fred's buckets, laid a towel on the bottom and put the coins inside. Then he laid the other towel over the coins and stacked the other bucket inside along with two more buckets he found. Later he'd find an even better place to hide his treasure, but for now ... who would think of checking a stack of empty buckets for a secret cache of gold and silver?

***

Back in his bedroom, Joe did another calculation:

149 x $1200 = $178,800 in gold
500 x $20 = $10,000 in silver
GRAND TOTAL = $188,800!

"Holy ...!!" *Where did Fred get that kind of money?*
Joe searched gold prices and found that gold hadn't always been so expensive. Not too long ago it had been down to two hundred dollars an ounce, and before the 1980s it was even

lower. So maybe Fred bought the gold back when it was a lot cheaper? Or maybe his parents had died and left him a pile of gold? All Joe knew was that he was now very rich!

The phone rang downstairs. *Kind of late at night for someone to be calling.*

Joe went to his door to listen. Whoever it was, Mom seemed to think it was a nice surprise to hear from them—like an old friend or something. Shortly into their conversation, Mom said "Oh, okay," then she went into another room and closed the door. Probably Grammy Jeanne—Mom always said she was a night owl.

***

Lying in bed waiting for sleep to come, Joe considered the possibilities. He could retire at the age of thirteen. Or he could go to the Ferrari dealership and get himself a very early sixteenth-birthday gift. Nah, *that* was thinking like a lottery winner: win big and blow it all stupidly. He could buy his mom her own private library … or he could hire some construction guys to finish the condo and pay them extra to keep quiet about it. He could put the money in the bank and earn almost nothing in interest and get a whole lot of questions—like where did a thirteen-year-old get so much money? He could put it in the stock market and watch it climb … or drop to nothing if he invested poorly.

Joe consulted Einstein.

You're pretty smart. What would you do with that much money?

The wild-haired man gave a thoughtful expression.

Would you tell your mom about it?

There was doubt in his eyes.

Should I share it?

The scientist looked wise and compassionate.

How long should I hang onto it?

Albert said, *I never think of the future. It comes soon enough!*

58

Going for the Gold

JOE COULDN'T CONCENTRATE IN SCHOOL. He couldn't imagine the other kids had to deal with these kinds of ups and downs in their lives.

The loss of Jun still put a lump in his throat. As much as possible he tried to replace thoughts of her death with thoughts of how he would prevent such tragedies in the future.

And of course, he was still wowed by the sudden increase in his wealth—but was even more overwhelmed with the question of what to do with it.

He knew he couldn't leave the coins as they were—he had to find a way to turn them into usable money, but how was he supposed to do that? How could he do it secretly and who could he even trust to help him? You couldn't just walk into a bank—especially if you were a kid—with a bucket of gold and say "Hi bank person, I'd like cash for this ... hundreds, please." Questions would be asked. Suspicions would be raised. Authorities would be notified.

Then came the question of where to hide it while he figured out what to do with it. As a kid, he'd been a natural expert at hiding things, but stashing away candy or even a wad of bills was a lot easier than hiding thirty-three tubes of large coins. And when he went down the list of places to hide stuff, none were both super-stealthy *and* accessible.

That's why Fred had it stashed in the secret compartment of a safe hidden in the concrete floor of his basement closet.

Then there was the question of what to do with it. There were more ways to spend or invest that much money than all the pimples on all the students at Halverson Middle School. No wonder people needed financial advisors. Mom would know what to do with that much money, but Fred's advice about telling Mom was probably correct:

> … Use it wisely. If you decide to tell
> your mom about it, she probably won't
> let you use it the way you want, if she
> even lets you keep it. Trust me on that.
> I know your mom …

Yeah, Fred was right. Mom might not mind her son having that much money, but she would definitely say it was wrong for Joe to take *that* money. So now he was keeping two big secrets.

He wondered: When did Fred put that note in the tree? He couldn't have done it after the accident … he was in jail. It was doubtful he'd had someone else do it. He must have planted that note somewhere between leaving the hospital and getting in the accident.

And that nagging question returned: Why was he giving away his money? If he was packing up and moving, why wouldn't he take his gold and silver too? Was he worried about someone stealing it from him as he travelled?

Joe considered the last part of Fred's note:

> … I might not be around to keep you in
> line when you break the rules, so when
> you do break them, imagine I'm there
> either yelling at you or cheering you
> on. I think you're smart enough to
> know which rules shouldn't be broken
> and which ones damned well should
> be. Take care of your mom, and take
> care of yourself. And remember rule
> #1.
>
> I'll be back. Someday.

The note was unsigned.

By the end of the school day, Joe was exhausted. Trying to understand the grown-up world was more taxing than studying for the hardest test ever. So he tried to clear his mind during his ride home. Mom would be at work and he'd have time alone to figure things out: Jun, Fred, Mr. Pruitt, the gold, the silver … the condo. Maybe he could use some of his new fortune to hire an advisor.

Joe rounded the corner onto Oak Street, and that's when he saw them: two cop cars and his mom's SUV parked in front of the house.

Joe pulled into the driveway and was greeted by an officer.

"Hello son, I'm Officer Scott," he said. "Are you Joseph?"

"Yes sir." He saw his mom talking to the other officer and his heart started to pound. "What's wrong?"

"Nothing serious, just a little burglary. Someone broke into your garage and took a few things—that's all. Nobody got hurt."

Joe's knee started to buckle. *The garage?* He felt the blood rushing to his face as he swallowed hard. He dropped his bike and stumbled over it, running to the open side door of the garage which now had a broken window. He ignored his mom and the other officer who turned and said, "Be careful son, don't touch anything."

Inside the garage, things looked pretty much the same as yesterday. All the big stuff was still there. The thieves went after small items: power tools (all of them, and there were many) and mechanic's tools—a couple drawers of Dad's big tool chest were empty and left open.

And the five-gallon buckets—all of them—were gone.

<h1 style="text-align:center">59</h1>

Easy Come, Not So Easy Go

JOE LAY IN BED AND STARED at the ceiling fan. He wanted to cry but this was far beyond cry-worthy. The officers had been polite and acted concerned, but Joe could tell they'd thought this robbery was small potatoes. They said there'd been a lot of garage break-ins recently—that thieves were mostly after tools and expensive bicycles. When Mom suggested it was probably just some kids getting into mischief, Officer Scott said he didn't think so, because kids usually feel the need to trash the place. These thieves just wanted to grab the goods and get out fast.

They'd asked Joe's mom what she thought was missing and if she could put a value on it. She'd told them she'd have to check, but on the surface it just looked like some tools were gone, probably no more than two to three thousand dollars' worth of stuff.

Yeah, plus about another two hundred thousand!

If the cops knew just how big a theft this really was, there'd be more than just two deputies there. They might even call the FBI. Of course Joe didn't say anything. Even if they believed him, he'd just get in trouble for taking the coins from Fred's house.

Joe felt sick. *If I'd have spent just two more minutes thinking about it I could've found a dozen better hiding places! I'm such an idiot!*

At the dinner table, Mom seemed pretty cavalier about the whole thing; in fact, it seemed like the burglary had lifted her mood out of the dumps. Very strange.

"Hey Joe, since you're such a handy guy, can you come out to the garage with me after dinner to find some wood to put over the broken window? It doesn't have to be a perfect fit, just something to make it secure until I can get someone out here to replace the door. I think I'll get something a little more solid this time—seems like city crime is making its way into the suburbs."

"Okay, Mom."

He didn't want to go back out there. It would be like rubbing salt in a wound to look upon the spot where his great fortune once sat. Still, after dinner he followed his mom into the garage, where she grabbed a broom and started sweeping the broken glass into a dustpan.

"Honey, can you bring me the trash can?"

Joe grabbed the can by the handle and dragged it over. It wasn't very full but it was strangely heavy. The glass clinked as Mom poured it into the bag-lined can. Joe glanced inside, then did a double-take.

Fred's towel! He took a closer look into the can. *Coin tubes!*

He thought for sure his mom heard him gasp, but she just kept sweeping. She was having a hard time getting the glass into the dustpan, so Joe risked another look. There they were: a lot of them—maybe all of them. But were they full of coins or were they empty?

Joe wanted so badly to reach in and find out, but there was Mom, getting ready to dump another dustpan full of glass into the can. Joe grabbed it from her.

"Here, Mom, let me take care of that. Why don't you find whatever piece of wood you want me to put up and I'll do the rest of the sweeping."

Mrs. McKinnon kissed her son on the forehead.

"You're such a good boy," she said. "I take that back. You're a good man … just like your father." Then she handed him the broom and headed to the other side of the garage where the wood remnants were stored.

As soon as Mom was far enough away, Joe reached into the can—and jerked his hand right back out when his mom turned around and headed back toward him.

"Probably need to measure it first, huh?" She walked by the trash can and grabbed a tape measure off the workbench. After measuring the window, she walked back to the wood storage area while repeating the dimensions to herself over and over.

Joe leaned into the can, put his fingers on one of the coin tubes and shifted it. It was heavy! He quickly grabbed the towel and tugged it over the exposed tubes. As he did, one of the glass shards nicked him.

"Ow," he muttered.

"You okay, honey? Be careful with the broken glass."

"Okay, thanks Mom." *This is the happiest cut I ever got in my life!*

Joe went to the table saw, swept up some of the sawdust from underneath it and poured it over the towel. Then he finished sweeping up the rest of the glass and any other debris he could find on the floor.

Mom came back with a piece of wood.

"Honey, I don't think the glass made it that far," she said. "Look, I found a piece just the right size. We won't even need to cut it."

They spent another five minutes screwing the wood over the broken window before returning to the house together.

***

First excuse he could make, Joe went back to the garage. This time, he found a pair of gloves to put on before picking through the broken glass.

He pulled out one of the coin tubes and opened it. Sure enough, it was full of silver coins! He glanced at the words on the tube: *1 ½" lead washers.*

There are *people that stupid!*

Joe continued to pull the tubes out of the trash until he had all thirty-three of them lined up in neat rows. He tilted his head up.

"Thank you!"

Now—where to put them …

60

Stress

YESTERDAY'S THEFT MADE it obvious Joe had to do something with the gold—and fast. But another thing became obvious: the clock was ticking on the condo. Days were going by with no progress. If he didn't get it done before the school year ended, its chances of being discovered would escalate. Nick was just a scout; soon there would be an army of thrill-seeking kids out there.

Joe thought of asking Mr. Pruitt to help him sell the coins. He was definitely trustworthy. However, even a respectable person like Mr. Pruitt couldn't walk into a bank with $189,000 in coins without doing some explaining. Besides, Mr. Pruitt had already gone out on a limb for him, and Joe didn't want to risk getting him in more trouble.

Off the top of his head, there was nobody else Joe could think of to help him. So he decided that once he got home from school and after he was done at the condo, he'd make a list of everyone he knew—friends, relatives, neighbors—and carefully weigh the plusses and minuses of each one until he figured out just the right person for the job. Whoever it was, Joe would offer them a percentage for their services (and for their silence).

***

When he got home from school, Joe discovered his mom's SUV parked in the driveway.

"What the …?"

The garage door was open and Mom was digging around inside. Joe pulled up near the garage and laid down his bike.

"Mom? What's up, Mom? Did we get robbed again?"

Mom emerged lugging a ladder.

"No, but after yesterday, I got to thinking: maybe it's time to clean out the garage, get rid of a few things—it's all just sitting here collecting dust and waiting to be stolen. I could use your help deciding what we should keep. Whatever we don't want, we'll have a garage sale and sell it. We could always use the extra money."

"Aren't you supposed to be at work?"

"I decided to take the afternoon off." She smiled. "Actually, the staff decided for me—because of everything that's happened."

Joe looked at what she'd done so far. There was a small pile of goods where she usually parked the car. He looked over at the box under the table saw—the one Dad built to catch sawdust when cutting wood. It was still there, and there was still a heap of sawdust inside it.

"You're not selling the big shop equipment are you?" he said. "The drill press, the jointer … the table saw?"

"Well that's what I need your help deciding. Do you think you'll want to use them someday?"

"Absolutely!" Joe said. "Don't sell any of Dad's tools. I'll use *all* of them someday!"

Mom looked taken aback. She hesitated, studying his face for a second.

"Okay—we won't sell any tools. I'll just keep looking for anything else … like those old ice skates that … don't fit you anymore, and that sled … things like that." She pointed to the pile she'd started. "And maybe I'll just straighten things up and do some vacuuming."

"I'll do the vacuuming!"

"Well good." She looked at her son like he had a zucchini stuck in his ear. "That'd be good."

"Can I do it after dinner, though? I just wanna do some other things first," Joe said.

"Sure, honey. I'll just keep finding things to get rid of—no tools—and we'll either donate it all or have a garage sale depending on how much we have."

Joe headed into the house, feeling a pang of remorse for being so curt with his mother. He dropped off his backpack, grabbed a snack, and was back out the door in seconds. As he hopped on his bike, Mom called out to him.

"Hey, where ya going?"

"Just out for a ride," he said. "Save the vacuuming for me though!"

"Wait!"

Joe stopped. "What is it?"

"Why don't you stay and help me out?"

"After dinner, I promise," Joe said. "I really just—"

"When you said you had to do other things, I thought you meant something here at home. I could really use your help—and your company."

"But Mom—"

"How often do I come home early enough for us to do something together?" She looked sad.

Oh, boy: a nicely executed triple jump of mom guilt. All the judges' scorecards gave her perfect ten-point-o's.

"Okay," Joe said. "Could I at least go riding for twenty minutes or so to clear my head first?"

"How about nineteen minutes?"

Joe shook his head. "Bye, Mom."

***

Before Joe reached the trail, a voice called out from his left.

"Hey Joe!" Mr. Pruitt was waving him over. "Were you heading out to the condo?"

"Yeah … right, sorry, I forgot to stop by to get you first."

"Well, yes, but that's not why I'm stopping you, Joe. Thought you should know to stay away from the condo right now. See those trucks?"

He pointed to two pickup trucks parked down at the forest preserve gate.

"Uh-huh," Joe said. "What's up? Who is it?"

"I'm not sure exactly, but they headed into the woods with something that looked like prefab shed walls and a roof, and one of those GPS devices on a pole. I didn't ask them what they were doing, figured I'd just keep my eyes open and see if they give me any clues as to what they're up to. At any rate, now would be a bad time to be making noise, and probably a bad time to be poking around out there period."

"Oh, okay." *Dang it, this is gonna kill my building schedule.* "Thanks for telling me, Mr. Pruitt."

"Just keep your fingers crossed they don't go out anywhere near the condo. If they find it, that's the end of it."

Just then they heard some distant hammering.

"I've been hearing construction noises for a while," Mr. Pruitt said. "Maybe they're building a remote weather station or something—don't know. But I don't think the sound is coming from the direction of the condo."

Joe thought it was coming from *exactly* the direction of the condo.

"You sure, Mr. Pruitt?"

"When you're down past my house, you can tell—it's a better angle. I think the sound's coming from closer to the area where we pretended Fred had his chainsaw accident."

Joe let out a long sigh. "That's a relief."

"I'll tell you what: do you still have the same phone you used to call Fred the day of his accident, when I answered Fred's phone at the hospital?"

"Uh-huh."

"Good, because I took the liberty of copying that number into my phone. Let's make a deal. Why don't you stay low until we're sure these guys are gone for good? I'll call you when it looks like the coast is clear, then we'll go out there together to make sure everything's kosher before we start working again."

"Kosher?" Joe said. "Isn't that like Jewish food?"

Mr. Pruitt laughed. "Yes, but in this case it just means everything's okay. Kids say the darnedest things!" He chuckled some more.

If those guys touch my condo, I'll definitely say the darnedest things!

61

Shut down … Open up

SATURDAY WAS AWFUL. Joe wanted to see the condo in the worst way, even if he couldn't work on it. He wore a virtual groove between his house and Woodside Lane, checking every hour or so to see if the trucks were still there. They were—sometimes three or four of them—and he heard the faint sounds of power saws and screw guns. What they were building out there? Was it really a weather observation station? Seemed like a lot of work for a small shed. Whatever it was, he hoped it wouldn't get regular visitors once it was finished.

By four o'clock the trucks were gone, but he was afraid to visit the condo for fear that someone might still be out there. He'd seen enough movies to know that whenever the villain seemed gone, he was usually just waiting to pop out and attack.

Mr. Pruitt emerged from the woods just as Joe was fixing to head home. Joe wheeled around and rode over to him.

"Hi, Mr. Pruitt."

"Hello, Joe, what're you doing here?"

"Just checking—wasn't planning to go out there or anything."

"You don't need to," Mr. Pruitt said. "I just did."

Joe's eyes lit up. "You did? What'd you see? Is the condo okay? What're they building?"

"The condo's fine—doesn't look like anything's been disturbed. But they're close enough that if you went out there and worked, they'd probably hear you."

"Yeah, but they're gone for the day, aren't they? Can't I go out there now?"

Mr. Pruitt breathed in through his teeth.

"Eh … not a good idea, I'm afraid."

"Why not? Weren't you just there?"

"Yes, and I saw something that very much concerned me," he paused. "Cameras."

Joe flinched. "What kind of cameras?"

"The spy kind."

"Dang." Joe thought for a second. "They didn't catch *you*, did they?"

"Could be," Mr. Pruitt said. "I guess we'll find out. But there's no sense in you getting caught too."

"I could go around the back way, from Drop-Point Charlie."

"Let's just play it safe for now. I'll tell you what: when the trucks are gone for good, I'll go survey the area and figure out what the camera situation is. Then I'll call you and we'll get back to work. How's that?"

"All right … I guess." Joe didn't like it, but didn't know what else to do.

***

That night after dinner, Joe retreated to his room with an ocean's worth of burdens, and every thought brought on a fresh wave of emotion. The most constant one was guilt for having started this whole chain of events. There was pain, too, from losing Jun … and wave after wave of confusion over Fred. Just when he thought one feeling had finally receded, another surged in and overwhelmed him.

Mom knocked and poked her head through the door.

"How's my Joe doing?"

"He's fine." He sat with his head propped up on his hand—his eyes fixed in a lazy daze on his computer screen—listening to an old man playing his flute.

"Pretty song," Mom said. "What's it called?"

"*Madrigal.*"

Though it wasn't quite near the end, Joe readied the mouse to replay the video. He felt bad that he was pushing his mom away, but thought talking right now would make him feel even worse than he already did.

"You look sad … or bored … or something. Anything on your mind?"

"Not really."

Mom sat down on Joe's bed facing her son from behind, but to his side.

"Would you tell me if there was?" she said.

"Probably not."

He knew that was mean, and that brought on a fresh wave of guilt.

"I'm just a little worn out," Joe said. "That's all."

"I'm not surprised," she said. You've been working hard the past couple of months: school, your *landscaping* job …"

Joe finally looked away from his computer.

"I had an idea," Mom said. "Tell me what you think."

"What's that?"

"How about we donate the money we get from the garage sale to the Song family—for the family they left behind? The cost for funerals and burials for three people will be astronomical."

"Yeah," Joe said with zero lilt in his voice. He hadn't even considered how awful things must be for the rest of Jun's family. "Sounds good."

"I know how bad you feel," Mom said. "Losing Jun … and Fred being the one who did it."

Joe shrugged. The music ended; the room was quiet.

"You have a tendency to keep things bottled up," Mom said. "Dr. V. said you're going to explode someday if you don't let it out."

"What am I supposed to do, cry in my beer all the time?"

"Have you been drinking?" Mom said.

Joe gave his mom the look.

"Just teasing," she said with a smile. "Since you can't drink beer yet, you can cry on my shoulder instead."

"I don't want to cry." He turned back to his computer.

"It's okay for men to cry, you know. Your dad cried sometimes."

"Yeah, at a funeral."

"Not just at funerals," she said. "Sadness, despair, feeling hopeless—happens to everyone. People cry."

"I don't feel like crying."

"Then how about talking?"

"About what?"

"About what's bothering you. Like, say … Fred … or Jun?"

Joe shrugged.

Mom said, "Fred's responsible for the deaths of three innocent people and—"

"No, he *murdered* three innocent people."

Mom sat up straight, putting her hands on her knees.

"So it's bothering you a lot."

"Of course it is!" Joe felt his breathing getting fast and uneven. "Doesn't it bother you a lot?"

Mom took a second before answering.

"It does," she said. "You saw me when we first heard the news."

He looked away but kept watching his mom in his peripheral vision.

"I know it was painful for both of us, Joey, but we've been through too much in the past year and a half to take on any more grief. We haven't even finished dealing with your father's death yet. Yes, we're going to grieve over Fred—and Jun. But we also need to talk about your dad."

"*Your* husband," Joe said, turning his chair to face his mom.

"What's that?"

"You always call him *my* dad. But he was *your* husband too."

Mom looked a little rattled. "Yes, he was."

"And that's just as important as him being *my* dad, isn't it?"

Mom remained silent.

"You talk like it's all about me saying how I feel about Dad's death, but what about you? Shouldn't *you* be opening up too?"

"Well, if I do, I shouldn't open up—"

"To me? You shouldn't open up to me?"

"That's not what I mean, Joey. It's just …" She paused, starting to show a pained expression. "It's just that a mom shouldn't lay her troubles on her son, that's all."

"Why not? Is it better to lay them on some stranger for a hundred bucks an hour?"

"It's my job to take care of you—"

"No, Mom. It's *our* job to take care of each other—our family is down by one!" Joe said. "You need me too."

"I do need you, Joey." Mom's voice cracked. "I need you to be a thirteen-year-old who plays with his friends and whose biggest worry is whether little Suzie will dance with him at the next sock hop."

I should have told Jun I'd go to that dance with her.

Joe lowered his voice. "I don't play anymore … and they stopped calling it a sock hop like fifty years ago."

Mom laughed, but there were tears in her eyes.

"If you want me to talk, I'll talk," Joe said. "But I can listen too. I'm not a kid anymore."

"No, you're not," Her voice broke and her face twisted up. "You're a young man now." She opened her arms to her son. "Come here."

Joe stood and wrapped his arms around his mother. She held him tighter and longer than he thought she could, rocking him back and forth. Then she held him at arm's length and smiled with teary eyes.

"What do you say we start with some milk and Oreos?"

Joe smiled too. "Sounds a lot better than beer."

62

Eagles and Legals

ON HIS WAY TO SCHOOL Monday morning, Joe stopped in the store parking lot and pulled out his phone. He'd prepared a message in case nobody was there, and as expected, he was greeted by an answering machine. He spoke at the beep.

"Hi, this is Joe McKinnon, I'm leaving a message for—"

There was a click as someone picked up.

"Hello, Joe, how can I help you?"

"Is this Mr. Fergussen?"

"Yes it is," Francis said. "What can I do for you, Joe?"

"Remember how you offered to help me?"

"Sure do."

"Well I have a big problem," Joe said. "And I'm hoping—actually, I'm *trusting* that you can help me out."

***

The lawyer wasn't coming over until four, so Joe took his time riding home. His meandering took him past Brain STEM Academy—the first time he'd been this way in over a week. The Brain had let out a few minutes ago and the usual stream of students was down to a trickle.

Joe felt his throat tighten as he remembered the last time he saw Jun.

I didn't know we were getting married … You are kind of cute.

He still had a perfect picture in his head of how she looked as they stood face to face while she played her flute. Since then, he must have played that song on YouTube at least fifty times.

He had to get out of here; the last thing he wanted to do was start crying in public. He was turning to leave when the door opened.

A familiar mom appeared, wearing sunglasses. She had armbands on both arms and carried a stack of books, papers, and a plastic bin. Using her back, she held the door open for a student with a peace-sign backpack, who was carefully balancing a bridge made of toothpicks in front of her. Under the bridge, a flute case dangled from her fingertips.

Joe gasped.

Jun!

Mother and daughter turned toward the parking lot, Jun's mom saying something he couldn't catch. Jun nodded and gave short answers.

Joe wanted to run to her as fast as he could and give her the biggest, tightest hug imaginable. If she was alone, he would've done just that. Instead he watched.

They pulled out of the parking lot. As they drove past, Jun looked out her window and caught sight of him. Their eyes locked. He smiled and waved to her. She gave a sad smile and a secret wave with curled fingers.

He stood there a long time, heart pounding, almost dizzy.

Jun's alive!

***

Joe sat on his sidewalk steps waiting for the lawyer. He was nearly delirious with joy, but also kicking himself. From the armbands Jun and her mom were wearing, it was obvious some of her relatives had died. The tragedy was still real, and it showed on Jun's face. He should have been there to help her through these tough times. But he didn't go by The Brain even once last week. So far his boyfriend skills sucked.

About ten minutes before four, the lawyer pulled up at Joe's house. He looked more composed, more like the Francis

Fergussen from the hospital. He reached out and shook Joe's hand.

"Hi Joe, how's it going?" He didn't look as down as last time.

"Pretty good, except for this problem I have."

"On the phone you said it was a big one. Are you in trouble?"

"No, not really. My problem is … I need you to help me get rid of something. Well, not exactly get rid of something, more like change it into something else." He was already second guessing himself on whether this was the right thing to do.

"Okay … do you want to tell me what it is?"

"You lawyers are good at turning valuable things into money, right?" Joe said.

The lawyer smiled. "Well, we're not exactly pawn shops or securities brokers, but we know the right people to take care of those kinds of things. We often help our clients cash in securities like stocks and bonds—"

"How about gold?"

"What kind of gold?"

"Gold coins … silver coins too."

"You can go to a coin dealer to sell those," Francis said. "I can help you find a reputable dealer."

"Not for this many coins."

"How many are we talking?"

Joe looked Francis straight in the eye, not wanting to miss a millisecond of the lawyer's reaction.

"Five hundred silver, one hundred and forty-nine gold."

The lawyer's smile faded.

"One hundred and forty-nine gold coins? Like some small ancient Greek coins or something?"

"Nope, US one-ounce gold eagles."

Francis scowled. "You have one hundred and forty-nine United States one-ounce golden eagles in your possession."

"Yup. And five hundred United States one-ounce silver eagles. Worth about one hundred and ninety thousand dollars altogether."

"You want to show me these coins?" There was skepticism in his voice, like Joe didn't know the difference between a real gold coin and a chocolate coin with a gold foil wrapper.

"Follow me," Joe said.

They went to the garage and Joe pulled out the box of sawdust from under the table saw. He batted the sawdust around with his hand until the tubes began to appear. He pulled one out, blew it off, and handed it to the lawyer, who seemed surprised at how heavy it was for its size.

Then he read the writing on the tube out loud.

"One-and-a-half-inch lead washers." He looked at Joe. "Why does it say that?"

"It's to fake people out."

The lawyer laughed. "No offense, Joe, but I don't think anyone would be faked out by that."

"Wanna bet? It fooled the thieves who robbed our garage just the other day."

He blinked. "You were robbed?"

"Yep."

"Well, they probably just didn't see the coins. You *do* have them hidden pretty well."

"They weren't hidden so well then. They were in a bucket. The robbers dumped the coins into the trash and then used the bucket to steal other stuff."

The lawyer laughed harder. "That's the first real laugh I've had since ..." His humor quickly trailed off. "Well, you know."

Joe looked down. "I know."

"I guess that's why they're criminals and not bankers or doctors." He hefted the tube again. "So how does a guy your age end up with such a treasure?"

Joe figured this would come up, and he'd thought it through. The only thing believable would be the truth.

"Fred gave it to me," Joe said.

"Really." Francis seemed surprised, but not as surprised as Joe would have thought. "Fred was always pretty thrifty, but I had no idea he was *that* thrifty."

"Can you help me sell it all and get me a bank account to put the money in?"

Despite Joe's abruptness, the lawyer was quick on his feet.

"No," he said.

"Why not?"

"Because," the lawyer said. "You can't sell it all at once. If you do, Uncle Sam will take notice, you'll pay taxes, and worse yet, there will be questions about where it came from. You'd likely end up losing it all. No, with gold you can only sell it a little at a time without the government being notified."

Joe didn't like that, but he was comforted that Francis understood the situation.

"How long would it take to sell it all?" Joe said.

"Do you have a pressing need for the whole one hundred ninety thousand right now?"

"No, but it makes me really nervous having all these coins lying around. Someone might find them."

Francis put his hand on Joe's shoulder and looked him in the eye.

"I can help you with that," he said. "But you have to trust me."

63

Missing Jun

ON HIS WAY TO THE BRAIN the next day, Joe was somewhat anxious—how could he explain to Jun why he hadn't come by her school all last week?

But as he approached The Brain, he noticed something odd: no kids. Next door at Algonquin kids were popping out the exits and milling around, but The Brain seemed completely dead.

He smacked his forehead. *Of course!* It suddenly made sense: all that stuff Jun and her mom were carrying yesterday was last-day-of-school, take-everything-home stuff. And now he remembered that The Brain started classes a week sooner than HMS, and probably had about the same number of snow days, which meant they'd let out about a week earlier than HMS.

Damn. He wished he'd thought to ask Jun for her cell number when he'd had the chance. Of course she might not even have her own phone—he'd never seen her using one— but then again, what teenage girl didn't own a cell phone? He could probably find her number and where she lived pretty easily, but he didn't want to seem like some creepy stalker.

Joe began pedaling home. He had to be careful with Jun now, or he could really blow it. It occurred to him last night that she might find out that the man who killed her relatives was a friend of his. If Jun found *that* out, she might never talk to him again. What if he told her up front about his friendship with Fred, then denounced him? No … that felt cheesy—even though part of him still hated Fred, he couldn't bring himself to do that.

And if she ever found out about Fred giving him that gold and silver, there'd be no way to explain that. He couldn't even explain it to himself.

But there was something Joe *had* figured out: how he was going to use his treasure. He already knew he couldn't keep it all for himself. In fact, the more he thought about it, the more he knew Fred hadn't wanted him to do that.

Rule number one: It's wrong to only be looking out for number one.

It was his mom's idea, really: what could be a more obvious, unselfish use for the money than to help out Jun's family? They definitely needed it right now. But doing it discreetly … that would be tricky.

Seemed like tricky situations were Joe's life these days, but he felt sure he could figure this one out.

***

He arrived home and let himself inside, after verifying that the garage was still intact. Milk and Oreos were a necessity for clearing the mind to think through important issues. Mom liked to keep the Oreos on the back of the pantry's upper shelf—a lame mom-trick to put less healthy foods more out of reach—*nice try, Mom!*

Would Jun someday share milk and Oreos with him? He hoped so … though it would probably be better to invite her out to The Shivering Cow, and maybe to a movie.

Joe set his milk down as a sinking feeling hit him.

I'm an awful person. I started that condo, which made Fred lose his arm, leading him to leave the hospital, get drunk, and mow down Jun's family. And here I am thinking of taking her on a date?

On that thought he lay on the couch for a nap. Ironically, right now—even with the turbulent life he was leading—he had the luxury of time. He couldn't work on the condo and he

286

had only a little more studying left for his last two finals, algebra and science, most of which he'd done yesterday.

It was hard to believe he'd be graduating next week. He wished Jun could be there, though he didn't deserve it. Last night when Joe broke the news to Mom that Jun was still alive, that was exactly what she'd suggested: that he should invite Jun.

"I'd *so* like to meet my son's first girlfriend," she'd said.

"I think she was heading back to China to visit relatives as soon as school let out," he'd said.

Mom frowned. They both knew that was just his way of saying, "I don't think I'm ready for that yet."

Joe closed his eyes and tried to focus on one redeeming fact: the same condo that caused all this calamity would someday prevent many more.

***

The phone's ringing woke him up.

Dogs!—one of those 1-800 numbers. That was another invention the world needed—a way to track down these people so you could call *them* in *their* homes and disturb *their* naps.

And now that he was awake, all his problems came rushing back.

The condo. It seemed impossible to get it done before school let out. His last final would be Thursday and then he'd have nothing but time on his hands. No way could he hang out at home doing nothing while the condo sat out there so close to being finished. He decided: trucks or no trucks, Mr. Pruitt's approval or not, he was going out to his condo after school on Thursday.

With that settled, his thoughts shifted to the lawyer. He was already impatient to hear back about the gold. The lawyer told him it might take a week for the first coins to be sold, and it was only yesterday he'd left Joe's garage taking all the gold and silver with him. Now *that* was a leap of faith. If Francis decided to keep it all for himself, there was nothing Joe could do about it.

He started to think about Fred, but that was too complicated. Next.

Jun. Maybe he was selfish for thinking of her, but he wanted to be near her again, be silly with her, be serious with her … see her face up close. This was almost as complicated as thinking about Fred, yet it was really simple: he was missing Jun.

64

Ha!

AFTER SCHOOL WEDNESDAY, Joe was in his bedroom reviewing how to solve systems of equations when his phone rang. Although he didn't recognize the number, he answered. Maybe it was Francis with some news about the coins.

"Hello?"

"Hello Joe, this is Clarence Pruitt."

"Hi Mr. Pruitt, how are you?"

"Good Joe, listen: the trucks are gone, I think maybe for good. Haven't seen them all day. Maybe you and I could go out and survey the situation. Are you doing anything right now?"

"Yeah! I mean no! I'll be right over."

***

Mr. Pruitt was waiting in front of his house when Joe rode up.

"Ready, Sparrow?" Mr. Pruitt said.

"Ready, Carson." Joe was nervous. "How do we avoid the cameras?"

"The cameras were just there during construction. I think we're good to go."

Joe left his bike at Mr. Pruitt's and the two walked alongside each other until they got to the wood-side path, where Joe took the lead. He was straining to keep himself from running ahead.

It felt like years had passed since he'd been out here. He hadn't realized how much he'd missed the woods this past week: the soothing sounds of nature, the sunlight flittering through the trees, the ground softened by centuries of twigs and leaves being dropped there.

But as they approached Ground Thirteen, it became apparent something was wrong. Ground Thirteen wasn't there.

Joe stood horrified, wondering if maybe they were in the wrong place. But no, there was the stump—it was unmistakable. The condo, the tarp, the backhoe, the piles of dirt, the carpet soundproofing—all of it—gone. But then why had Mr. Pruitt said everything was okay when he'd gone to check on Saturday?

He looked to Mr. Pruitt for explanation.

The old man was wearing the biggest false-teeth smile Joe had ever seen. He held up a lanyard with a key on the end of it, then offered it to Joe.

"Go invent something wonderful, young man."

They stared at each other. The disbelief in Joe's eyes was the polar opposite of the twinkle in Mr. Pruitt's.

Mr. Pruitt put the lanyard around Joe's neck.

"This is for the inside door lock," he said.

Joe walked around. There was no sign anyone had ever been here. It looked just like it did the day he found this spot— the day he'd surveyed the woods looking for just the right place to begin working on his dream.

Joe walked over to the stump and tried to open it. It wouldn't budge.

"Other side," Mr. Pruitt said.

Joe stepped around the stump.

"Right there. Now, there's a latch release inside the hole at the bottom of the stump, just to the left. See it?"

He looked down and saw the hole. It looked natural enough.

"Yeah, I see it." He was almost shaking with anticipation.

"Put your toe into the hole and lift up. At the same time, there's a narrow groove in front of you under the top of the stump. Lift up on that."

Joe did as instructed. The top of the stump lifted open. It was really heavy—must have weighed fifty pounds.

"You can open it all the way. It has a chain stop to keep it from flipping all the way back." By now Mr. Pruitt had made his way over. "But it has nothing to keep it from slamming down on you, so be careful."

He showed Joe all the details of the entrance: the hidden light switch, the best way to get in without scraping up the bark on the stump (any wear on the bark would start to look suspicious), and the best way to go down the ladder.

Joe climbed down. "Wow!"

There was an abundance of recessed lighting. The walls were finished, textured, and painted—there was even a ceiling fan! Upon the patterned linoleum floor was a two-cushion couch, a small entertainment center with a TV, a stereo system with speakers in the corners—there were even some fake plants on top of them. There was a card table and four chairs with a Chicago Bears rug under them. There were some posters on the wall: the solar system, the periodic table of elements, and a poster of Einstein. On the wall behind the couch was a framed painting of dogs playing poker—the same one dad had in his office, and his favorite. A floor lamp next to the couch had a round table built around it. Except for the Bears rug and the posters, the furnishings were all older with some signs of wear and tear, but still, everything was clean and well put together.

The wall outlets had built-in night lights. And something odd: there were fire extinguishers everywhere. He looked around and counted. There were at least eight fire extinguishers, four flashlights, two smoke detectors, and a gas mask.

"Holy cow!" Joe said. "I'm not a smoker or anything. Why all the fire stuff?"

"It's dangerous to be completely underground with only one exit. A fire marshal would condemn this place in an instant. So we made sure that if there ever was a fire, you wouldn't be more than a couple of steps—or a couple of crawls—away from a fire extinguisher. And don't forget, you don't have plumbing, so the only thing you have to put out a fire are these. So check them regularly to make sure they're always fully charged."

It was eerily quiet except for the sound of a fan—not the ceiling fan, but something else.

"Where's that sound coming from?" Joe said.

"That's the vent fan. Remember we talked about getting some outside air in here? It's right up there in that box. Goes out a hole in the roof to that fake rock we talked about." Mr. Pruitt pointed to a box in the upper back corner of the condo. There was a pipe going from the sump pump to that box. "Works pretty good too. If it wasn't for that, we'd be choking on paint and glue fumes right now. But I also made sure they used low-odor paint and only glued down the edges of the linoleum to minimize vapors."

"They?" Joe's expression darkened. "Who's they?"

"You didn't think I did all this myself, did you?" Mr. Pruitt laughed. "Even Tom and I working twelve hours a day together couldn't have done all this so quickly."

"I know …" The reality was sinking in. "And it's really nice and everything but—"

"But you wanted to do it yourself," Mr. Pruitt said.

"I kinda did—I mean, except with you and Tin Man helping."

"Sit down Joe, please."

Joe sat at the card table.

"Joe, I know how much you wanted to be involved in every stage of the project. That shows just how ambitious you are." Mr. Pruitt sat himself at the table next to Joe. "But you did the important part. You did all the planning and you got it started. You did more than get it started; you shaped it into its final form. The drywall, the flooring, the painting—those are all simple tasks most anyone can do. But not everybody can come up with the idea. Not everybody has the initiative to get the idea rolling."

Mr. Pruitt reached over and put his hand on Joe's shoulder.

"You should be very proud of what you accomplished here," he said. "I doubt there's another young man your age in the whole state of Illinois that could even think through all the details of such a project, let alone do so much of the work himself. You should be very proud of that."

"Who helped?" Joe was uncomfortable with so much praise.

"Friends of Fred. The day of the car accident—before the accident—he came over with a list of contacts. He'd already called and asked them all if they'd do the work—for pay, of course. He asked me to be the general."

"General?"

"General contractor, you know, like your dad was. Basically, I told the guys what needed to be done, and they did the work. The women went shopping to furnish the place. They did a real nice job, don't you think?"

"What women?" *Is there no end to the list of who's been down here?*

"Just a couple wives of the workmen. Nice ladies."

"The condo looks great, Mr. Pruitt, it really does. But now half the town knows about it. How do I know they won't tell other people, and then those people won't tell more people?"

"You don't." Mr. Pruitt sighed. "You just have to trust."

Where had he heard that before? Joe got up, went to the lamp, and turned it on. Then turned it off again.

"Joe, those people are busy with their grown-up lives. Not to belittle what you're doing here, but they have bigger things to worry about than what some teenager is doing in a hole in the woods."

Joe plopped down on the sofa. He felt a little insulted at the insinuation of his condo being just a play space—a fort— but at the same time he was reassured knowing that nobody would really pay attention to it.

"Why would they do this for me?" Joe said.

"Not so much for you as for Fred."

"Then why would they do this for him?"

"Loyalties run deep, Joe," Mr. Pruitt said. "If your mom made a mistake and killed someone by accident, would you stop loving her?"

Joe shook his head.

"Fred's guilty—that's obvious—and he'll pay dearly for it. But it doesn't mean all his friends are going to turn away from him. Did you turn away?"

The question caught Joe off guard. He averted his eyes from Mr. Pruitt. Even after all Fred had done for him, it felt dishonest to say *Yes, he's still my friend*. Joe would have to come up with a new word to describe his relationship with Fred; *friend* wasn't the right one anymore.

"What happened doesn't erase whatever kindness or good deeds he did for them in the past," Mr. Pruitt said. "Of course, it also doesn't hurt that he's paid them handsomely for their work."

"How did he pay them? He's in jail."

"He gave me money along with that list of contacts," Mr. Pruitt let out a heavy sigh. "You know, Fred was planning to leave town—he was going to California, didn't know if or when he was coming back. But he wanted to make sure your condo got finished. It was important to him."

"I didn't know he was leaving." *I kinda did.* "Was he really not coming back?"

"Depended on his son ..." Mr. Pruitt searched his memory.

"Phelps," Joe said.

"Right ... he said that if he couldn't reconnect with *Phelps*, he was going to ... disappear."

"Disappear?"

"That's the word he used. Not exactly sure what he meant," Mr. Pruitt paused. "But that's where you came in."

"What would I have to do with him disappearing?"

"That treasure you got from his house."

"Wait—you know about that?" Joe was starting to get freaked out.

"Don't know the amount, but yes, he told me he'd be leaving you something and if it seemed like you needed help getting it, I should help you."

"That's why you were willing to drive me there."

"And why I watched you cart away those buckets without asking questions."

Joe nodded. "But wait—he left me instructions at Drop Point Charlie for how to get the coins. How'd he do that while he was in jail?"

"He didn't," Mr. Pruitt said. "He left them *before* he went to jail—the same day he brought me the money and the list of contacts. He wasn't going to tell you about it unless he was sure he wanted you to have the coins. The car accident forced him to make that decision earlier than expected."

"But I still don't know why he gave it all to *me*," Joe said.

"If I had to guess?" Mr. Pruitt said. "I'd say it's because he felt you were more of a son to him … than his own son."

65

Secrets

JOE HAD ALWAYS PICTURED himself jumping up and down and yelling, "Yippee!" when the condo was finished, but now that it really *was* finished, all he felt was a sense of relief. Other things were weighing on his mind now, one of them being the coins.

It'd been hours since he'd called the lawyer's office and it was long past closing time. Joe knew his call wouldn't be returned until tomorrow at the earliest. So he'd have to spend at least one more night wondering if he'd ever hear from Francis Fergussen again.

What was to prevent the lawyer from putting all that gold and silver into a suitcase and taking a one-way trip to Switzerland? Maybe Francis was feeling ripped off. After all, the treasure came from his brother. Maybe he felt like that money should stay in the family.

Suddenly, Joe's phone vibrated. It was a text from Francis.

Joe, give me a call at your convenience at this number.

Joe sped downstairs. "Going outside for a minute!" He didn't wait for Mom's reply, just went into the garage and hit the callback button.

"Hi Mr. Fergussen."

"Hello, Joe. Thank you for calling me promptly," the lawyer said. "Are you able to talk now?"

"Yes."

"I have something for you," he said. "When would you like me to bring it by?"

"Tomorrow after school." Joe liked that—calling the shots.

"I understand. You can't really talk much now. How about four thirty tomorrow at our new meeting place?"

"Sounds good!"

***

Joe was waiting at the Criminy Coffee Café the next day at four fifteen. As a meeting place for covert operations, it was perfect. First off, Criminy had a diverse clientele, from high-school kids, to local businessmen, to old coffee-shop cronies, to beret-topped right-brainers—nobody looked out of place there. Plus, it had indoor and outdoor areas, both hopping with music, banter, and shrill bistro noises—no single conversation stood out. And people brought in computers, books, and backpacks all the time, so an exchange of goods could easily go unnoticed.

Joe ordered himself a Dos-sized Criminy Cocoa Caliente topped with Crystal Cream (Criminy's coveted extra sugary whipped cream). Criminy drinks came in sizes Uno, Dos, and Cuatro. Nobody seemed to know what happened to Tres.

Ten minutes later, Francis arrived. He bought a drink, came over to Joe's table, and shook his hand before sitting down across from him.

"You have a great handshake," Francis said. "I'm guessing your father taught you that?"

Joe nodded. "He said it was important to have a strong handshake."

"Good man, your dad," Francis said. "Met him only once, but he left a great impression on me. I meet all kinds of people in my profession. People would say it's wrong, but I can size up a person within two minutes of conversation with them—sometimes even within ten seconds. Ninety-nine percent of the time that first impression is correct." Francis sipped his coffee. "I could tell your dad was a good man."

I know that. "Thanks—do you have it?"

"Right here." The lawyer put an envelope in front of Joe. "There's three in there."

Joe pulled the envelope toward him. Nobody seemed to be listening, but there was no sense advertising that a kid was carrying three thousand dollars around in his backpack.

"The rest of the first exchange went to the bank," Francis said. "As we do more exchanges, we put one hundred percent of the proceeds into the bank, as we discussed. Right?"

"Right."

The silver, Francis had told him, could all be sold in one or two batches, but the gold could only be sold eight coins at a time so the government wouldn't be notified. Where or how he sold them, Joe didn't know. What bank it went into was also a mystery. As far as Joe was concerned, the money was going into the "Bank of Frank"—that's what the lawyer called it. He said Joe was better off not knowing the details. That way if anyone ever asked him where he got that much money, he could just say it was between him and his attorney. Joe carried one of the lawyer's cards in his wallet just in case there was trouble.

"That ought to keep you going for a while, I should think," Francis said. "The amount banked is written on a piece of paper in that envelope. If you ever need to know the current balance, just ask and I'll tell you." He changed his tone. "Now we talked about this already, and I just want to make sure we're on the same page. Getting large sums of cash like this shouldn't happen very often—right?"

"Right," Joe said. "But there is one more thing."

"What's that?"

"I want to make you my official lawyer."

Francis smiled and studied Joe for a second. "I already *am* working for you. Pro-bono, too—that means free. Why would you want to make it official?"

"I guess so what I tell you stays a secret between you and me."

"I won't tell anyone your business. Any good lawyer is also a good secret-keeper, whether or not there's a contract. It's just the nature of our profession. Besides, you'll run out of money pretty fast if you start paying me my standard rate."

"Yeah, but I don't want you to work for free," Joe said. "And I have something big for you to do for me—and later on, probably even more things."

The lawyer smiled. "Why don't you just tell me, and then we'll figure out if we need a more formal arrangement."

"Okay … are you ready?"

The lawyer leaned back in his chair.

"Go ahead, shoot."

***

At home, Joe pulled out $40, then put the remaining $2,960 back in the envelope. It was a pretty thick envelope since he'd specifically asked for mostly twenties—if he started shelling out fifty- or hundred-dollar bills, people were bound to get suspicious. He put the envelope inside his guitar amp. He was pretty sure Mom would never check there.

He went down to the kitchen, to where Mom kept their cash jar. Mom had a credit card, but hated using it—said it was dangerous. But she didn't feel safe lugging around a large sum of cash in her purse either, so she just kept some cash in a flour jar and pulled out only what she needed before she went shopping.

Joe placed the two bills into the jar under the other cash, trying not to disturb the top bills in case Mom remembered how it looked. Moms could be sneaky that way.

He'd have to do this little by little. If he had the opportunity, he'd also slip money into her purse. He'd have to get some change so he could match whatever denominations she happened to be carrying.

Joe chuckled to himself. His mom was probably the only parent in Illinois whose kid was *giving* her money behind her back.

66

The Beginning

EVERY JUNE THERE WAS a neighborhood picnic held on the opposite side of the woods, sort of an end-of-school/beginning-of-summer celebration. The Edward A. Corley Forest Preserve picnic area had been the site of the Palos Ranchos neighborhood picnics since ... well, since before Joe was born.

On more than one occasion—at Mr. Pruitt's or someone else's place—someone showed a few old movies of past picnics where kids and grown-ups played games all day long: horseshoes, an egg toss, races, softball ... even mummy-wrapping with toilet paper.

They still did those, although their initial enthusiasm for physical games was somewhat lacking. In recent years, kids kept getting drawn back to the benches, where their thumbs hovered over their smart phones, and fingers slid across their tablets. Interaction had become exchanging tips on how to raid a neighboring clan, or sharing new apps. The adults sometimes had to shoo the kids away from their electronics.

Still, it was nice to see them come out of hibernation and to see how they'd changed in the last year.

Nick was there, casting an occasional sideways glance at Joe and Mr. Pruitt. He was rather quick to turn away whenever Joe looked at him.

Mom appeared to be her happy self again; having the neighbors around made her laugh and smile a lot.

Mr. Pruitt sat near Joe and his mom for a while. They talked about the weather—specifically the unseasonably early heat and humidity. And people confessed they were already spending a lot more time in their basements to keep cool.

"Sounds like everyone's going underground," Mr. Pruitt said, throwing a sly wink at Joe.

But soon the talk turned to Fred. Joe merely listened, trying to gauge how much his neighbors knew.

It sounded like everyone still believed the story about Fred cutting off his arm while taking down a tree just inside these very woods, though it was still a mystery as to why he would be over here when there were plenty of woods by his own house. There was universal sympathy for the Song family, who everyone now knew were first- and second-generation Chinese Americans who'd come to Chicago from China by way of San Francisco. It was assumed they were in the restaurant business, but nobody knew their occupations for sure.

There were mixed emotions about Fred. Joe's mom talked about how hard he'd taken his divorce, his limited access to Phelps, and just how much he'd missed his son the last few years. Couple that with losing his best friend (Joe's father) and his arm—well, didn't that warrant at least some sympathy? A lot of people didn't think so, and felt he deserved the harshest punishment allowable by law, but Mom and Mr. Pruitt had more empathy.

One new facet to this whole soap opera was Fred's brother, the lawyer. Apparently, everyone said, he'd started up some kind of relief foundation to compensate the surviving members of the Song family.

It's The Song Family Aid Fund, Joe wanted to say. *And it's not to compensate them—it's a charitable organization meant to help them with funeral costs and other expenses that resulted from the accident.*

At least that was how Francis explained it to Joe when they set up the fund. Of course the surviving family could and probably would sue for the suffering of their beloved who died in the accident, but there was something different about taking money from the person who hurt you versus someone giving you money out of the kindness of their heart.

Suddenly, Mrs. Smith pointed. "Look, isn't that some of their family over there?"

Sure enough, across the parking lot, a slew of Asian people were getting out of their cars and heading toward picnic tables. They all wore the same armbands like Jun had on that day at school.

A moment later, Jun emerged from her mom's car carrying picnic items with both hands. Her hair was tied to one side with a yellow bow. Despite the armband, she looked cheery in her bright summer clothes. If it weren't for all the people around, he'd run over and give her a hug.

As time passed, Joe glanced over at Jun more often than might be considered reasonable. This didn't go unnoticed by Mom.

"You keep looking over there. Any particular reason?"

"That's Jun," Joe said.

"Ohhh," Mom focused. "Which one, the one with the red shorts and the yellow bow?"

"Yeah, that's her."

"She's very cute. Why don't you go over there and say hello?"

That was ridiculous, of course. Joe *did* want to talk to Jun. He just couldn't think of a way to do it that wouldn't breach the complex rules of the boy/girl protocol.

***

The afternoon waned, and the picnic was drawing to a close. Jun's family was putting things away—Joe's window of opportunity was closing. If he didn't act soon, he might not see her until school started again—and even that was questionable since he'd be going off to high school. He had no idea what his schedule looked like yet.

Son, when opportunity knocks, you should at least crack open the door and see what it looks like.

Without a word, Joe began walking toward Jun. It was almost involuntary, like the Jun-crazy part of his brain had taken over his body. The distance between them was closing. Joe's false appendage wasn't obvious—he wasn't limping—but he *was* the only one on the picnic grounds wearing long pants on a hot day.

One by one, Jun's family started taking notice. They threw him suspicious glances, but nobody appeared to feel very threatened by his approach.

Finally, Jun turned around. Upon seeing Joe, she began stepping in *his* direction and when their eyes met, he slowed. Jun's mom said something. From the tone of her voice and from how she kept glancing back and forth between her daughter and Joe, it could only have been disapproval. At the same time, another woman was speaking to Jun what might have been encouragement, judging by the way she smiled. Jun's mom turned and spoke harshly to that woman.

Although he had the words in his heart, Joe really didn't know what he was going to say when he reached Jun. There was so much to say to her … and he wanted so much to hear *anything* she had to say to him. All these people, their lives had been affected, some possibly ruined, by the boy who was coming their way. One teenage boy and his pickup kills a father—a husband—and ruins his own life. One drunken Fred does the same.

When Joe was about ten feet from Jun, he stopped.

Once upon a time, Joe was just another kid she knew from school. But now, he was part of her family. They didn't know it, and probably wouldn't like it, but that's how it was. They quieted themselves and waited for whatever it was Joe was bringing their way.

Tears filled his eyes and spilled over.

"I'm sorry," he said to Jun. His lips trembled. He looked at Jun's relatives. "I'm very sorry for what happened to your family. I wish I could do something for you."

The lady that had been smiling wiped tears from her own eyes. An elderly woman, maybe Jun's nai nai, sought translation while the rest of the family stood silent and motionless. Jun started to move toward Joe right when he turned to walk back toward his own family—his mother and his neighbors, who'd been watching him and were no doubt wondering what had just transpired.

When he reached his mother, he fell into her arms and sobbed.

***

Since the Palos Ranchos picnickers were packing it up, Mom decided it was time for her and Joe to leave as well. They said goodbye to their friends and walked to the Sequoia. Mom opened her door, but suddenly stopped.

"Uh, Joe?" Her eyes motioned back behind him. When he turned to look, there was Jun.

"Here." Jun held out a container of food. "It's from my family."

Joe took the container.

"Thanks."

She gave him a quick hug, then backed up two steps.

"You're very sweet." She gave Joe a long look with caring eyes. Then she turned and ran back to her family.

***

On their way home, Mom said, "Someday will you tell me all about that?"

"Yeah, sure Mom."

"And will you tell me about your *condo*?"

Joe snapped his head toward her. He felt his eyes bug out. "You *know*?"

"Of course I know," she said with a smile. "I'm your mother."

"Who told you?"

"Mmmm, let's just say a little birdie told me."

Joe's surprise persisted. "How long did you know?"

"I only found out near the end," Mom said. "Did you see the dogs-playing-poker painting? That's the one from your dad's office—he always liked that painting. It belongs in your condo now—that's *your* office."

Joe stared at his mom for a few long seconds. She didn't seem mad—in fact, she seemed … pleased. She also wasn't driving straight home, but was instead taking a scenic route.

So he told his mom about the condo: the whys, the hows, the dream. Mom listened, and she told Joe some things *he'd* never heard before too: the mischief Dad had gotten into as a kid, and *his* dreams. Joe listened.

The St. Christopher's medal swung from the rearview mirror. Maybe tomorrow he'd ask his mom if they could go to mass.

The feel of Jun's hug still clung to him.

Dad, I think this is the start of something really good.

Acknowledgments

The author would like to acknowledge:

My family for giving me breathing room, tolerating my writing stuff lying around, listening to me carry on about pretty much everything, and not laughing at me (at least not in my presence)—especially my wife, Jackie, who brought home the bacon while I "played."

My friend and neighbor Lopa—the "give me any date and I'll tell you what day of the week it was" savant who taught me about Indian customs, and that people from India would most likely not do the Charleston after a puja ceremony.

My friend Monica, who encouraged me to keep writing, provided insightful critique on some passages, and linked me up to my first unbiased teenage alpha reader.

Krishna, my first unbiased teenage alpha reader, who has wisdom and communication skills beyond his years (and I'm not just saying that because he liked my manuscript!).

Mary Simonsen, who advised me along the way about the non-writing aspects of the writing business.

Amber, for helping me understand social media.

My parents, whom I may have lied to once or twice as a teenager. They loved me anyway.

My editorial team: Shannon Roberts (the creative writing teacher I never had), Julie Miller (there *is* a real reason—

possibly subjective—behind every punctuation choice), and Jane Ryder (my go-to person whose clever wit and kindness are unsurpassed.)

My eighth-grade English teacher, Mrs. Foley, whose strictness scared me straight and who could pick apart sentences like nobody's business.

Our family cat and writing muse, Reese's, aka "Crazy," who sat next to me much of the time—listening to my clickity-clack and reading aloud—trying to convince me that I'm not really a dog person.

All the writers who've come before me who role-modelled what good writing is supposed to be … and the few who role-modelled not-so-good writing … just as important.

John Penteros is a math tutor and former engineer who resides in the thermal nightmare known as Arizona. As an engineer, he wrote long and tedious specifications, procedures, and reports peppered with "unprofessional" artifacts to see if anyone was paying attention. The occasional chuckling response lit a small fire within him, leading to other writing endeavors like the annual Christmas letter, which received mostly five-star reviews.

John is also full of make-believe, and when he makes a statement to people who've known him for at least ten minutes, they know to ask themselves, "Wait … is he just kidding me?" Put those things together and you get someone who writes fiction.

Visit John Penteros at:

Website: http://www.JohnPenteros.com
Facebook: http://www.Facebook.com/JohnPenteros
Twitter: http://www.Twitter.com/JohnPenteros

If you enjoyed this book, please take a moment to leave a review with your favorite retailer (or wherever) or send a note to the author through his website. He'd love to hear from you!

You've *been* down. It's time to go up …

TWELVE FEET UP
(The First 5.6 Feet)

… it doesn't end underground.